Little Nine

For Alice Webster

Little Nineveh

Dexter Petley

Polygon
Edinburgh

© Dexter Petley 1995

Published by
Polygon
22 George Square
Edinburgh

Set in Palatino by WestKey Ltd, Falmouth, Cornwall
Printed and bound in Great Britain by Short Run Press Ltd, Exeter

A CIP record for this title is available.

The right of Dexter Petley to be identified as the author of this work has
been asserted by him in accordance with the Copyright, Designs and
Patents Act 1988.

ISBN 0 7486 6190 5

The Publisher acknowledges subsidy from

THE SCOTTISH ARTS COUNCIL

towards the publication of this volume.

Chapter One

That Saturday when Partridge strangled Yvonne Sharpe down Little Nineveh I was eleven and a quarter. The November sky bulged above us – a grey sack of angry crows, the trees had all been nutted weeks ago and the air smelled of pencil sharpenings. All concurrence between us stopped like an unwound clock. Daz and Skinny eleven that September. Milky White a year ahead.

Childhood was too tremulous an age to consider the languages of fiction. Honesty and innocence are finally trampled underfoot in the first term of Secondary School by older boys; the way they always strip the unripe fruit from every tree. Truth was a windfall; my sudden use of it an accident. I should have left it in the ditch where the winter would have made an end of it. Didn't life always find its way back into the tree? Didn't winters always end?

Time in those winters of ours was measured in Saturdays, half-terms, frozen puddles and punctured footballs. November opened with conker fights and bonfires, closing on wetted gloves, quagmires and pike bungs. The last tench from down the pond had long been hooked, boasted and disputed. The first winter jack from the Rother at Bodiam had yet to fall to one of us. The goalmouth up the Playing Field soon churned with clay and sawdust as our village team failed us and sank at the bottom of the East Sussex League by their half dozenth fixture. The skylight died earlier after the clocks went forward and the school bulbs twilit the afternoons. Air grew colder and we knew that Saturdays were God's only gift to children.

By the Saturday it happened, Partridge had, as far as we knew, gone with summer. We thought we'd seen the last of him; he never entered our minds, we who lived down Barratt's Road among the hundred brick-orange council houses built just after the war. There were twenty boys our age to choose gangs and teams from, a few squirts or brothers, plenty of sisters. And we were many gangs of duos and trios, meeting up at the Two Trees where allegiances shifted like the wind. We knew our village backwards too, but the common haunt for all the village children was the recreation ground up Church Hill. It was here that Partridge first appeared to us the opening week of the summer holidays, riding through the wooden gates on a racing bike. I hated him from first sight because he rode my bike. I couldn't imagine why at the time, or believe how, but I knew he'd been down Little Nineveh and stolen it. Of this there was no question. So perhaps it had originated there – only Little Nineveh had always been mine and had no existence without me.

In fact, I'd never told the others of this place. Its single atmosphere could only be secret in one boy's mind. At Little Nineveh the Victorians had built a sunken garden and Edwardians abandoned it for fifty years until I found it, overgrown, at first a place to hide the things I nicked from shops – or conjure up, indulge the otherwise unthinkable and even voice these things forbidden at home. It became a place which understood my needs, a place which gave freely.

The surrounding estate of Great Nineveh had been in decline all century. I'd first encountered it on one of those unexplained visits ten-year-old boys make with their fathers. You don't know why, but it's Sunday morning and has something to do with sparking plugs and an old Smith's speedo-meter for the Alvis. Lower Nineveh was the farm and stables with its fields spread along the Gunmill Valley. Upper Nineveh had a cedar driveway and Gothic lodge, the manor house converted to St Dunstan's Preparatory School. We drove into the farmyard and I stood in the stone yard while my father gave a ten-bob note to a red-faced man with quick, fat hands who'd been leaning in the farmhouse doorway.

Back home I looked it up on the Ordnance Survey and saw this other Nineveh, Little Nineveh. A footpath cut between the farm and school. There was an orchard, a copse, a kitchen garden, and on the edge of this, outside the wall, a little round dip with a tiny pond. *Little Nineveh* it said, in delicate italics. The map was ancient so I didn't think the pond would still be there but I took the first chance I had to sneak off and find out, one Saturday morning three weeks after our visit to the farm. Daz and Skinny had buggered off on a bike ride with the others so I found myself unobserved with no one much to play with.

'I'm goin' up the shops t' spend me pockit money,' I lied to my mother.

Instead, I soldiered down the lanes well out of bounds with eyes in the back of my head. The footpath was easy to find. It ran behind the Lodge, marked by a bent iron fence and shrivelling bracken. Spring was a few weeks yet. The kitchen garden wall was unscalably high, but through an opening I found a well-raked gravel path, greenhouses, a huge beech and monkey puzzles. The man with the quick hands was easy to dodge as he paused several times to light his pipe on his way to the compost with a wheelbarrow. Through a broken cuckoo gate down the far neglected end I entered the sunken garden, in sight of nothing and no one. A half acre round, it dropped like a soup bowl under my feet as I thrashed my way in, ripping ankles and pulling threads. Four brick pathways met at the centre, each pole of a sludge-green pond: a black stink beside the sundial, telling birdshit-moss time, shadowless all year. Timeless. Such strange hairy shrubs, wild spikes, bindweed thick as wire wool. Trees which looked made for coconuts or pineapples blocked the entire sky. I imagined parrots and beat paths and hunted out the beasts, so that by dinnertime I had a world of my own.

It was a world in which to relieve the other hard-done-by world, balance the grievances. My father not letting me have a bike was the sole, worst grievance left by the time I was nearly eleven. Every boy and his sister had a bike too. If he caught me having a go on theirs, my father skinned me with the flat of his hide-thick, dry hand. At least it didn't matter to the others if I never had a bike. I was much too good and indispensable at football, fishing, lobbing and scrumping for them to worry. It worried only me. It really mattered. Not that I couldn't occupy myself when deserted and left alone all afternoon because of bike rides to Bodiam or Bedgebury Forest. I went fishing alone quite happily; only the 'bike ride' was an important ritual from which I was excluded. In the minds of everyone down Barratt's Road my existence was incomplete. Then, because of Little Nineveh, I discovered I could own a bike in secret. So I stole one, trying to kid myself I'd found it.

By then it was mid-June, a month before Partridge appeared. Primary School was nearly done, my eleventh birthday was a week away, the fishing season was nearly upon us. Thus my mind was occupied: which of four ponds should I fish first? I was on my way to look at one of them, passing the black carriage gates of the Tudor Arms Hotel. A few yards down the lane, parked in the ditch, was a racing bike, glistening silver-blue, catalogue-perfect as it leaned like a photograph against the green bank, wild strawberries in the spokes, five gears, white drop handlebars. I admired it, wondered briefly whose it might be, then with better things to do climbed the five-bar gate to survey the pond at the back of the hotel, a tiny clay pond half-choked in rushes and teeming with four-ounce tench.

Come June the sixteenth Daz and Skinny decided to fish the pond down Barratt's Road, so I set off without them long before the milkman to the Tudor. The sun had risen on cold, wet grass, a fisherman's dawn. The racing bike was there too, wet with dew, webs slung between the spokes. To me it seemed unwanted and abandoned so I touched it, set it upright, pulled it onto the road. It was far too big and I knew I couldn't hope to ride it anyway, but I dumped my fishing gear behind the hedge, stood on the pedal and freewheeled down the lane as far as Little Nineveh. By then I was possessed; I had no choice. I pushed it along the footpath, into the field which skirted the kitchen garden wall, then through the opening into my darkened, evergreen world. The bike was mine, as if it had never been otherwise.

For a month I kept it under an old tarpaulin I dragged in from the field and camouflaged with bracken. When able, I polished and oiled it, slowly working up the guts to take it for a spin down the lane. I named it Bluebird. What with Daz and Skinny coming round for me all the time plus school, fishing and cricket, I only managed to see Bluebird a few times, but I felt Bluebird waiting. My ownership was irrevocable – I was a fox alright, foxing the dogs. No one had found out. No one had said anything about their bike getting pinched. The village copper didn't knock on the door at teatime. So I even imagined the years passing until one day I would simply ride Bluebird up to the Playing Fields and no one would tell the difference, or wonder where I'd got it.

First week of the holidays I didn't worry over Bluebird. Up Church Hill we organized two-a-side rush goalie knockouts on Wembley grass or shrieked French cricket and flew ludicrous gliders. Then, one afternoon, Skinny looked up to scratch from batting and said: 'Ooz'at jis come in the gate then?'

Partridge glided Bluebird round the boundary line then leaned it on a bench and sat there blowing smoke through his teeth. Bluebird's hero. She didn't move unless he made her, Bluebird's rider, careless and sneering at my useless hanging fists, my stump of tongue. As he stood and switched his dog-end for a blade of grass, Bluebird leaned against his thigh and seemed to say: I'm his now. He *knows* how to ride a bike.

After this he appeared up Church Hill most days we did, nameless for at least a week, spotted nowhere else in the village. I learned to live with his presence which in fact resolved my ambiguity by placing Little Nineveh out of bounds. He had been there, seen me hiding Bluebird, heard me talking to her. So Little Nineveh was a broken secret, a Gethsemane, an empty place where I had been betrayed. So what? He couldn't be everywhere and summer promised us the earth . . . then bid us share it.

Partridge always chewed a fresh Bazooka Joe with every fag so we looked for his wrappers and dog-ends wherever we went. Up the Playing Fields he usually sat and watched us from the swingboat, his green baseball cap back-the-front, white sailing jeans and an egg-yellow pullover against bare skin even on the hottest days, making us critch ourselves for the itching he never did. As sweat strained through his face he grinned with his top lip and watched us through his mouth, running a finger under the cap rim, flipping it off to rake his fingers to the scalp through his slicked-back, Brylcreem-packed hair.

One day he threw our ball back really hard, so hard it tore through the hedge into the vicar's field, so we nicknamed this tennis ball and invented a new game. Greaseball. Whoever it touched was it, Greaser. 'Ugh Grease-er, Grease-ball, uuuggghhh-you're-Greaseball . . . '.

Everyday I hoped to see him pranged, sharp-corner-elbow-skinned across the road, Bluebird buckled under him like an old pushchair off the dump.

On Wednesdays we saw real cricket when the shops shut for the afternoon and family doctors, shopkeepers, farmers and milkmen met for the two o'clock toss. We'd join them heaving iron-wheeled sunscreens into place like shunting traction engines with our shoulders. The creosote-planked pavilion came to life as the shutters swung out and released the smells of batting pads exhumed from wooden trunks, tea-cakes, deckchairs and the women's eau-de-Cologne. From our observatory between pavilion and scoreboard we listened to the throaty, half-made words of idle cricket men, the fluting of the vicar's wife beside the rumble and glug of the tea-urn. Butter would melt through dry scones, a few runs scored, clapping like a handful of wooden bricks gently toppling over. It fascinated us, this world of sprawling about while playing sport. Our speculations on what they were paid for this grew wilder. Our true sport was football. Our actual empathy was with the village heroes whose laces snapped in six inches of cold mud. Toothless, bloody men who rose at dawn and waited for the works van coughing in the fog under my window, winter after winter. How they hawked on half-time Old Holborn, swearing the bollocks off at the ref as we echoed and acted their every word and deed. But these white village cricketers were more like schoolmasters so we kept quiet and sucked grass as the poplars rustled along one boundary. Once or twice we'd get to chase a good stroke lost in the rhodedendrons. Our village always played a man short and lost but we stayed until the stumps were pulled when they reached our length in shadow . . .

Then one Wednesday Partridge skidded to a standstill at the gate. He looked over the cricketers for two seconds then snapped the bike round on its back wheel and flew down the path in a raging hurry.

' 'E prob'ly don't loike crickit,' Skinny chirped in his high pitch. By the time I'd sprinted to the gate the road was empty both ways.

Next day he was back again, pushing Bluebird along behind three girls. Caroline Monk, Jennifer Gibbs and Yvonne Sharp. He pushed Caroline Monk forward with the bike. She needed no prompting and came on haughty.

'We wanna play . . . Flower Petal!' My surname was Lily. Yvonne hung behind, Gibbs toothpaste laughed.

'Fuck off, Monkey,' Daz said, but Partridge flipped Bluebird onto her stand and snatched our tennis racket.

'Bowl it, ratface,' he said at me.

I didn't hesitate. The ball was sticky with my sweating hand and fell halfway, so Partridge launched himself forward, took a threatening run and swiped. He missed and Skinny giggled.

'SHUDDUP, FOUR EYES!' Partridge sweated through his pullover, veins like drainpipes on his neck. He belted my next ball over the pavilion roof, into the vicar's brambles.

'APES!' Monkey and Toothpaste yelled after us as we scrambled after it, 'you lot couldn' 'it it that far between yer.'

Partridge was rubbing and spitting on his hands. 'Huh, they won't find it if they try neever.'

Mounting Bluebird at a run he slapped his thighs cowboy horse way: 'LEZGO LEZGO LEZGO . . . '

Two moments and he was skimming down Church Hill with three girls running after him, Gibbs and Monkey screaming 'WAIT!'

'Crikey, wha' a bastard,' Daz said. Skinny was shaking, terrified. I was nursing fists. We never did find the ball.

Those girls were our age. Partridge, we found out later, was nineteen and lived with his gran between our village and its neighbour, like a monster would. We only saw him now when the girls were about, like down at the swing-boat, him pushing them so high the chains slacked and the bars thumped as they came down screaming. Yvonne didn't swing, she sat it out and sucked her pony tail in the shade or sat dream-eyed a whole hour at the top of the slide with her knickers showing. We wondered why she stuck it.

'Soppy face,' the other two called her. Yvonne still said 'lickle' so Partridge called her 'soppy-lickle-Yvonne-lost-her-lickle-doggy'. She lived down Donkey Lane in a farm cottage; at least *we* called it Donkey Lane. We all said her mum and dad never washed because they stank of hops or cow clat all year. Living down there meant Yvonne had no one to play with so she hooked herself on that diddyguy Gibbs. Then Partridge began to take more notice of us than Yvonne or the other two, egging us on, too. One day he pushed Bluebird across as I was mucking around with a sixpenny glider and Daz was behind a tree having a slash. Skinny was miles away with Dodge down at the see-saw, scrooping like chair legs on the classroom floor. But Partridge came up close so no one heard, nodding at the bike. 'Cummon, where'djer ged it from?' I shook my head and looked for Daz, but Partridge wheeled himself in front of me again. 'Nicked it, di'nyer? Cummon, own up. Yer pinched it, yer liddle tea leaf.'

'Did not.'

'Lyin' l'il cunt.'

Daz came out from behind the tree and hesitated, so Partridge backed away fast then shouted 'Wanna backer?' at me, his eyes pinching my face as they squeezed shut against the sun. 'Betcha scared. Diddums might fall off.'

'No I aint,' I said, walking forward, and in spite of my fear and hatred of him and Bluebird I touched her mudguard in what had been my own, special way. 'It's me,' my fingers whispered.

Partridge straddled it. 'Ged on then, yer dopey prongo.'

He yanked me round the boundary, hanging onto his waist shit-stiff with air gushing into my ears ten times faster than running, more like tree swings or motorbikes. He threw a skid as I knew he would and over we went, green elbows and grazes, the jelly-wobbles and a thick ear where the ground punched up. He might have killed me but he just laughed. Perhaps that very afternoon he'd decided not to strangle me. He must have chosen Yvonne for being most alone.

The water fight came next, sometime in August behind the pavilion where the brass tap was bound to the standpipe by all makes of string and wire. Partridge started it, coming upon us as we sqwarked a cheek-bladder of bulge water on each other's plimsolls.

'Girlz 'gainst boys,' he shouted, hogging the tap. He filled a Tizer bottle and threw it at me with a twirling lob. I ducked and it smashed on the cricket-pitch roller.

'You're the girlz,' he was mocking, mocking, mocking. 'We're the boyz.' He stuck a thumb up the tap and turned it on full, soaking himself instead of us.

'Come 'ere, goo on, COME 'ERE!'

We weren't looking when he climbed onto the pavilion roof.

' 'Ere twerp features!' he called.

I looked up. 'Know yer fuckin' name then,' he said and pissed full in my face, catching Skinny on the shoulder and Daz in his hair.

Next time he appeared we cluttered off. He stuck his fingers up and shouted but the wind was against him. After this we hardly saw him, just odd sightings or some rumour that he'd been and gone. We stayed clear of Church Hill and went fishing a lot, following the stream for miles east of the village.

The last time I saw him that summer was August Bank Holiday. I saw him smoking fags with Basil Latter up the crossroads, jossed up astride the railings watching all the cars come back from the coast and jam on Highgate Hill. He held a massive radio on his shoulder like a coal sack, the music–innards scraped out into hot, dry leaden-dust air as Partridge jerked his neck and shoulders like a chicken, half chewing, half singing:

> 'He-rode-into-the-night
> He-sateracton-his-mo-torbiii-ike
> I-cried-to-him-infright
> DONT-DO-IT-DONT-DO-IT-DONT-DO-IT . . . '

Then he saw me. 'Whatchew lookin' at Lillywhite-'ad-a-fright? Wet yerself agen? Gone over yer 'andlebars? Goo on then, TAKE OFF!' Autumn came, a new school, and Partridge vanished.

The Saturday after Guy Fawkes, Watson's knocked tuppence off a box of bangers so we exploded them late morning by the gas tank, then chucked sticks into chestnut trees. Only the brown, empty husks showered down. Dinner was sausages and beans. I licked the cake dish and went out. There were four of us wondering what to do that afternoon: me, Daz Ashdown, Skinny Wickham and Milky White. Hawks versus Ninfield was cancelled after three days of rain had waterlogged the pitch, so there was no point going up Church Hill.

'I know, le'ss go down the Lanes.'

We golloped and dawdled in our wellingtons as far as the Tudor Arms, the way the road took us, plunging into the lanes. All the windcocks were still and pecked north from the previous day and the telegraph wires hummed at the poles. We left a trail of boot droppings and rusted shads dug up from under. Our moods tipped up and down. We huffed a lot with Milky White, who was a snag as usual. I resented any reminder of Bluebird (for this was Nineveh Lane) but other things commanded our attention. We dammed a running ditch with a bale of clung grass which hadn't hayed. We skated on crushed husks, bunged acorns at milk churns and weather-vanes. Three pikeys shot an airgun at us. I stuck a '2 pints today please, milkman' sign in a cowpat and Daz hit a Landrover at over thirty yards with his catapult strod.

We didn't know where we were going, we couldn't know what we might see. There was nothing to put us off the scent as we followed lanes edged in thin brown streams running inexorably downwards. The air was tinged with woodsmoke too damp to make a flame. Slurry smells stewed up our nostrils. Our lane grew recent with tractors but we saw no one. A dog barked twice, a shotgun in the lag flung its pellets at the valley mist, and a wedding church bell came from very far away, like finding an ice-cream wrapper from last summer at the bottom of a trouser pocket. It was Little Nineveh we stopped at, just as St Dunstan's clock plinked three times in the damp.

From here the reconstructed truth becomes uncertain, a shadow of a thing, not the thing itself. The others cast this shadow, a distorted form bearing many, unintended resemblances. So this memory has become mine alone, a version they might not recognize. The iron cuckoo gate with its fluted post marked the entrance to the footpath. Even from the lane the existence of my sunken world seemed so obvious. For allowing its own discovery I hated it. The dead ferns were trampled flat as if half the village had thrashed their way along the path with walking sticks. Daz, Skinny and Milky nudged their way along, trespassing, creating states of mind for which none of us were ready – the danger seemed obvious to me. This was a dark place now because Partridge had already been there and made it so, and only I knew this. And he was here again. We stopped dead before it. Three yards up the path, leaning against a tree, a silver-blue racing bike.

' 'S Partridge's,' I said.

'Nah 'snot. Carn be,' Skinny said, hoping hard it wasn't.

'Bet 'eez watchin' uz,' Daz said to scare us stiff.

Little Nineveh held us in the palm of its hands. The game began itself. Spies. Commandos. Enemy country. The footpath signposted in German so we skiced along it fingering rifles. Skinny threw a grenade at a cow. 'TANK!' he said. Milky called him a twit and said we were all stupid. He cut a stick and walked behind us. Excited now, I saw an airfield up ahead, behind that hedge – we had to creep on hands and knees because of sentries. Already jumpy, I looked first, remembering that Partridge must be somewhere. There was definitely something, even if I couldn't see it, I could feel it.

'QUICK! IT'S 'IM, SCARPER!'

Didn't take much to scare us so we scarpered in a blink. Skinny had been halfway up the path the second I'd said QUICK! A murder of crows suddenly rose on our yelling. We ran the wrong way, not back towards the road but inward. My mind threw up an eyeball looking through the hedge the way a stomach throws up a bad dinner. As I ran behind Daz I sensed that Milky wasn't with us. I looked behind. He hadn't moved an inch. He just stood there rigid, staring through the hedge, shit-struck. I called his name. Nothing. But the second time he was up with us at once as we slashed and bullocked on, our faces blenched, our noses dripped. We weren't making this up now. Something had got to us. I mean we'd played scare games before, ghosts and monster-demons. At Halloween we all put candles in the pumpkin's eye and skreeled with the lights out. Only this was different. We were running for our lives and only Milky knew why. I saw Milky see it, and I could hear his pounding boots behind me, his pounding breath like pumping up a heart. But for this, a chain reaction all the way to Skinny, we would have stopped and burst out laughing. Milky kept us running, like an engine, till we climbed a fence and stumbled across the farmyard, safe amongst the rusted tractors and empty barns. Skinny was the first to talk as we bent forward and sucked wind.

'Blimey you lot, what we runnin' fer?'

'Christ, Skinny,' I said, 'don'tchew know?' I didn't want Milky to think I hadn't see it, expecting him to tell us quick.

'Nah,' Skinny said, 'know what? Ooz comin' after us?'

'Partridge,' I said.

The other two said nothing. Daz spat a long trail of knackered gob on the clinkers. Milky kept his back to us, resting his hands on knees. Skinny wiped his glasses on his sleeve.

'I never saw nuffing or no Partridge,' Skinny said. 'Scotch mist if y'arse me.'

'Nor'd I,' Daz said. 'You said scarper Lily, so oi scarpered.'

'Musta bin Partridge,' I said. 'Whaddabout the bike then? Ask fuckin' White, 'e were standin' there longest.'

'I'm fed up with this,' Milky said. 'I'm going home.'

'Whaddabout the bike?' I kept asking.

We'd reached the lane by then, walking up the farm track, down the slope from where we'd started at the footpath.

'Alright then,' I said running up to the iron gate, 'I'll prove it's Partridge's bike, see.'

The proof had gone. I stood and ran my hand along the shape it left in the dampened air like feeling a dry patch where a car had parked during rain. The others were silent, certain of nothing, estranged by my mood. Milky walked home alone. Daz trailed him. Skinny trotted beside me like a silly dog, showing off the bogies on his handkerchief.

On Sunday morning church bells pealed across three valleys in the cleared and cold bright air. A woman on a horse from Lower Nineveh picks up the story, coming upon the body of a girl. The Murder Squad came down from Maidstone. Everyone in the village come Sunday dinner knew Yvonne Sharp had been strangled.

By evening the house-to-house was underway. Our story, or mine as it became, arose. Yes, the police detectives had seen our footprints. They'd found a fragment of a tyre track and went round asking: 'Whose footprints? Whose bicycle? Whose children?' My father strapped me with his belt for going down there in the first place. The policeman bid my father postpone his wrath, then asked me how I could be certain it was Partridge's bike. Strange thing was, we didn't know his Christian name.

'My goodness, boy,' my father said, 'if I find you've been anywhere near that blessed bicycle . . . '

So they put me, Daz, Skinny and Milky in the same room without our dads. Skinny said the bike was green, but anyone could see he was making it up. Daz said he didn't know what colour, so Skinny admitted he didn't either. Milky said he hadn't seen any bicycle. He even denied looking through the hedge and it was my word against his. They wrote it down, we held our knees and read the WANTED and MISSING posters in our PC Wyman's tiny little police house, our mums and dads under the trees outside with their glowing fag-ends and smacked torches. Then Daz said 'Nope' when the detective from Maidstone asked him for the tenth and final time if he'd seen the bike.

'Do you know this Partridge fellow?' he asked Milky.

'No, sir,' Milky said, 'I've never heard of him. Lily started going on about him just to scare them two . . . '

'Yeah, thass roight,' them two said, ' 'e said Partridge first. We never.'

No matter, the police knew all about our summer playmate. By midnight Sunday they were sure of their man. Partridge never stood a chance, and even though they couldn't find the bike they said he would have been arrested anyway. Partridge said that someone nicked the bike Saturday dinnertime, from against the pillar box at Four Throws. The village said he was a liar, like his gran. 'Nicked it 'imself, more like,' Skinny's mum said. Partridge's gran was an old bag who got on people's wicks. Misanthropic, not from round here neither, Hastings way she were from. She hung a face like a six-inch nail, a sneer like a hammer driving it home. No one was laying a finger on her grandson if she could help it. She swore blue he'd been indoors with her all day in any case, but villagers are quick when roused and soon remembered seeing her up the shops at three o'clock, a mile's walk from home. And we knew her grandson had only lived there since July because he'd been at a 'special school' till then.

'Learned 'eez letters in a nut'ouse,' we were saying Monday morning.

It had all come out, knowledge for the common: ' 'Angin' 'bout them kids fer the luvva God . . . pissin' on their 'eads . . . oh 'e did it alright the freak, no bones about that . . . '

We were none of us safe from the lists of other stranglers our mums and dads compiled. Village idiots, farm labourers, anyone who lived alone had better be watched or put away. Caroline Monk couldn't keep her mouth shut either, hogging the griefless limelight, swearing blind that Partridge had got Yvonne to take off her knickers once, then twice. 'Wanted a butcher's at 'er wick, 'e wantid.'

Dodge called her 'Wicky Wantid' for years after that.

The inquest was held in the Toc H hall. My milk-and-pyjamas voice rose like a winter moth among a packed house of candles craning forward on their brown canvas chairs. My mother wrung her handkerchief while my jury-faced father held his jaw. This was not the school nativity nor *The Lion, The Witch and The Wardrobe*, my only previous appearence in the Toc H hall, my one line coming at the end: 'Long live the King!' So I described, as requested gently and kindly, the bicycle I'd seen and where I'd seen it. My prescribed description of our one collective minute on Saturday afternoon. That I recognized the bike seemed to matter not, because Jennifer Gibbs agreed with Doctor Parish that my description fitted the bicycle Partridge used to ride. His gran denied he had a bicycle at all, but Mr Vynall said he'd sold Partridge a puncture repair kit for just such a bike. He'd walked outside his shop and seen it with his own eyes.

Daz, Skinny and Milky were never mentioned. The previous evening our village sergeant had called for a friendly chat. As if trying to tell me kindly that the three kittens had all died at birth, he said my three friends wouldn't be there in the morning and that I must try not to mention them too much. They'd be at school and, well, I were rather bettermost for facts. Partridge was committed for trial at the Maidstone Assizes and his name was never mentioned in the house again, forbidden ever after. For months I was treated like the criminal and kept strictly in the garden, until they found him guilty as charged on the evidence. His first life-day in prison, we played five-a-side in the road with the drains for goalposts. Yvonne's parents moved away.

A distance came between me, Daz and Skinny. I didn't care about Milky. He was a year and a mile ahead of us in any case, so we'd never had much to do with him. Neither had he been long in the village, whereas I'd grown up with Daz and Skinny. Little Nineveh was hardly mentioned during new cold spells in our friendship, only bobbing to the surface when we were our old selves, which wasn't often. We might be bored, perhaps, phlobbing over old Mr Miles's wall after school and something would start it off. Most likely we'd be sick of chasing Monkey and Gibbs round the deserted bus station, playing Lurgy on their new friend Gaynor, an ugly crumpet with a scab on her lip who always told her dad on us. He'd come round teatime after a day on the dustcarts, whacking our knocker and losing his dobbin at me old man.

'It's sight more'n sauce, Mr Lily, when your boy's gone an' bin chuckin' dog mess at our Gaynor . . . '

She'd taken Yvonne's place two years now. Daz would holler across the bus station: 'You've even got less tit than ol' Monkey features.' Skinny, reminded of the dead, would say: 'Cor, even that ol' Yvonne Sharpe'd 'ave tits boi now, oi betcha.'

We'd bicker about this sort of thing, but never at the real cause of all the mistrust between us. At school we led our separate lives until the murder brought us back together. When boys reached the fourth and fifth year they wanted to hear about it again; they were bigger boys with sisters who were fascinated by things horrible, especially during those wet dinnertimes when confined to classrooms under prefects. By then we'd nurtured exaggerated versions with which to entertain and excite the pilgrims who came to listen. We might have been a puppet show or story Tuck Shop. The progress of our sexual lives determined the scripts. As third years we began to accumulate a few rudimentary deeds both in and out of school. We'd grown new, curly hairs and split some in mutual discoveries on the white rims of school urinals. We thought we knew what shagging was. So the old, true story turned stale with time and at one point the sole remaining interest any of us had in it was the chance, which soon became fact, that Partridge 'musta shagged 'er first'. Boys would gather round as they would for a fight and the debate went on until the bell rang. But no one ever mentioned the bike except in passing, as being equally present as the sky that day. Nor was my significance attended to.

Then death also came our way from quarters other than Yvonne's. Cogger left the fourth year to join the Merchant Navy and was burned to death in a sea of blazing tanker oil off Panama. Norris had his head torn off at Cowden Cross where it landed thirty yards from his Royal Enfield. Babbidge died of gangrene and Butterworth cupped a discus to his brain while wandering unheeded in athletics. Besides these, Yvonne's became a baby's death; stationary, not caught in the act of adventure. None of us had been to school with Yvonne or even spoken to her. As if she hadn't noticed us either, our interest in her vanished. Then just before Daz moved to Paddock Wood he settled our matter in his own mind.

'Nah,' he said, 'Lily prob'ly fought 'e saw 'is own reflection. Thass enough t'scare anyone that is.'

Milky had left the fifth year and won an entrance to the Grammar. None of us had spoken to him in years. He wouldn't even look at us at school and you wouldn't know he'd still lived down Barratt's Road. But at last, like sleep, the very final term arrived.

Long jump practice. Thirty-a-side football at dinnertimes on the mowed fields. Dull cricket inter-house. Dull swotting for the CSE. By then I hated school and hated the moron teachers who had severed their connections with us years before, disinterested, victimized custodians. I went inside myself, split away from the others, and spent more time alone than ever I had before. All

Skinny and me had left in common was Barratt's Road. We'd hardly spoken to each other all year. Now we were to be boys for just a few weeks longer; life to come was suddenly undeniable and forced its way onto our faces. I'm sure we didn't know that we were really growing up this time, that all the signs were in place. I'd been to youth clubs a few times. Some of us had even fooled the doorman down Cranbrook flea-pit and got into *Virgin Soldiers*. Most of us had shoved at least one cold, chip-smirched hand down Jane Brewer's tit up the bus station bogs or round the back of the pavilion. Memory was a reminder of inexperience, so I tried to leave it alone. Skinny didn't. In the very last week of school he grabbed me in the playground, yanking at my shirt tail like a first year. He had a new theory of Little Nineveh based on a real-life experience shinning up the drainpipe outside his sister's window. She was going steady with Basil Latter, Partridge's shadow up the crossroads that Bank Holiday. Sundays were their day, when Skinny's mum and dad went up the cemetery.

' 'Ere, guess what oi saw Bazawl do to'er ven,' Skinny said.

I didn't wish to know, but other boys came like maggots round the meat.

'Wha'd 'e do then, Skin? Cummorn Fore-Skinny, wha'd 'e do, yer woman?' I pushed myself away from them. ' 'Ere, watch where you're treadin' Lily,' they said.

'Wha's wrong wiv 'im?' I heard Skinny ask.

'Take no notice of 'im, Skin. Sin eez self in the mirror mose loikly.'

'Yeah, 'e doan know nuffing.'

They were right too. I knew nothing and was fed up knowing nothing. It troubled me that I should even feel my ignorance and long for some method of expressing it. Until, that is, I thought of Milky White and realized that he must have felt the same and pushed himself into Grammar School because of it. His mind was looking after him.

And here was Skinny Wickham, I could still hear him, delving into childhood when childhood was over: '...Nah, listen, Partridge an' some bird huhuhuhuhuhuh, ged it? Whadyer fink? Ol' Gibbon an' Monkey, they musta come along wiv Yvonne all tied up, like ...nah, shuddup, I know, listen you lot...'

A week later Skinny was down the Labour Exchange and I went strawberry picking, blackcurrant picking, raspberry picking. My skin peeled raw week after week as I fidgeted through back-breaking rows like a locust, a piece-work failure earning £1.50 a day at my peak. I had not considered the purposes of education until then, neither had I questioned hierarchy and class or the social effects of Milky White from a council estate going to a fee-paying Grammar School with boarders whose fathers drove Bentleys and Jaguars and lived in massive houses up long driveways.

In the village they were soon saying I was an odd one. This doesn't take long to occur in villages, the moment they see you've broken with their ways. In many ways they likened me to the weirdos they'd picked on after Yvonne Sharpe's murder. In simple terms I hadn't found a job or saved up for a moped like Skinny. He thought I was weird because I didn't even want a moped. Instead, I jacked in fruit picking, grew my hair, took long slow walks in second-hand clothes, one book stuffed in a pocket, another open in my hand. I was abused by former playmates and pelted with mud pies by enemies who hadn't been my enemies for two years. I didn't trust anyone; I didn't want to talk with anyone. I hated seeing even the ghost of a smile on anybody's face. Milky didn't show himself all summer. If he had, I might have broached the subject, or formed my question . . .

Something I was able to consider as 'me' gradually emerged, dating from my estrangement with the football team. My name was posted on the list in the Draper's window. Evening training. I didn't turn up the first Wednesday and nothing was said. The following week the captain came round our house and asked me why I hadn't turned up again. Didn't I want to play for the team this year? Didn't I like football anymore? Keen on girls now, is it? I just said I didn't know but I'd turn up next week.

Training fell in two halves: an hour's physical, exercises, jog-ging round the pitch, press-ups, sprinting on the spot. Then the kickabout, which lasted half an hour. This particular Wednesday evening was sultry so I didn't bother going for the physical half, just the kickabout. The other players were fagged out, slow as donkeys. Puffing and so soaked in sweat they could hardly stand. I felt fresh and alive. The men had worked all day and Vic had trained them mercilessly. I'd slept half the afternoon so I ran rings round them, not making the slightest concession, delighted by their fury as I ball-hogged and outsprinted them, walloping goals and teasing them into falling over. I'd never felt so fit or brilliant, so convinced by illusion as fit men turned old before my influence. Of course it couldn't last and nearly came to blows when the captain grabbed me by the shirt and said who the hell did I think I bloody was? If I wasn't going to train like everyone else I could piss off. 'You ain' no law unto yerself, Cedric.'

But that was suddenly my point: I was a law unto myself, I had to be. Surely there could be no other way. I was so exhilarated by the discovery which had already helped me demolish eleven men single-handed that I shouted: 'Oh yes, I bloody am!'

For this I was dispensable of course, but I was reading poetry books by then and college was only a few weeks away. Education here we come.

It's a fact that if you're working class and your mind has separated you from the pack you are truly alone and your need of a language is greater than it would normally or can ever be. Likewise education. So before another year was out my hopes and energies collapsed because I aimed too high too quickly, over-sensitive and friendless among fellow students who'd been to public school. To compensate I changed my accent, exaggerated my abilities and poverty, acting out my loneliness and confusion as true artistic despair, a fraud among intellectual dead-beats who I treated to the same display I gave the footballers, with similar results. Soon, knowing less than before, my ignorance over-whelmed me. That Milky White, successfully eluding self-consciousness, would learn of my failure precipitated it and I dropped out at a time when dropping-out was considered subvers-ive and anti-bourgeois. It went unnoticed by everyone but two fed-up parents.

Milky left the village in quiet triumph. No one actually saw him leave, but the *Courier* printed a modest article: LOCAL BOY TO READ HISTORY. The photograph showed a scrupulous swot in his new university scarf: the first pupil from our boys' County Secondary Modern ever to gain a place in Higher Education. That autumn was like widowerhood. On the first day of Milky's university career I felt like nailing a wreath to his parents' front door. They didn't seem to realize we'd lost him. My jealousy became insomnia. The only books I read were detective novels, one after the other until I fell asleep, chain-reading. In a recurring nightmare Milky stood like a marble statue by a hedge, screaming so loud you can't hear it.

Chapter Two

Mr Lee-Lee lived in a tin bungalow under mvule trees in the compound of an up-country missionary school in East Africa. Every morning a boy called Kintu walked from his village in the bush to sweep my floors with a broom stump while I was in school. He stole my sugar, salt and dead batteries. He'd not been asked to enslave himself; I was powerless against his expectations to become houseboy, trained and fostered by priests. Morning school was Empire Made, teaching boys called Hyacinthe Burton and Winston Churchill correct elocuted delivery of 'Dover Beach' and 'The Hound of Heaven'. One daily duty was the confiscation of all Mills & Boons from girls with names like Faith, Hope and Charity. Mills & Boons were otherwise the sub-text for my lessons on *Wuthering Heights* so my duties were derelict. These were reclusive years when life, unchallenged, made sense. After other years in Italian cities, coming to Mbugazali healed many differences. This crumbling village once marked out for township by a railway was abandoned to swamp and forest by colonial bankruptcy. In such a place you don't falsify your nature for the social good. All that Italian passion for the moment. Ten-minute friendships you could poke a finger through. Mbugazali people didn't expect to be loved if you chose to live among them. Neither do they demand you try their ways until satiated and bored. At Mbugazali either nothing mattered or everything had equal importance, from the patching of mosquito nets to the monthly ration. So I was left alone as governments came and went. Some mornings when filling my bucket at the river, bodies floated by and the villagers said there'd been a revolution in the capital. Other mornings cigarettes were thirty quid a packet down the village duka. My only link with England was the BBC World Service, coming over short wave like mud from the bottom of a well. I shaved at monthly intervals and the minutes lasted an hour in the heat, but I kept healthy. My pupils died of malaria, tick fever, abortions or the half-cooked school meals. The best of these were mouldy beans which made everyone fart bad eggs through the mouth in class. Our students said I lived on ice-cream and chocolate flown specially from England. How could this be? I said. When does it come? Where do I keep it in this heat? I catch a fish for my evening meal. I eat matoke and beans for weeks on end like everyone else because we have no choice. They clap their desk lids and laugh. But, sir, how do you, a relative of the Queen of England and the Commonwealth eat matoke and beans?

Life at Mbugazali could have gone on and on. I might have died there happily if I hadn't written that first page, if it hadn't split open within me like an aneurysm or ruptured spleens do in other people. In fact I was genuinely horrified that it must have been there all the time, monitoring the system. I always thought Milky White would get it, not me. Same way you know that someone in your class is going to die in a car crash, drown in a river, kill themselves. It frightened me because it forced itself into consciousness, wanting life, blaming me for its silence the way I blamed Milky White for my former unhappiness.

I describe it medically because it begins with sickness. I even know the exact moment we exchanged blood. Falling asleep one afternoon on the verandah, a half-eaten mango rolled off my lap onto the concrete floor where sugar ants blackened it. An open book lay face down. The heat was like a rope twisted round my throat. Vervets clashed and swarmed through the trees stripping fruit and showering the tin roof with bark and cocoons. From a throbbing doze I awoke to see a mosquito settle on my arm, sink its proboscis into a vessel and drink, the way you'd watch a kid with a straw and milk bottle. Gorged, it rose slowly into the air and clung to a dark corner of the roof. I knew I'd been contaminated. Had it been a deliberate act of submission, to allow something vile into my life? Why hadn't I slapped it flat? I wish I could say it was a great moment.

A week later the first sign was a beating in my head like heavy rain on the hard earth. Within an hour I was feverish and sent for the school nurse. She diagnosed malaria and left me a few chloroquine in a twist of paper to see me through five days of delirium in stages.

My train of thought began with the idea that life was a wire you're attached to. Mine was a thousand miles long. I could reel out the coil inside me and discover how long I'd live. But perhaps I'd die because my death was at one end. So if I pulled the other way I'd discover who held it because somebody always holds your life in their hands. But the wire made a grid and there was warp and weft. Pulling one way upset the grid. The grid was the matrix. Little Nineveh. My strength had gone. Skin burning like oil on water. From inside the matrix in the next room it came, dragging itself across the floor day and night, drumskin-pounded eyeballs, blindfolds tightened by ratchets. Those last few inches nearly killed me. Dry scraping shadows hauled into the doorway. Got it. I collapsed back against the bed, my mouth a drought of scream as all that wire whipped and lashed about the room, gashing corners, gutting slits out the dark. Dawn revealed the born thing, this other person, the white marble statue of Milky White, mooncuts on his sharp face, the sound of scuttering lost-voice cockroaches in a cold mouth . . .

The nurse stood in the doorway, daylight flooding in behind her. She said I was alright now and shook her thermometer, smiling. You were shouting like a priest, she said.

My position at the school took on a new significance. The previous significance had never bothered me – the fact that I'd obtained the post with a forged degree. This hadn't even mattered. No one else had wanted the job: no foreign exchange, the country overrun by guerilla warfare, food in short supply, the school cut off for months by mud or lack of fuel or the power station blowing up. In fact I was the only applicant. There wasn't actually an advertised job. I simply made myself available when travelling through. The school's good fortune guaranteed me against procedure.

Convalescence meant living by a thread on two hours' sleep, closing my eyes on a snubbing candle just to impose conscious thought onto sound, like Milky turning into the dry slither of monitor lizards crawling over the roof. Weak, light-headed, I'd waste a whole box of dud African matches prolonging the candle life so I could stare blinded at the jumping shadows in the doorway. Pacing the bungalow was fruitless too, so I began to write these stammerings down, stripping time and begging for language like a tramp begs for meths, wishing I could pour it down the drain; only desire made me greedy, reckless, my simple world transgressed by another. So I begged for memory too as the stinking oil-lamps belched black smoke from bare rag wicks doused in paraffin and stuffed by a nail into a hole in a tin. This way, exhausted, I'd sleep at dawn and wake with the morning half over, the roof clanking me awake as the sun hit ninety. Nothing was said if I missed assembly, but then I missed first morning class three days on the trot and went back to bed instead of going to a staff meeting. The Headmaster decided to intervene at this point.

He was a priest from Yorkshire was Father Grimble. An unlikeable man after twenty-five years in the bush, a man of unholy pleasures he took great delight in sarcasm. His victims were Ugandan teachers, poor, hard-drinkers, barely shod, all terrified of being kicked out of a job with a house. They'd do and say anything for Grimble, the priest whom Idi Amin made a Corporal, gave a revolver. He clepped himself an intellectual, a hierophant, but in practice was nothing of the kind. He was ignorant, unhygienic, dictatorial and twisted. He'd always baited me but now he was like a wasp on a fallen apple. In staff meetings he was relentless without ever raising the actual matter or issuing a conduct warning. Instead he'd say things like: 'And how are the S6 progressing in *modern* literature, Mr Lily?' in his Spiritus Sanctum voice. He knew I wasn't teaching 'modern' literature. The A-Level syllabus was the work of priests and dead bodies in Oxford, dominated by Shakespeare and Dickens. *Wuthering Heights* was the other novel, Shaw the 'modern' playwright. Against Grimble's principles I began teaching the African option: Nigerian novelists, Senegalese poets, South African playwrights. We read Ngugi's *Petals of Blood* as central to my project on Imperialism. I obtained the keys to the book room and discovered an African literature dump moulding in a dark corner. Piles of Okot p'Bitek and V. S. Naipaul invaded by scorpions. My S6 became a radical forum overnight. Its notoriety spread throughout the school. Fuelled by Grimble's sarcasm English literature became the target for our 'new reading classes'. Marxist criticism, the ideology of Church and State in the literature promoted in Africa by the British Council and the A-Level Board. With his Presidential connections Grimble was nervous. Anti-Obote Marxist guerillas were operating not twenty miles from Mbugazali. Then one of my S6 boys ran away to join them. Grimble was out of his depth but planning. I was about to answer one of his sarcastic S6 enquiries when he put his spectacles on as usual and said, leaning forward for a closer inspection: 'Would you mind my asking you a personal question, Mr Lily? Are you growing a beard?'

The rest of the staff stared at their broken sandals made from old car tyres. 'No,' I said.

'Then I request you shave, Mr Lily. Your, uhm, stubble . . . has the effect of lowering morale, hmmmmm? Morale is the missing link at Mbugazali, among other things like Godliness.'

'And razor blades,' I added which at least raised a titter from some teachers. But seeing Grimble's expression I sensed I'd gone too far. That evening he sent his boy round with an invitation to dine at the Headmaster's table. When I arrived he castigated me over my lateness and ordered my apologies to other teachers present. I said I'd come within five minutes of receiving his invitation, so he pretended on my behalf to humiliate his houseboy in front of us, accusing him of failing in duty. My defence of the houseboy rendered the meal a silent one. We chacked on the slop from twelve tins of out-of-date Red Cross baby-food served cold over yesterday's potatoes.

In the morning I was woken by the school secretary banging in panic on the door. Grimble's note requested my immediate presence at assembly. I asked Tinka to wait but he hurried away saying, 'Oh, oh, Father is angry.' I didn't bother with finding socks. I simply threw a shirt and trousers on and shoved smelly feet into canvas shoes. Tinka limped badly so I managed to catch him up. 'Oh,' he wailed, 'Father is so angry he has made a special announcement. It is a *decree*.'

Assemblies were outside in the quadrangle, staff one side of the flagpole, students opposite. A thousand sulking faces, Father Grimble in the middle, his sheeny black vestments caught the early sun on worn surfaces. As I took my place behind him he looked over his spectacles and down his nose.

'I demand *so* little of my expatriate staff that I am considerably hurt when they fail to display their courtesy by inappropriate dress.'

The focal point of this assembly was the plume of smoke rising from a pile of books in the centre of the quadrangle. Thirty rows of eyes popped up at the end of prayers, not for the cultural loss but the price they'd have fetched down the market in Jinja. Grimble kept his eyes shut during a particularly extended 'Amen' pause, snapping to and jumping us. 'Now listen to me, please,' but unexpectedly his languid, hooded-eye voice glanced over the shoulder to make certain I was listening.

'All of you, please.' Raised eyebrows dropped like guillotines. He stepped forward to poke the flames with the stick he used to beat his dog. 'The deplorable condition of the book room has been most kindly brought to my attention. I need hardly remind you that hygiene, so to speak, is a state of mind, hmmmmm? Certain seniors are in arrears, under the influence, I am sorry to report. I intend to ROOT IT OUT. There are causes of diseases, and with your co-operation there are cures, yes? Is your co-operation too much to expect, hmmm? Well, is it?'

'No, Father.'

'I do not hear *all* of you.'

'NO, FAAAAATHERRRR.'

'Better. I blame myself of course, hmmm? I have always stood aside to allow for the inroads of a liberal education. But, *Nemo mortalium omnibus horis sapit*, hmmm? I have been reminded that your spiritual welfare is incumbent upon me. My task commences. A number of books have also been removed from the library . . . '

He pointed with his stick as flames opened pages and whole passages detached themselves, whorling over the quadrangle, escaping into the air like wounded birds. He unfolded a sheet of paper and fiddled with his spectacles, which hung from his neck on knicker elastic. After separating stick, elastic and paper, he quoted Scripture, read the Law, and said 'Woe betide any of us who mixed politics and education'. Then he recited his list of banned authors in his daily penalties voice. My bibliography of course. The burning of African books angered me most. I nursed the anger until he announced me responsible for collecting and disposing of all remaining copies. On the chair beside him was the Bible presented at his ordination. I stepped forward, opened it and threw it face down into the fiercest flames. Some girls in the front row screamed, others clapped. Two S6 boys cheered. Father Grimble was rooted in silence. The school watchman rushed forward and flung himself upon the burning Bible. A teacher dragged him off and doused his smouldering trouser leg with tea. Grimble raised his voice above the crackling Bible and added my name to his list of forbidden authors.

Half an hour later Tinka knocked on my door as I was packing. He'd booked a seat for me on the next flight to London.

Chapter Three

It was snowing a blizzard at Heathrow and under these conditions one place seemed as bad as another so I stayed in London. Sam's address in Hackney proved fruitless. Sam was a traveller I'd met in Africa, but, after ten minutes hammering on the door, a woman stuck her head out the upstairs window and said he'd moved without trace two years ago. Gone to Africa, she thought. I had no winter clothes and London was one place I'd never been. All I owned was in a rucksack. My life had emptied like a bucket of slops down a drain. You just feel like closing your eyes until something happened.

In Mare Street I found a dingy Bed and Breakfast. My Ugandan bank draft didn't bounce so I had two hundred quid to find a bedsit with. Two days before Christmas I moved into a dirt-cheap freezing scum-hole of a bedsit in Shoreditch. There were mice in the grillpan and the wallpaper came away in soggy lumps if you pulled at it. I counted two hundred and seven empty miniature gin bottles in the wardrobe and found the TV Times for the last fifteen years in the shower cupboard. Coming home from a café on Christmas Eve I found my door kicked in and the fridge gone, my milk, cheese and eggs with it. Christmas Day was spent wrapped in a blanket with a runny nose staring at my new life through the one blackened window; a sheeny, rubbish tipped, ill-lit street, one pub and a murderer's railway arch.

It wasn't long before Desmond, who lived in the room below, came to my threshold. His door had been kicked in so many times I'd already glimpsed him through the permanent three-inch split, sitting on his crummy bed wearing headphones, drinking a mug of tea with his eyes shut, an art book of English landscapes propped open against the wall. He tapped on my door late evening on New Year's Eve, smelling of beefburgers and nylon-shirt sweat. His flared trousers were fastened with a safety-pin and his stomach bulged over the waistband. About my age, Desmond looked friendless to the core like he must have washed his hair in cooking fat and shaved with a breadknife. He introduced himself with his foot against the door, nodding and cocking his head back down the dark passage. 'Having a knees up on me own,' he said. 'Fancy comin' down?' With a throat full of snot he kept snoring to clear it, taking deep breaths like a hiker in mountain air. When I didn't answer he tried to peer inside my room.

'Not shacked up tonight, are yer? Not going to a party then?'

I said I wasn't so he said, 'Oh right then,' and clapped his hands in settlement. 'I've got a nice bottle of the ol' dago vino. Good film on.'

This was a language I'd forgotten and my face twitched with embarrassment, but I managed to stutter that after ten years abroad I was not exactly top of the London guest list. He was not interested in the slightest, so I said I might as well because my room was cold, the noise from the pub drove me stupid and my shortwave radio had packed in.

'Yeah-yeah,' he said. 'I know who wogged yer fridge too,' he whispered on the stairs.

His room stank, the walls streamed and there were dinner plates congealed in a stack on the only armchair. 'Me ol' man's armchair,' he said, 'but works for sitting on.' He lowered the plates to the floor and threw me a pouch of tobacco after I'd picked bacon rind or dried-up lobworm off the cushion.

'Burn chum? Fag-a-rooney?' he asked. 'Go on, yer c'n roll a joint if you like, I'm Baron tonight. Dope's inside, like.'

'I don't smoke dope,' I said, handing it back.

'Jesus,' he said, 'how dyer get lifted out, then?'

He swivelled the television my way and lay on his bed. We watched a western, stupefied but warm. I had to pull my jumpers off while Desmond sweated huge rings under both armpits on account of the three electric fires he'd switched on.

'Used to be me ol' man's room this,' he said during the adverts.

'These are his shirts I'm wearing too. Drunk himself to death in here, the ol' man did. Silly bastard couldn't take it after me mum pegged it.' I just kept nodding, then the film resumed and he shut up till the next bunch of insane adverts.

'She died of jaundice, see. In Birmingham. 'S where we lived. Got bitten by a patient in the home where she did the dinners for thirty years. Can you believe it? What a way to go! Bitten by a spastic, shit! I'm suing the Health Authority for ten grand but they said no way. Should get her pension though, the bass-tards . . . '

Now and then my eyes would wander in fascination round the room. Wasoga in mud huts lived cleaner lives than he did. At one point I was looking at the door for no particular reason when Desmond caught me. 'Oh that,' he said. 'They kicked it in after the ol' man choked . . . huh, six days after he choked. Took his room after the funeral, didn't I. Always fancied London. Been here five years now.'

There were two easels in the corner. On one a half-finished still life. On the other he'd copied a postcard scene of a Scottish glen. The still life was arranged on a table in an overturned cutaway grocery box like a toy theatre. A tea cup, a plastic rose and a leather-bound prayer book on a white cloth. He said he painted in the mornings and busked down the tubes of an afternoon. 'No light in the afternoons. Course I sign on too. Good dodge that. Have to keep an eye out though. Fuckin' dole supervisor came by once an' give me 5p, the cunt. Didn't recognise me did 'e. Either that or I was singing 'is tune: Hey big suspender! YEAH! Loads o' money. Look!' He undid his shirt to reveal a T-shirt with Loads-a-money written on it.

I hardly said a word but I don't think he expected me to.

Midnight came. He opened his bottle of sweet, sparkling perry and we toasted out the old year, then Desmond yanked his guitar out from under the bed and sang 'Auld Lang Syne' like a Mississippi Blues number. He was very good at this. I continued to fill a saucer with dog-ends.

'Oh well,' he said, 'another fucking year up the drainpipe and down the sewer. Know what me resolution is? Get the door fixed and marry a rich widow. Won't get the door fixed, I know that much. What's yawn?' I hadn't meant to tell him my resolution, but I suppose that by saying it aloud I made it real and created a relationship with it, an attitude towards it now it had a witness, an existence. 'My resolution', I said, 'was to finish something I'd started writing'. I regretted saying so immediately because Desmond probed and picked at me but got nowhere.

'Come on, what's it about? It must be about something? How can you write a book and not know what it's about unless you're Samuel fuckin' Beckett?'

In the end he gave up and confessed his interest was because he'd written a book and wanted to see if I'd stolen his idea because he couldn't find his manuscript. He began hunting in the cupboard again but it was fruitless. 'I lended it to me sister once. She's probably still got it.'

'Well, what's it about then?' I asked, more sarcastic than interested.

'Oh well, I tell yer it was fuckin' brilliant. Get this, right? This bloke, he's the only bloke in the world what really knows, I mean KNOWS about the fourth dimension . . . '

His activation of the plot continued for two hours until at five in the morning I crawled back to my room knowing that if I had any sense I'd pack my rucksack and move elsewhere and apply for a VSO posting back to Africa. So I have to admit I relied on Desmond that winter. My life at the time needed someone in it, someone I had no feelings for. It was essential to hold no illusions about people, to know exactly what they were and where you stood with them. In this sense Desmond was perfect.

The New Year began with three days of chill drizzle and Desmond helped me through the intricacies of the DHSS. After twelve years away I didn't even consider finding a job. This would have meant admitting a certain permanency into my life at the time, drawing attention to myself as a human being in need of an employer. Unemployed, I remained anonymous, ready to move on (my only hope, or back) when I decided, without anyone but Desmond and the VSO knowing. It was vital I remained untouched by the life around me, inpenetrable, undrawn, like a winter bulb under frozen earth. Desmond was the perfect darkness through which no light shone. My hard earth. He had no inclination to see me prosper, nor any spare life he wished to introduce me to. It was in his interest that I remained as dead as I'd become, a deadness he couldn't see I was wholly conscious of. He didn't like me, and that was essential too because I couldn't have remained there otherwise. He daren't lose me either as I was his only companion, a fact which made him dislike me even more than he did others. Before I went to London I'd always found it preferable, usually imperative, to have no friends at all rather than just one single good friend whom you end up hating for being your only friend. Under these circumstances me and Desmond were able to sit in each other's rooms fairly often, saying little at times. In Desmond's room I'd flick through art books while he painted, putting up with him saying: 'Put the kettle on, moosh.' I was always an unsatisfactory companion in any case. 'Don't give much away, do yer?' he'd say. 'Don't get much per gallon do we, eh?'

His problem was that his girlfriend Fay had chucked him. He'd only come to London because of her. She was a nurse. In a rare moment of insight, Desmond told me that she hadn't chucked him because of the way he lived. 'I wasn't a slob then, you know. Ohhh, she's bea-u-tiful. I did my best for that girl. It was afterwards the trouble started. Hey, that's when I wrote me book I told you about. Yeah . . . never thought of that before.'

Then he looked at me and thought he understood.

'Who *is* she then?' he asked, dancing on the bed.

After this he never believed a word I said. Everything I'd done was due to 'the mystery woman'.

'Don't worry, I know what it's like. Hits some of us right here,' he said, thumping his heart. 'Just look at me. Still not over it. Bit like the ol' man in that respect, God rest his bollocks.'

Ours was a relationship which couldn't endure beyond winter. It was too derelict, barren and dark. As soon as the spring light flooded London we left our rooms simultaneously and spent our time elsewhere. I sat in the park reading once more and everything lifted at once. What I'd written seemed cramped and incomplete so I rewrote it. Once or twice I met Desmond coming down the stairs on his way out, clean shirt, haircut, squirting mint deodorant into his mouth, whistling or pretending to chew gum.

'How's it going?' he'd say, walking off down the middle of the road admiring his shoes.

One evening I came back after dark and noticed a blanket stuffed in the split in Desmond's door. His bed was creaking and I heard a woman's voice: 'Ugh, that's cold. Lick it off, will yer Dez, for fuck's sake.' 'I'm going to,' he said. 'That's the idea, innit?'

In my room that evening I conceived the idea. Life could be guided by writing up the scene as it occurred. And then I decided I had to move once I'd discovered where Milky White was living. That was all. I made no real connection between the two thoughts, content to imagine Milky's present life while occupied with writing about him during May. Then a letter from my parents arrived, in reply to a spring card of mine which informed them of my whereabouts. They intended to visit me at two o'clock on the afternoon of my thirty-second birthday.

It was a terrible day when it came, heat like a dirt storm, flat, sultry, choking air, the London sky heavy with the scent of brewery and factory, every pore of skin clogged in grains of sweat. Eighteen hours of dust, dry June greylight. Restless all morning fretting over their visit, I hadn't seen them for twelve years. Whatever they thought I'd become there was nothing I could do to prepare them for their disappointment. Appearances meant everything to them and they had always judged the moment at hand.

By dinnertime I was shoving my body round the streets, trying to make it walk, hoping to draw strength for the afternoon. But in England there is little you can do to protect yourself against the emotional embalming done by parents, especially in a new era of radical conservatism. What I saw around me increased my gloom. Steam pipes hissing from windows among the terraced houses, where Turks heaved bundles of cheap labour sweat-shop jackets

into vans from Oxford Street department stores. KARHOLSUN FAC-
IST DIKTATÖRLÜK scrawled in red paint along the walls. The surrounding streets were paved in bronchial gob and dogshit, with
white Golf convertibles parked outside the new jacuzzi parlours,
plastic phone-cards littered the gutters, and I couldn't understand
a word of what passed for communication. To me London
sounded like a cry of pain at the speed of light.

I paced the room listening for the doorbell but heard my name
thick as a plume of smoke shouted in the air. Some people, it's
said, bring the weather with them. My parents carried claustro-
phobia.

When I opened the door I was surprised to see the street because
my father's voice had re-created in one deep instant the room in
which I'd most heard it calling me. So I expected to see him swivel
his orange chair round like a gunner taking bearings. Instead he
was standing in the road looking up at the windows.

'Why didn't you ring the bell?' I asked.

'You heard me, didn't you?' he said.

He pointed his big finger at the car, at my mother who sat with
her window still wound tight, a suppressed smile rubbing over her
teeth.

'Aren't you coming in?' I asked.

'Yer ma doesn't want to,' he said. 'You c'n come and sit in the
car.'

Several important things took place that afternoon, conscious
links in the chain of events. As I stepped into the car with them I
realized I could only face the tension of the event by fictionalizing
it as objective/subjective opposition, a live novel. For the same
reason that policemen arrest suspects at six in the morning, my
father bunged me into the back of his stuffy two-door car where
I'd be their version of *son*, according to their creation of our pasts.
If I could not step outside of our combined thoughts, they would
distort my intentions, my circuit of memory. The problem was that
for a year I had been wholly concerned with my own version of the
past, one in which my parents were denied a point of view. The
meeting had therefore become a test, the first ordeal that my
writing had to endure in its struggle for a subjective existence; its
first confrontation with any of its original characters, as opposed

to those like Desmond who come into contact like insects against a car windscreen.

I began by observing details with a detective's fascination. I saw that I had neither of my parents' looks: my father's bacon ears and thin flat hair, eyes too far apart tightening into grey strips like buds which never catch the sun, large pitted nose like a fist showing through a thin sock. His mouth had one passionate and one mean lip. His brown polyester blazer was done up with flat, gold tin buttons and his legs were almost bandy. After twenty years he was still a traveller in plastic gutter and waste fittings with the same firm. I thought my own looks had probably formed for other reasons – a thin face on a long neck, eyes darkened and sunk by years in Africa. My looks now were, if anything, bookish and peaky, the kind of thing aunts always said, but even though there was no doubt I was almost unrecognizable as the boy who'd left England, another look at my father and a close scrutiny of my mother via the driver's mirror revealed my physiognomy as an amalgam of theirs. In any case, they'd recognized me without hysteria.

My mother was still big-boned with a mouth the size of a letter box. Scone-faced, hair permed into a monthly fleece, she even sat three inches taller than her husband, bag-eyed, stern, always farting at inappropriate or emotional moments. She called me the family rasher from the moment I was born.

'Well then, boy?' she said.

'Well what?' I answered.

'Are we alright then?'

'I'm perfectly alright. Why shouldn't I be?' I said, because I could see her disapproval, the way she'd wound the window down and sniffed. I'd even put on a tie and my tropical flannels but they'd gone unnoticed. It was the filthy street and the disreputable building which they'd found me in. They didn't need to ask me what I did for a living. I began to weaken already, probably due to the car, the way they made it smell like all their cars – airless, mothballs, the cheapest Yardley. They'd pulled in somewhere on the way up too, for a fag and a cup of tea from the Thermos.

'What d'yer mean: *why shouldn't I be?*' my father said, irritated.

In the same breath he passed his blazer over and told me to put it on the back seat and pass him the *Daily Express* which he flipped through until with a grunt of satisfaction he found what he sought. My mother asked me over her shoulder what I'd been doing since Christmas and I said nothing much.

'Can't yer get a job?' they both said.

It was as if I'd been nowhere and done nothing. Twelve years had not passed in the world. I'd simply gone upstairs to my bedroom and come down again twelve minutes later to find them still sitting in the front room.

'There!' my father said, handing me the paper, 'read *that!*' They'd never been abroad. Once a year they went to a guest-house in Truro where my mother had a sister married to a dustman she'd met in the war. The *Daily Express* informed me that Hackney was Britain's poorest borough, had the highest crime rate in the land, the most unemployed, the highest population of immigrants . . .

'So what?' I said, and my father began to dogmatize about doing better for myself, how ashamed they'd been that I hadn't come home, and what on earth did I expect them to tell people when they asked about me? Didn't I know how to behave yet?

'What do you know about anything?' I said. 'You haven't been anywhere or done anything; you've only read two books in your whole bloody life and they were Westerns . . . '

'Don't think you're past a clip round the ear, my lad,' he said, then my mother intervened, bringing down the silence. I could have closed my eyes and gone to sleep in a second, sucked dry, and never felt so alone. Years in the African bush were nothing to one minute in the back of the car with my parents. My mother restored a moment's peace by unclasping her handbag and lighting a cigarette from the dashboard gadget. She wound the window down an inch, fiddling with the ashtray.

'D'yer still smoke then, boy?' she asked.

'No,' I lied, dying for a fag.

My father had returned to his paper. My mother blew smoke as hygienically as possible through the one-inch gap. I undid my tie and heard the slow tock of the mantle clock above the fireplace down Barratt's Road.

'Wanna cuppa cha, Cedric?' my father asked at one point.

'There's cow-juice in the basket there, under the flask. Have a cow-cumber san'widge, goo on.'

'Good Gaaawwwwd,' my mother kept exclaiming when anyone passed by, 'look at the state o' that!'

It was my father who finally caused that moment of transgression I'd allowed for. He asked me what I intended doing with myself. I looked him firmly in the back of the head and said: 'I'm writing a book.' We were all suddenly frightened, like we were driving in that car and an oncoming vehicle swerved into our path. I wanted to escape but I'd have to climb over them and wrestle for the door handle. After all, I was the boy, whatever their version of the past omitted or contained, who'd stood before the assembled villagers and coroner and given evidence which not only sent a murderer to prison for life but linked me with this murderer. Supposing, they must have wondered, he still remembered that? 'Whatyer mean writing a book? What sort of book've you got to write about?'

Down Little Nineveh when I'd been ten, I'd imagined a time like this, when I'd tell them I'd been nicking stuff from shops for yonks, that since I'd found somewhere trespassed to hide it I'd become ambitious, daring and greedy. I'd imagined in great detail their shame and anger, their lifelong secret fear and awe that I could be capable of this. And at the same time I rehearsed smashing up my mother's collection of sacred glass and china cows just to see her face when she came in from Christmas shopping and saw what I'd done. Then my father would come home from work after a cold, trying day among his worst customers only to find the matchstick models he'd spent every evening for twelve years making were matches once more, piled upon the tea table . . . I tried to remember all the things I'd nicked that were still, to that day most likely, buried under the fallen leaves down Little Nineveh. The worst thing had been the Missionary Box from the chip shop – and Bluebird of course, but only Partridge knew this. The idea seemed fantastic. Would he remember me? What would they say in the village? Was I not in the process of admission? And to whom, Partridge or Milky White?

I think my father really knew I'd been a thief and a liar. This was what must have worried him about me writing a book. The fact is, knowing I'd sent this man to jail for life, my father still accused me of a crime I hadn't committed. Aged sixteen, I was experimenting with stuff you could get a buzz with from smoking, like cinammon, nutmeg, bay leaves, banana skin, only to puke it or get a splitting headache. I shoved a pouch full of the dried remains of my 'boy's' drugs under my clothes in a drawer, plus Rizlas, matches and joss sticks, only to forget about it. A month later my mother found the pouch while cleaning. My father accused me of being on drugs. I didn't see the point of denying it, certainly not after he said, 'Don't bother to lie, I can read you like a book, Cedric.' So I admitted it and he phoned the police, making me stand beside him while he said, 'I want you to arrest my son on drugs charges. Will you do that?' When they evidently refused or asked awkward questions he slammed the phone down in a temper without giving our names. Then he made me go outside into the road with him as he went from drain to drain till he found a good deep one. He handed me the pouch. 'Goo on. Drop it in.' To this day he still believes he caught a drug addict, though the matter, like all matters, was never referred to again. We must have hated each other very much.

Now my mother broke the silence in which she'd remembered these things too, with her own anxiety.

'Whatyer wanna be wasting yer time writin' for, son?'

I felt I'd just woken up but another dream was taking place. My father said he had a splitting headache. I could see their thoughts like pictures on the windscreen, the way home, best be getting back. My eyes opened, a voice rose in my throat.

'D'you ever hear much about Milky White these days?' it said. 'I just wondered where he lived, that's all. Don't you see his mum up the shops or anything?'

My mother was astonished. She said Milky White's mother worked in the butcher's, if that's what I meant. And what would they have to talk about 'cept the price of them fatty chops that butcher sells? As for Milky White, well, he was a stuck-up little twerp whose father always thought the world of him and still did for all she knew, or cared.

'Alright, alright,' I said. 'Blimey, keep yer hair on.'

My father said you ought to give him his due. He'd done well for himself, you have to admit that. My mother grunted and stubbed her cigarette out, wiping her fingers with a handkerchief.

'Yerse, I suppose so. Works in some museum, doesn' 'e? I seem to remember readin' somethin' about it in the *Courier* recently.'

My father said he hadn't the foggiest. 'Oh, might yer go and see him then, Cedric?'

'Whatever's 'e wanna do that for, father?' My mother snapped her handbag shut, catching her handkerchief by the tail. 'Never did you any good, did 'e?', addressed to me, I assumed.

'Well, if you must know,' I said, 'I'm writing something which concerns him as much as it does me. That's all. The first bit's about that Little Nineveh business. You remember that, don't you?'

Their head-backs said nothing. My father put the keys into the ignition.

'Well?' I proceeded. 'Do you?' I imagined them driving off with me still in the car. My mother made a loud fart and shifted about the seat. My father asked for his blazer, opening the door and stepping outside to put it on, the headache in his mouth now. 'You've no cause draggin' that muck up, Cedric. Yer've upset yer mother now.' Her lips began to smack as she sucked a mint.

'Now yer've upset yer father,' she said. 'There's no need to go upsettin' yer father after he's drove all this way up to this . . . this Black Hole of Britain.'

I was still trapped in the car because my father resumed his seat, dabbing himself with a folded handkerchief, opening his wallet, my mother opening her handbag simultaneously. By now the shirt stuck to my back and my mouth was dry.

'Get enough to eat, do you?' she asked.

'Course I do.' We were our normal selves again. My father cleaned out a dirty nostril with his handkerchief then put his fingers in the wallet.

'Well, 'e y'are then Cedric. Happy Birfd'y.'

It was a five-pound note. 'I 'spect yer ma'll give yer one too if y'ask 'er.'

It was already there, in her purse, also folded like the other, two brand-new fivers with consecutive serial numbers.

' 'E y'are then, boy, 'Appy Birfday.' It was like a puppet show for the Sunday School treat.

A minute later I stood on the pavement and watched them drive away, my relief the most intense I'd ever experienced. Everything the village represented was encapsulated in that car. And there they went, taking it away with them again. Too late, disappointed, I'd failed to penetrate it in my self-protection. I clutched at the five-pound notes, hearing my father's grudging toot on the horn, watching my mother's sullen wave. Gone, back to each other. So Chapter Three closes as I trudge upstairs past Desmond's sealed door, thinking of museums and old Milky sealing up the past quick as he could knowing I was after it.

Chapter Four

There was a flat blue sky the morning Milky White first came to Barratt's Road, first week of the summer holidays when me, Daz, Skinny, Dodge Smiff and Dennis Packham were bored to death, perched on the wall and drumming it with our heels, flinging stones against the kerb, scratching SHIT in the brick with the sharpest ones. By elevenses our mothers had their feet up with cups of tea and Woodbines, lines sagging while the washing dripped, Skinny's mother first to roll her stockings down. We gobbed on passing ants, the bubbles popped and dried on a hot pavement. It would soon be flippin' hotter. Back gardens white with butterflies on cabbages as we waited for the flying ants to rise from nesting-cracks between the kerbstones, each suggestion leading into argument.

'We could git some worms an' go darn Feobalds. Caught masses o'roach lars' toime, di'n we?'

'You never, Skinny. Anycase, you said you 'adn' got no 'ooks left an' you still owe me 'alf a dozen o'them Mustards . . .'

Skinny walked to the corner to see if there were any bloomers on Edna Haunt's clothes line.

' 'Ere, you lot!' he shouted, pointing up the road, 'removal lorry!'

We jumped off the wall prepared to run after it, either down the hill as far as the pond or up one of the cul-de-sacs, but Daz said what we all knew: 'Oany firty-nine's empty.' He was right because it turned our way, shifting gears and stopping at our feet.

'Bliiii-mey.'

Huge and old green, dented by low bridges, it was the size of a whole house. BARNEY & SONS MAIDSTONE. We perked up and looked for boys among the newcomers. They came up behind in a black Humber Hawk, emerging like cubs into the wild, one about our age, one a squirt and a sister, who didn't count. We swaggered for their benefit, if swaggering means three-foot dribble or lobbing handfuls of gritshot on the lorry roof; for we were eleven, we were nearly at Secondary Modern, where big boys sprouted whiskers on their lip. We rearranged ourselves upon the wall for an all-round show. The path sloped upwards behind us; thus the wall rose higher, high as the lorry, to the empty house at the top, number thirty-nine. They all went up there as the men began to open the lorry doors, so we stayed and there it was: these newcomers' sitting room as it must have been in real life, all ready to sit and read comics in.

The oldest boy came down first to cart his own belongings up the path. He wouldn't let the men touch them. Under one arm a remote-controlled boat, under the other a big Scalectrix set. We forgave him that, you had to show something off, but this boy swamped us. Up and down he came and went, like a moving toyshop at Christmas – Dan Dare Radio Set, fibreglass fishing rod, air gun, boxing gloves, telescope and more and more, all preserved like new.

'Blinkin' big 'ead,' Dennis said, gobbing in the dust and rubbing it in with his plimsole.

The boy was back again, clapping dust from his hands, an upright soft-treading boy, his lips compressed with purpose, his face not one of our faces. We didn't bother disguising our contempt as wonder when he wheeled his bike out, the perfect bicycle; like a girl's first pony, he led it from the lorry and down the ramp. Light blue and turquoise, white saddle, white-walled tyres, 3-speed twist grip gears, white rubber pedals with reflectors. Its sober handlebars were for steering on straight, clean roads. Its mudguards knew no mud. Dennis had a tracker made from bits off the dump. Daz had a chopper with cow horns and one brake. 'Namby pamby,' they said.

'Andy Pandy more loike,' Skinny said, whose bike had one pram wheel and you stopped it with the hole in your shoe bottoms, and we laughed just as the boy's dad came down to the lorry to give orders. He sounded just like all our dads, so we thought they must have won the pools.

'I dunno,' Dodge said, whose bike was even worse than Skinny's, as the removal men put a washing-machine on the trolley, 'we got one o'vem washin'-machines. Come out the ca'alogue.'

'Fuckin twit you are Smiff,' Dennis said. 'Yer doan git fings out ca'alogues if yer won va palls, yer buy 'em.'

When the lorry was empty and the beds in their rooms, the man stood with his eldest son by their new front gate. 'Those boys look your age, Melvyn,' we heard him say. 'Goo on an' make friends with them.' Melvyn. We didn't think much of that name and smirked. Melvyn pouted, but his dad held the gate open, fiddled with the catch and said he'd better fetch the lubricant and toolbag.

' 'Ere comes Mouw-vyn,' Skinny said. We pretended to ignore his coming, all but Dennis, who did ignore him by eyeing the kerbstones closely.

' 'Ere-curmes the jurdge, 'ere-curmes the jurdge. Righdy-righdy righdy-righdy 'ere-curmes the jurdge,' Daz chanted in a yankee neck hoarse drawl. The judge was upon us, his jeans like trousers pressed to a knife edge, checked shirt glimmering, his baseball boots just out of tissue paper, his walk straight-foot perfect, coming to rest like a knitting-pattern boy, that hair combed into waves and corrugations you could stand a model ship on. There were even little daisy fields of freckles either side of his snub-snob nose, but his mouth was set hard for the ordeal he could see we meant it to be. We looked sideways now, acting jealous, bored and sullen, our ears like open traps set to catch his span-new words which blinked at us. The words of a boy whose father has ideas for him and tells him always mind your words when all our dads tell us is wash yer mouth out with soap and spit be'ind yer wick.

'Do you live down this road?' he pronounced, but he sounded

council house nonetheless to us detectives. Dennis reacted biggest. He sniffed and passed his fists under his nose making it sound like a boxing match.

'Woul'n be si'n 'ere if we didn', would we, yer twit,?' he said, rubbing his palms together, making cat-kits into sausages two inches long because he never washed his hands. A BEA Trident flew south overhead, common as sparrows in those days so we looked up at it in silence till the sun bled our eyes. Melvyn took our silence for ignorance and saw his big chance with words. 'That's a VC10,' he said.

'Bollocks,' I said.

Skinny got nervous and jumped down off the wall. 'Ow, me poor feet. 'Ere, show yer where the field is, mate?'

Melvyn nodded and we went with them, following in a single line behind as if the school bell had pealed the end of break, reluctant, a creeping dustcloud which had no wind to shift it. From the corner Skinny pointed up the road too eagerly as if our Mouw-vyn might evaporate before we got there. 'See where vat gate is? Thass the fild. Use-ter be an 'ouse vair once, di'n vair, Daz?'

Dennis made the same mistake. 'Gelz 'in allowed in va fild . . . '

'Oo you callin' a gel, Packham?'

'Not chew, Skin. 'Im! Vat big twerp!' Dennis said, jerking a grubby thumb half-nailed at Melvyn.

The fight took place beside our marbles hole under old bag Aida's hedge. Dennis never stood a chance. He even looked defeated, the way his bum stuck out the back pocket of his hand-me-downs, the soles of his Empire Made plimsoles flapping like a pair of jaws, his dish-cloth T-shirt blobbed with dropped baked beans. Sure he was twelve, but so was Melvyn who didn't flinch at the challenge, just stepped forward and squared his fists with a military precision learned from his dad at the punch bag. Yes, Melvyn boxed. Dennis stoached like a cow in mud, trying to yank his hair and kick him in the arse till Melvyn one-two'd him nose and guts and tipped him up. Dennis slobbered like a bulldog and Melvyn, with distaste, without gloves or groundsheet, knelt on Den's tit and banged his head up and down on the marbles hole.

'Submit? Submit, you great oaf?'

'Year, yer bastard . . . su'mit . . . ' His handkerchief was a ripped square of old bedsheet, two twisted ends of which he screwed into his bloody nostrils. Melvyn brushed Dennis-matter from his person with clean hands swiped red at the knuckles.

'Mummy's boy,' Dennis said in a funny voice. 'Getcha nex' toime, yer cun'.'

'I'm not scared of you,' Melvyn said. 'You're licked.'

'I'm not scared o'you neever,' Dennis shouted back all the way from his front gate as Melvyn did a dummy run after him.

'Jump in the lake, you fat dunce,' Melvyn shouted.

So then we stood picking Aida's hedge as Melvyn looked up and down the road and round at the houses. Dodge said no one had beat up Dennis before. Skinny said he'd never seen no one smack no one on the nose like that. 'Whass yer names?' I asked him.

'Melvyn White,' you said, looking through me when I said I was called Sedge. I was suddenly very sorry for Dennis. We all were then, and this was the beginning, Melvyn White, of our hatred of you.

That same afternoon you refused to let us ever have a go with any of your things. You wouldn't even bring them out to show us, saying if we'd seen them come out the lorry we didn't need to see them again. You weren't the slightest bit interested in our things, so we took you down the pond, our half-acre paradise. 'There's tench an' roach,' we said, pointing through the scum and oil slicks into its few stinking feet of green water. We loved our pond, its rats and stunted fishes, moggies, frogs and sticklebacks.

'Whaddya fink?' we asked, genuinely hoping your clever tackle might hook its best.

'It's just an old dump,' you said. 'Christ, I've fished in bigger puddles than this dirty old rat-hole. Look, it's full of old prams.'

'So what?' I said, not bothering to tell you about the sunken car.

'Well,' you said, '*I'm* not fishing here for a start. I bet it's full of disease. I can fish in Moat Park Lake, Maidstone, whenever I want. It's over a mile long . . . '

You weren't even a seven-day wonder. By teatime even Skinny loathed your guts. You called him a clot and shot him up the arse with his own catapult, snapping the elastic and saying it wasn't much cop in any case. It wasn't your place to humiliate and criticize. Our village was not your place at all. You were from the town and you'd already done a year at Secondary School. You kept telling us to remember that. Top of the A Stream, you said, and only our ignorance prevented us from asking how come you'd failed the Eleven-Plus and weren't at Grammar School. The fact was we'd sat the Eleven-Plus without even knowing why.

After this we tried not bothering with you, but childhood knows few resolutions. Boys spin like weathercocks and have more faith in the moment than the principle. Though our everyday life excluded you by nature, I remember you joining in now and again: up the field or the wreck where you wearied us with your ball-hogging and wild shots at simple goals; or bowling unsporting yorkers for Australia against us MCC, boasting about googlies and leg-breaks, but you never showed us either, preferring to say 'I did that on purpose' when the cricket ball veered or skipped off a lump in the grass. Then once or twice you got up a bike ride or a fishing trip. Daz said you always rode like Cycling Proficiency, barking out the rules of the road, coming home alone and ostracized. Once the convoy deserted you *en masse*, but like a missionary you reached the destination alone. You never did fish down the pond. Instead, you told us they were going to fill it in because your dad said it was dangerous and had complained to the Parish Council. Down Ockley Pool you had a bite everytime we weren't looking. Down Bodiam *you* always lost a biggun. Anything we caught you called a tiddler. Our cane rods warped, our unoilable reels clacked like a *fluck* of ducks. You and your ball-bearing, silent, fibreglass precision shone with the sun.

What gave you authority? Why could I never, even then, settle you in my mind, carry an image of you as one of us? Why did I wish to? Because your existence removed me from mine, with that linguistic superiority and the radical humour it thrived on. I felt you were educating us. It was a strange humour, schooled rigidly by your father. You confounded us with backslang straightaway, mocking our blank faces as you gave us new names in a whining, cowboy drawl you always used for being funny with.

'Ol' Sinned Mach-kap,' you called Dennis after he'd gone in. I was Cirdec Yill, to become Sir Deck Yill. I didn't get it, so you called me a gib loof.

'Ask me where my dad's been,' you'd say.

'Where?'

'No, not Ware, Hoo.'

'But you said where.'

'No, I didn't. He was in Ware last week. Yesterday he went to Hoo.'

We'd heard of none of these places. You were beyond us and you knew how far. Our ignorance only served your increasing obscurity.

'Ynniks tog a wen skid-lid morf retap Ynniks.'

We had no use for this big language. We spoke directly in our own tongue, which until then had never let us down. You made us doubt ourselves, as if our flies were always undone and you were looking down and catching us out. Your self-importance justified itself, making fools of our families' ways and means. Your dad even let you say 'bloody' as long as it wasn't said in anger but in humour, in that cowboy accent. You'd point at Skinny's feet on the turf and say: 'Sod,' with intended results: the English lesson which always followed hurt argument. A magician of meaning you were. 'I loave you, Sir Deck,' you'd say, and Skinny'd go, 'Ugh'omo, you love Lily . . . '

'Oh mo ah doan,' you'd say in cowboy hoarse. 'Ah sayed: ah loathe you, Sir Deck, loave yer guts . . . ' And your whole family seemed to thrive on such exchanges.

I must step back now, away from this apostrophe, finding myself overdrawn at the point where I wish to capture some aspect of the homogeneity of this family, without addressing any one of them in particular, by describing a picture I have carried in my head as in an album: a human still life, a family portrait in the manner of Zoffany or Devis of a family which remains as mysterious to me now as it did then, a family which seemed content and independent, making me feel a child excluded when the feeling was irrelevent and premature. The external connections of this picture reflect the unknown nature of its internal life: an annual holiday in Cornwall or The Broads (holidays were unknown to us in those days), a relative who owned a shop, an uncle in Australia. It has no beginning or end, it just is.

I am standing outside the Whites' garden gate. Milky is the other side of the gate. An ambulance has drawn up in the road below us bringing home his little sister with the hole in her heart mended. The image is at its strongest point when she is wheeled up the garden path on a trolley stretcher. Milky has stood aside onto their tiny strip of lawn, hands clasped in front as he looks down at his sister's long-chinned, yellow face which pokes a suffering smile above the edge of a blood-red blanket, a smile which makes her close her eyes with the effort. Milky's is the family smile, but of similar hue. His eyes thin down in scrutiny instead of opening in joy, conscious of all they see, lips widening but still straight, neither turning corners of pleasure nor welcoming his sister home.

At the backdoor stands his younger brother, sharpening arrow points on hazel sticks with a sheath knife. He has already fixed cardboard flights on the other end and bound the slits with white cotton. He calls out: 'Watcheer, maggit,' and carries on whittling. The front door has opened and Mrs White is coming through, one hand crumpling a yellow cotton apron, the other outstretched to take something from the nurse who has come along too: a shiny steel kidney bowl a-tip and tilt full of very liquid travel sick. She has carried this so carefully, without spilling a single drop, all the way from the ambulance, up the long concrete slope to the front door. From the front room window Mr White's smile is genuine and broad with humour. The window is open wide and his smile has its source in a home-made joke.

'Well, well,' he says, 'so you get free bowls of soup with every ambulance ride, eh Margaret? Haha, can't be bad, can it? No, not the soup – don't can that!' The two boys laugh with him and sing a well-known advert jingle for Campbell's Soup – Campbell's Soup in their American cowboy mouth. And here the image ends. I must have gone home . . .

I don't know why I was even outside the White's front gate. I rarely crossed their threshold and *never* went into their house. Once he made me stand at the backdoor and wait for him to fetch something he wanted to show off. What made the White's house different to ours was the backdoor. It was at the front, separated from the real front door by a porch and dustbin cubby / coal bunker. As they had a back garden too, they had a pseudo backdoor, a back garden gate and cinder path linking up with the concrete path to the shops, so unless they'd come home by car the Whites hardly ever used the two front doors. The pseudo backdoor was entry to their inner sanctum. Outsiders were stood at the front/backdoor, which was painted blue. Strangers went to the front door, which was pale green till the council matched it blue. So I waited at the front/backdoor, which Milky left open two inches, but footsteps gave it a closing shunt. The long wait magnified that closure, but I was rooted there, wishing I could walk away instead of granting Milky his material power. He showed me a pair of shoes in their box. Trackers. Animal tracks on their soles and a compass under a leather flap in the heel.

Which brings me to the one thing I can never understand about Milky White, always so predictable in behaviour and aloof in his manner towards the rest of us. Why did he come with us to Little Nineveh? We never invited him that Saturday afternoon. By then, me, Skinny and Daz did not even pretend to like him, be friendly with him or even know him. We denied his existence as vigorously as he denied ours. Secondary Modern had sorted this out for us, where Milky had found his own species of boy, considered long extinct, which he belonged to – a handful of clean, law-abiding, master-loved swots who sat in the front row with their hands up eager to answer the question or wipe the board, looking forward to homework with conscientious gratitude. Anyway, being a year above us, our natural contact was at a natural end. Yet he forced himself upon us that afternoon. Must have done, knowing we loathed him and did not want him with us. In spite of all this, he still came along?

His best friend at school and in the village was Wormhole and sometimes we saw the two of them up Church Hill. In summer Milky and Worm'ole went on bike rides together like girls on their ponies. Worm'ole became so associated with Milky that we ceased to consider Milky a separate character. Right from the first term they'd stand aloof at the coach stop where they met, the only two boys to own briefcases. They were last on, seats at the front, and first off. We all slung our duffle bags onto the shelf. Milky and Worm'ole kept their briefcases on their knees like taking cats in baskets to the vet. So throughout the school years Milky remained a speck in the distance, avoiding, ignoring, disowning us whenever the occasion demanded – in the playground, up Church Hill, or the village shops. Then, during his fifth year, he won his place at the Grammar School and passed out of our lives altogether and into the Lower VI. Our school was proud of Melvyn White; even Worm'ole, who was left behind, blushed at the mention of Milky's name. We hardly saw him then, this grey sixteen-year-old, expressionless but for his determined retreat along the back path of a Saturday morning in his snob-grey flannels and new scholar's briefcase with its gilt MW-brandished hide.

Within two years, university had taken him from Barratt's Road the way the hearse takes everyone else.

And then, by accident, we met. To my shame and perplexity I was living at home after my intellectual downfall, saving up to go abroad, working long hours for meagre wages at the local builders' merchants. I had my Transalpino train ticket and my departure for Italy was imminent. It was the first week of a New Year and I went to Hastings to buy a rucksack. Milky White was at the bus stop.

Escape crossed his mind, but he was too slow. I looked him over – sensible shoes and a dimpled, square-edged tie with grey woollen shirt, the collar of his short blue macintosh turned up against the cold sea wind, his beige scarf flapping loose and ineffectually. He held his rolled umbrella as if it were his scrolled degree. I hardly knew what to say. I felt like asking if he remembered me, or: Weren't you once Milky White? He'd never liked this nickname so we'd always called him it, this discovery from Physics with Popeye in the Lab, who said that carbon dioxide breathed through a straw turned distilled water milky white. As it turned out I baffled Mr Melvyn White BA with my manners, saying hello quite nicely, asking him how he was. His face fumbled but he said fine, thanks, and managed to enquire into my present doings. Quite proudly, I said I was working behind the trade counter up Durgate's. What about you? I asked.

'I'm reading for my MA,' he said.

This didn't entirely destroy me as there were books sticking from my pocket and self-educated words sticking from my mouth, forcing him to notice them like he would mud on turn-ups, but he quickly established his eminence by making some reference to the British Museum reading room. I mentioned the future. The British

Museum, he repeated. In the meantime he was 'honouring' his parents with a visit. I said I was dishonouring mine by my presence, to be rectified by departure in a few days for Rome, where, I anounced grandly, I had a position teaching the English language. Milky's only comment was his concern that I did not have a degree. There are ways round that, I said. Yes yes, he said, he'd been to Rome anyway and it was not a pleasant place, full of thieves, very corrupt and had been for over two thousand years. Then the bus drew up to await departure. I could see Milky contemplating another hour in my company. He looked at his watch and found he had ten minutes to spare. Forgotten to purchase one of the books he'd come to Hastings for, Hastings being a fine pantechnicon of antiquarian books. I knew this better than he did and I also knew what sort of bags they wrapped the books in. All Milky had with him was a pair of trousers from a sale in a Debenhams' carrier-bag. He bolted into the crowd with an ambiguous farewell, leaving me to mount the bus and travel home alone.

For some peculiar notion of her own – perhaps pseudo-maternal or anti-husband – my mother phoned me on the pay-phone downstairs the day after their visit. As soon as she spoke I could tell from her manner that she only dared to because my father was under the car or cutting the back hedge. She tested the sound level necessary for me to hear by coughing my name, then she said: 'Yer father's up the back yard clippin' the hedge.' She waited, and I knew she'd left it too long, that he was probably working his way down by now and next thing he'd be alongside the window at the front hedge. So I listened too, the exchange dialling in the telephonic depths like the sound of snicking secateurs.

'I found that article, boy,' she said. 'Yer know what I mean, don't yer? 'Bout Melvyn White,' she added in a whisper, tweaking the curtain, making trouble with her glasses, keeping back from the window, only the shuffling meant she couldn't see well enough to read the article. I was beginning to get nervous, like I'd staked my entire property on a horse and had to listen to the incompetent commentator on the radio who'd lost the runners in the fog. By the time she'd got halfway through the opening paragraph which told us nothing yet, my father came in the back door and she hung up. Melvyn White, educated locally, whose parents still lived down

Barratt's Road, who'd gained an MA at Aberystwyth in Museum
Studies and worked in various museums as an assistant, had been
appointed chief curator of a museum . . . I waited, but she didn't
phone again.

Directory Enquiries gave me the Whites' number. Milky's
mother answered, another whisper in an empty house, surprised
by the sudden ringing. She didn't recognize my voice so I said I
was an old colleague of Mel's from university days, lost touch,
went abroad and so on. She was flustered, her voice jacked up a
register in case I was some high-up. Well, I must have been –
university! How nice, she said, it would be for Melvyn to hear from
somebody . . . She knew what she'd implied and couldn't correct
it without getting herself in deeper. Clearly, he heard from no
one, or she suspected he didn't. He was still adrift, like me. I was
soon fed up being polite about him. 'Well, where *is* he?' I
asked. 'What museum?' She'd mentioned no museum but
failed to notice, her agitation risen to a new pitch. 'To tell you the
truth uhm . . . uhm . . . '

'Adrian . . . '

'Uhm Adrian, I don't rightly know, not rightly. I mean I have
an address, like.'

His museum was in the far north of Scotland but his address
was c/o the Estate Office. She didn't know, exactly like, *where* he
was living, that is, he hadn't written . . .

This was the proud mother who'd sent Milky's story to the local
paper, or was it his father, brother, sister, the whole proud family?
Or had Milky sent it in himself? His mother's voice seemed to come
from the same great hollow in Milky's past life as my own mother's
had from mine, only moments before. Had Milky too sat in the back
of their car, suffocating from their pride or hurt over broken
chains? Is this why he'd given them no phone number, no address,
at the summit of ambition? I couldn't bear Mrs White's shame any
longer and as I thanked her and said goodbye, it struck me that for
the first time ever my voice had entered Milky's house, just a few
doors up the road from where my father had probably returned,
after gulping a pint of tap water, or running a cut thumb under it,
to snicking the privet with his well-oiled shears as my mother stood
by the phone knowing it would never ring.

Chapter Five

Under the whitened sky, wind spun and whistled up the High Street, the sea snored in from somewhere round the back and the coach disappeared as if I'd imagined it. Not a soul. Shops all closed, every house window in deep, uninhabited darkness. Beside me, the windows of Kildaggie Village Post Office were shuttered, and the clock said three-thirty, September the first. North, the road stretched by a row of cottages, an acre of grazing, rounding the bend at the old white Kirk. The only signs of life were the smell of coal smoke in the air and a smell of perfume in the phonebox.

Mrs Cormorant answered the phone with a sharp hello like a beak on a cliff edge. I said I was the winter tenant, just arrived. How did I get to the cottage, please?

'Wait,' she ordered, only she might have said *wheat* or *wet* or *twit*. I wheated, cold and shivering, tired from a sleepless journey on the night coach from Victoria.

Ten minutes later a snuff-brown Granada with a tank aerial pulled up beside me. A small girl grinned from the back seat as Mrs Cormorant walked round to the boot like a taxi driver with shit on her shoes. In her forties, tight blonde curly hair, blonde fluff on a face of coarsened, broken-veined skin, she tottered on high cork soles, a freshly-lit cigarette between two fingers, dirty yellow stripes down the front and arms of her black nylon rally jacket, the hems of black corduroys riding high above bare red ankles. She shook hands reluctantly, the cigarette poked in her mouth the instant she said, 'Marine Cormorant.'

'Cedric Lily,' I said, trying to heave my luggage into the boot as she stood, arms folded, looking me over through the bottoms of her eyes. She didn't like me. I didn't like her. Only I was there at her mercy, and she knew I knew it. She didn't like the way I put my luggage in either, so she heeled my rucksack over like kicking a dead cat off the road she'd just run over.

'Is it hoose bricks y've goat in there?'

We drove in silence out of Kildaggie, past the Kirk and up the hill. A container lorry from Wick hurtled down towards us well over the white lines. Marine Cormorant didn't flinch. She accelerated to sixty. Thirty tons of tinned pilchards vacuumed the air to within three inches of us joining them. A black rabbit scampered off the narrow road and into the broom, joining more black rabbits. After a mile we turned up a rough track under the single railway line. HOME FARM, it said on a lichened, grey wooden signpost which had keeled into hedge. The little girl was rolling something along the parcel shelf.

'Ah've no bin t'school t'dee,' she said, and I would have asked why if her mother hadn't told her to shut up and sit straight.

'Aye, so y've no bin t'these parts b'fore then,' she stated, as if I'd done something like leave a window open.

'Weel . . . ' she continued, pleased with herself, 'ah've a mind ye'll be pullin' oot yer hair in a week o'two. Y'll no luss the wunter alone, thuss f'sure.'

I tried sarcasm. 'I don't need a wife to pull it out for me . . . '.

She said nothing, slowing for the cows, udders bulging on their stog to the milking shed. The cowman raised his stick, an old man in a blue boiler suit, mud-coloured cap, muckle-mou'd, sharney faced, hands like shovels. Marine Cormorant waved back. The girl tapped on the window. 'Haloo, John.'

'He'll be yure neighbour, muckle John,' Marine Cormorant said.

A way cleared through the cows and we drove into the yard

over thin stodge and flint. She pointed at the farmhouse fifty yards right of the milking shed, saying something I didn't catch. We turned left. Tractor shed, long gosk-grass in a quiet corner where a war-grey van sunk down on rotted tyres, long hatch up on stilts to reveal a Ministry of Defence Wartime Information Unit. Behind it, a derelict stone house, brambles growing out of its empty, downstairs windows. A tin sign on the door. HAZCHEM. Skirting the cow sheds, we passed another group of derelict biggins – stables, grain store. Beside a row of three, east-facing stone cottages, the track climbed upward, whitening as it went, twisting into the pine forest, dark green, loose topped under a whipped sky. Ben Daggie loomed higher still, whinned a desolate yellow.

She parked outside the middle cottage. Both neighbouring chimneys smoked, their gardens tended, so neat and tiny with painted fences. One had a high hedge running up the side, the other had rose-bushes like granny's birthday card. The middle cottage was the ugly sister. Dumped on the carpet-sized lawn lay a plastic crate of empty Guinness bottles. Nylon cord on the front gate instead of hinges. A modern, blue council-house door with aluminium letter box. Standing at the car boot I listened to the wind chasing silence with each fleeting swish through the trees, my first real sense of actually being in Scotland.

'Ken I opp'n the dour, Mommy?' The girl skipped up the path in four goes and turned the key which lived in the door.

'Is it your farm?' I asked Marine Cormorant as she slammed the boot down.

'Aye.'

'Were you brought up here?' I was pleased by the place and felt like knowing about it. She didn't like questions and flung her dog-end down without bothering where it landed. I frowned as sparks flew across the long grass. She was shaking her head.

'Noooooh,' she sounded angry. 'Ah'm fr'm fisher folk at Wick.'

Inside, the cottage smelled unaired. Mouse shit, damp nylon stretch covers, a stale cigarette stub. In a cold kitchen with blue and yellow square lino, the Rayburn stood like a neglected family vault beside a modern electric cooker with the oven doorknob missing. The girl just had to run to the backdoor and jostle it open while her mother peered in the empty fridge. I stood beside a glass-topped table with its tubular chrome stools topped in black padded plastic. A brown viyella curtain rode high above the sill, the light coming through like skin beneath a worn sock. I drew it back and found a plastic fern in a jamjar and a view which reached the sea.

I followed Marine Cormorant into the sitting room, the source of all smells. The last guests had tried to light a fire and failed, leaving charred newspaper, an empty cigarette packet and some stubs in the grate, nuggets of coal scattered angrily over the hearth. This clag of smoulder also rose from the chair covers the colour of dried blood and the pale straw beauty-board walls. On the mantlepiece were two orange and turquoise fluffy dogs, asphyxiated. Above them, framed in plastic relief, wide-eyed Pedro played his four-stringed guitar sitting on his asthmatic donkey. Marine Cormorant pointed the dogs at each other and straightened the picture.

'Naw television,' she said.

'Never watch it,' I said.

She saw me looking at the four-castered trolley and the square in the dust where the TV had sat till she'd removed it. She poked an unlit cigarette back in the packet and said there was nothing else to do up there.

Upstairs, there were two tiny bedrooms either side of a four-foot landing, one crammed with beds and cots, skeel ceilinged to a foot above the wainscot, tiny deep gabled windows. The girl was excited, pointing at the walls and saying when she was a bebby they'd lived in this room and Jairny put the Micky Mouses on. These assorted human-size Micky Mouses floated round the walls thanks to Jairny's amateur marker pens.

I decided on the other room, papered in blue vinyl flowers, a double divan blocking any space, a leg's width from the white dressing table with its fly-blown, heart-shaped mirror. Across the window sill a blue fluffy donkey pulled a plastic jewellery cart, its trail marked with dead flies like tufts of grass. I said I'd have to move things if she didn't mind, to make the place suitable. She'd lit a fag by now and stood smoking it furiously, blocking out the light while the girl did the stairs with an insect spray, 'whoosh-whoosh-shhhhhhh.'

'Aye, most folks move inta the kitchen f'r the wunter.'

Downstairs she counted the glass teacups in the kitchen cupboard, ensuring the notice pinned inside the door was visible: *If you break it Please replace it.* Outside, the tall grass shook and splayed in a rising wind.

'I don't have any food,' I said.

She drove me to the only open shop, a laundrette-looking co-op on a bungalow estate above the village. She smoked all the way there in silence. On the way back the girl whispered in my ear, loudly. 'Ah doan't huff to weir a stewpitt sitbelt i'the buck sit.'

Her mother told her to sit straight or she wouldn't be able to sit down for a whole week. Outside the cottage gate she switched the engine off and gave me no sign that I should open the door and get out. I watched a blue rugger shirt flap on next door's line and listened to the car keys jangling.

'Noo then, Cairdric,' she began, folding her arms, 'scaffymen come Mondays, collmun t'morrer, aye an' suitym'n's due, grocer vuns twice a week. If y'll be wunting t'noo much else y'd better usk me noo.'

I asked what scaffymen were. She looked at me, her jink for the winter, rolling eyes, a sigh full of bonfire smoke. Scaffymen, she explained, took scaff away. And she'd be over for the rent eight o'clock next evening. Thinking that was it I opened the door and put one foot outside the car. The girl was humming 'Pop Goes The Weasel' and Marine Cormorant fuddled with a yellow, disposable lighter which wouldn't light. 'Weel noo, Cairdric,' she said and I felt the ground pulled out from under my foot, 'an' jess what is't y'll be doon in ma hoose th'wunter? Ah'm nort say'n ah mind or ah wouldnay lairt y'in the fust place, on'y ah've a reet t'noo when a young marn coms all the wee fr'm London toon tah live in ma hoose. Marine, ah says t'maself, y'd bairst be noon a thung o'two fust.'

The car rocked. It might have been the wind or the girl in the back seat throwing herself forward.

'Um sairv'n years auld,' she said, 'an Roover's nairly fife, an' Mommy's sixty-four.'

Marine Cormorant grabbed at the girl's hand but crashed with the head-rest and the lighter fell on the floor in the back.

'PICK THAT UP AN' BELT UP! Ah'll no tell y'agen!'

She tried the lighter several times, like sparks from her own dry tongue of flint, each rub falling between the snap of that rugger shirt on the line as it caught the long rush of wind turning off the slopes and hurtling through the huge elm towering above the old stables.

'Well,' I began, not knowing what to say, 'I'm, I suppose you might say, researching . . . this book, you see . . . '

But she wasn't listening. The lighter went back on the dashboard.

I stepped from the car, embarrassed by my inarticulacy. 'It's alright,' I said. 'I'm from country folk. I've been abroad, that's all. Not from London *me*.'

'Aw, an' that shaird doon there,' she pointed to the back of where the kine were milked, 'yer c'n gairt mulk yonder through the green door.'

I went straight to bed, waking once to find it still light, an hour after London lighting up, the wind butting its way over the roof. Then I slept the hot, blood-eyed sleep of the night and day traveller.

It was three-thirty in the morning when I made my way down to the kitchen with raging thirst and hunger, crick-necked from the bed which had been moulded by other shapes than mine. Cold like a mist hugged low over the linoleum, the cottage feeling so empty and homeless, I sat dejected at the glass table listening to the kettle crank up, smelling toasted dust as the grill heated and the wind clattered the loose flaps and hooshed down the Rayburn. Rain swiped at the window. The all-glass backdoor rattled, the outhouse clung together like shipwrecked sailors, all rotted wood and plastic-sheets jacking. Opening the front door I listened to the sea roar half a mile away, lights winking along the Dornoch Firth. A cold, empty but familiar experience. This Kildaggie was a far-flung, bleak, unwelcoming place, which set your own doubts at you like a pack of dogs, driving them up to the door with wind and rain. Just what had driven Milky White to such a place? Had he mistaken it for sanctuary? I did not imagine so because Milky White knew his history and would have recalled that Scotland was a land where Macneill, after allowing his enemies to gain the sanctuary of a church, burnt the church down with his enemies inside.

Chapter Six

I'm an ungrateful traveller, frustrated by the experience but not from mental apathy or blunt vision. My problem is even simpler: my *whole* being absorbs new places so rapidly that I feel I've always been there, or seen it before. My digestion is the same. I was once told by a nurse that if I took a poisoned meal with ten other people, my digestive system would absorb the poison so rapidly I would die first, warning the other ten and leaving them plenty of time to reach hospital and save themselves.

So when dawn arrived and the wind dropped, my first day in Kildaggie became my second, and Milky White's presence there felt so substantial I took it for granted. It could only be a matter of time before our paths crossed. I'd lived in anticipation of this so long now that everything I did, or thought, had become to feel a daily occurrence even when it wasn't. Thus, I stood at the window that morning awaiting the familiar daylight. If what I saw were in reality unfamiliar, it would not be beyond my imagination. In that sense it was inevitable and part of *me*, not the world. I was there to write down what I could distill from it.

This organic potential of the writer gave me authority, the right to project myself onto the landscape, or withdraw my meaning into the undisclosed behind the language and the moving pictures.

The long faint glimmer of dawn turned the farmyard blue before the sun rose through clouds like anvils. The cowman was up and unhitching his gate as seagulls yammered out front after a long night. Automatically, I began to prepare for the days ahead. Each new place is the same. Previous tenants leave no love behind them, only signs of failure and carelessness, flight or filth. Encrusted bath, the carpet round the toilet turned green, hair clips with yanks of hair, toenails with the dirt still under them.

By midday I'd cleared a home in the leftovers by dragging the bedroom carpet down to the kitchen floor, replacing the glass table with an armchair and sofa, scrubbing the Rayburn of its black fleece, finding a wooden table for the window and arranging my few books along the sill. It began to look similar to everywhere I've ever lived: a lamp and a radio, a blanket instead of a curtain. Bedroom floorboards bare, single lamp beside the mattress on the floor, my clothes in a box, a chair for undressing. The coalman filled the bunker with a month's supply so in the early afternoon I put my jacket on and set out for the village.

Outside Kildaggie Post Office I phoned the Social Security in Wick and soon found myself driven towards the sea, away from human assembly, but reluctant to stray in case I crossed into Milky's territory. As with everywhere I'd ever found myself, the first essential was to make some part of it my own inviolate centre.

To reach the sea I had to retreat the way I'd come as far as a lane which left the main road opposite the white Kirk, passing a row of cottages trigged up for a chocolate box with their white window boxes and freshly-painted blue gables. I heard the runneling of a burn and the sea wheezing in a light sleep, low tide like a fallen blanket.

There was a two-storey building further on, its frames and cornices painted in red-fearing sober maroon, God's own colour in Kildaggie. Here, the duty or work had continued silently and meticulously for a hundred years, the double oak doors containing all purpose, their glass head displaying the three gilt words I had already memorised to the point of meaninglessness, the address Mrs White had given me: NORTHINTERLAND ESTATE OFFICE.

I hurried by, the lane following the burn to where it entered the sea, chuckling over reddened stones. On one side the path led back along the beach to the village, joining a concrete promenade which skirted the backs of High Street buildings. Behind me stood a wind-break of high fir hedge. I stumbled forward over the debris washed up below, along the point, up onto land the other side of the burn. Cat's-tail grass flushed yellowing along the length of shoreline as the breeze swept and flicked across two visible miles of wild coastline. Above it rose Kildaggic Wood, oaks, beech and pine tips as the land rose. Far away the wood came down to the very edge of the waves like a flock of trees to drink. Some had fallen in the years, great heavings of rock had split them to the root, sea worn to tinder and balsa, greying, coming and going with the tide until nothing but splinter. The point is I had found my place.

Hurrying forward I came to a slight bend beside a thicket and looked up to see a castle where the trees had cleared, a castle I'd not expected because I'd not researched, preferring to arrive in Kildaggie with a blank page. An ambiguous castle hewn by clans, some with conscious grandeur, others with Victorian brickwork after fires had gutted the wings. A huge wall enclosed the formal garden. The kitchen garden was in ruin, the wrought-iron gates snared in bindweed, peeling blistered cartwheels useless as old pennies, smothered by the long grass. Benches for sea viewing were cut into the stone wall. A jetty of great slabs had collapsed years ago onto the sandy run where boats had once been hauled above the tide.

I was grateful for no sign of life, no beer cans along the sea wall or fag packets in the grass, only scuttering hares and six Blackface rams snitching grass on their knees in a long strip of paddock. Then the hares bolted when they saw me and my mood vanished.

A dark, cobbled carriageway sloped upwards between the castle and kitchen garden walls, bringing me to a wide, beech-lined driveway leading from the castle to the main road, which meant I'd almost walked full circle. I could see the traffic flashing past the gates. I became a reluctant spectre on the edge of a Dutchman's snapshot. Three strikes on the castle clock. Chimneys smoked but windows showed no sign of life, a Scottish custom perhaps. I thought of Milky watching me from one of them, doubting his own eyes and wondering who this person was. I pulled my collar up and ran down the track to my cottage, all the dogs in a frenzy.

When the wind picked up, the Rayburn roared. I drank tea, ate toasted sandwiches and settled back to wait for Marine Cormorant, kettle on the hob as the Rayburn creaked with heat, the kitchen in a cosy fug, lamp on in a lingering twilight. There was nothing I wanted to ask her. A train rumbled down the single track and crossed the bridge below. From the window I could still see the woken, unmade sea, greying now. The weather vane out back spun faster and faster. From the garden gate I looked above; Ben Daggie standing knuckle topped, down to its skin in heather, a black outline worth a shudder when you look over your shoulder in this halflight.

I expected footsteps as I waited at the window, but the glare of headlights stopped outside instead. Marine Cormorant had driven up a short cut across the farmyard between the sheds, less than a hundred yards from her own front door. She lit a fresh John Player on my path and stepped into the kitchen like a cold draft in an allegory, perched on the edge of the sofa, her nose searching the kitchen as her ash fell to the floor. An icicle on a waterfall. I gave her a month's rent. She signed the receipt.

'If y'll be wuntin' me,' she said, 'doon come inta ma hoose alone or the dog'll have ye.'

The next day cowman muckle was leading his cows across the road into the track, leaning on the gatepost once he'd stopped the traffic, grinning at me while his bow-legged bawtie sniffed my turnups.

'Y'can cummon, lard. Ma coos wouldna hart ye.'

'I'm not scared of your cows.' I was standing reading a sign-board staked to the verge which said KILDAGGIE CASTLE CLOSES 30 SEPT.

'Aye,' he said, hitching the gate with bale twine as the last one shunted through.

'Do you know, is there a museum in Kildaggie?' I asked, but he shrugged his shoulders and went with his cows, so I climbed a stile and followed a footpath which ran alongside the railway track through a pine thicket, plunging down a long muddy slope through bracken, to the burn which tumbled ice-cold, rust-coloured down the tiny gorge, emerging just below the Kildaggie sign, at the ancient rallying stone of the Northern Clans.

I ducked into St Bartolph's Charity Shop to avoid Marine Cormorant's Granada parked outside the co-op stores. I was ignored by two women who scumped black bin bags from the stock room so I browsed along the books reading titles like *After Death: Conversations with Julia* and *Well-Known Prayers for Meetings*. The women spoke in faded accents, genteel Bromley, pre-war grammar gells, and I stared at them when they weren't looking. 'Were you looking for anything in per-ticular?' one of them asked.

She was gone sixty in her kilted skirt and green padded anorak, a tuft of black hairs under a falling chin, eyes overshadowed blue, pink clip-ons the size of shilling domes.

'No,' I said. Her suede ankle boots were brand-new and fleece-lined so she kept looking at them after each scuff with this big cardboard box full of curtains. 'Actually, I'm looking for heavy curtains. To keep out draughts.'

The other woman, hearing voices, dropped her bin bags and squeezed between us, untying the bags she'd already shoved aside. She was frail grey and moved like a wire puppet. 'Were they for your, uhm, camper van perhaps?'

There was no point evading her. 'No, I've just moved to Kildaggie. They're for doors and windows.'

'Oh really?' the other one said. 'You've moved to Kildaggie? And whereabouts would that be to, if you don't mind my asking?'

I told them exactly where.

'Not one of those cottages at the back, you mean?' Tufted chin was more than curious.

'Oh, which are those ones, Millicent?' grey face asked her.

'You know Ethel. The one I was after, I expect.'

'The middle one,' I said.

'There! It is, Ethel. What did I say!' Her voice dropped to a whisper. 'You remember what *she* said, of course!'

Ethel remembered alright. Millicent was haughty with me now. 'Well, are you working on the farm then?'

'No,' I said, 'just a winter let.'

Ethel clicked her fingers. 'Aren't you the geologist chappie?'

Millicent's anger had not run its course and she butted in at neither of us in particular. 'Hmmph, I'm surprised you need curtains up there. The Tourist Board ought to check these things properly, if you ask me. Hasn't she got any at all?'

'It's the draughts,' I insisted, looking from one to the other, two faces occupied by scandal. 'The curtains are so thin the draughts come through.'

'How long are you there for then?' Millicent asked.

'The winter.'

This time she seemed grudgingly relieved. 'Oh, I see. She's still turning you out then? For her couples? Not that there're more than two ever go there that I know of.'

'Quite,' Ethel said. 'Cows aren't my cup of tea either. Now young man, these curtains an improvement or not?'

'Only bedspreads in this one Ethel,' Millicent said turning out another box.

I noticed a pair of stout, olive-green corduroys on the trouser rail so I pulled them out, which prompted Millicent to ask if I'd met Donald yet. Assuming she meant the previous owner of the breeches I wondered if he was the tractor driver on the farm or Marine Cormorant's husband.

'Heavens!' she rolled her eyes. 'Don't you *know*?'

'No, I don't. Does he own the farm?'

'Good gracious! *Lord* Donald, that's who I'm talking about, Lord Northinterland, Crumwyel-St Rex, 8th Duke at Kildaggie! Of course, they only have a flat now in one of the wings, and his brother Andrew, the Marquis, he's had the dairy converted. Hasn't he, Ethel?'

'Oh yes. Lovely men aren't they, Millicent?'

'I'd say. Yes, indeedy. Not stand-offish at all. Donald in per-ticular. You'd think he was only one of us at times.'

'Comes in here then, does he?' I asked, still assuming they were his breeches.

'In here? This shabby old rag and bone shop?'

'Aren't they his breeches, then?'

'Oh, they're Donald's cords alright,' Ethel said.

'So you're neither of you from round here then, are you?' I asked.

'No nooooo,' Millicent said. 'I moved here with Ted twenty-five years ago. I've only been down to London twice in all that time. Once last year, in fact. Ohhh shocking. Harrods isn't what it used to be. I preferred Marks to be honest.'

I paid a quid for the Duke's breeches, a bigger man than me, reached for the door handle and having faked a bored air asked my question: 'Oh, uhm, you, er wouldn't know if there's a Mr White lives in Kildaggie, do you?'

'White did you say?' asked Millicent.

'I said you wouldn't happen to know if . . . '

'Yes, yes, I heard what you said, but did you say *White*?'

'Yes. *White*,' I said, as if I insisted the shirt were that colour.

'It rings a little bell, doesn't it with you, Ethel?'

'White?' Ethel repeated. 'Yes, now you come to mention it, I do believe there's a Mr White does the chiropody clinic for the old folk on Wednesdays, only I believe he comes in from Helmsdale . . . '

'There *was* a Mr White of course, years ago now,' Millicent said, 'lived at Glencoe with his sister. She was from outside at one time. He, poor man, went a wee bit simple in his dotage . . . '

By late afternoon the wind had shifted, coming off the hills, the wind propeller on next door's weather pole trilled on its nail. With the cottage door shut behind me, time slowed again and things reverted to the way they'd been. The minutes lingered, finally passed, failing to illuminate the beginning of the next. During one of these minutes I watched a hawk gliding on a lifting current, twisting like a slow thread for two hundred yards, but when I reached the front gate it had gone. I'd made no plan beyond belief in my idea: my presence in Kildaggie. But this was insufficient to heal the contradiction between my strategic aimless persona, which hoped for revelation, and my reluctance to step beyond these restraints into direct enquiry. This was my line of thinking as I sat in the window or wandered to the gate and back, watching the sky change, unable to stay in or out, uncertain of my faith in waiting, yet forced by fallacy to confer or seek significance upon all events, so I'd be forced to act in a particular way, and write in a particular direction by forcing resolution upon a previous and now connected event. Narrative arrogance aside, it did seem an effective balance between the random and the structural, especially when the next pseudo event occurred that afternoon.

At 4.30pm the postman parked his van outside my gate and walked up the garden path. Middle Cottage, Back Street, Kildaggie, an anonymous address if ever there was one. I was at the doormat before the envelope landed. In fact it stuck in the letterbox and I tugged it through, this fat brown envelope from the Social Security in Wick, containing forms and a signing-on booklet, each slip headed DECLARATION OF UNEMPLOYMENT. Because of the distance between Kildaggie and Wick I signed on by post. Problem was, each signature of mine had to be witnessed on the given dates by either a family doctor, clergyman or solicitor who knew me personally at the place where I lived. This witness signed on the understanding that they confirmed my status as unemployed. A witness, it said, could also be any professional person known personally to the claimant.

I let the blanket fall over the window and stuffed things under the doors as the draughts grew colder. I cooked a vegetable broth, then wrote half the night, ending Chapter Six with the question:

Where is the most likely place for a museum in Kildaggie?

Chapter Seven

A printed dream, clear glazed white and immaculate, me walking along the shoreline on a dry path, wind dropped, tide a way out. Fridge washed up among the broken lobster pots. Seals black as fat slugs stuck on rocks. Far away the waves sounding like tyres on a wet gritty road. Here, below the castle where the beach half-stone, half-sand, I see footprints. Expected them, but puzzled nonetheless, they lead from rock to rock, a pod of seals upon each rock, eyes at me. Milky's footprints, shoes with animal tracks on their soles (I know the compass under flip in the heel) Clark's Trackers, their name. But there Milky went now, a gap in the sea wall, up into dark low paths where pine needles snip softly under your feet, larch roots boney toes to tread on. Take no offence tonight, I've no time to step politely, Milky is a hundred yards ahead on his bicycle still listening as I talk quietly to him.

Can I pay you next week? I'm a bit frozen over today.

He'd gone. Through a door into the castle, with stick-on letters from that hardware stores. ME USE-M funny joke, said Milky, metaplasm. I said: Mallachie White, Mallachie White . . .

Once awake I felt afraid of a dream having spoken so closely like it had come into this room, empty but for me asleep on the floor. Milky was in his museum. The museum was in the castle.

My sense of time had weakened and I didn't know what day it was, being a midday riser whose few responsibilities are irksome. I found the sink cluttered with dirty plates and the Rayburn clotted in grime and ashes. By the time I'd scrubbed and tidied and fired the Rayburn the afternoon was almost over, so I settled at the table with tea and toast, staring at the sea. There was dust along the book tops already and I had no clean change of clothes. I washed a shirt and socks and as soon as it was dark went back to bed, waking to find the sun shining through the curtains. You can always tell a Sunday by the yellow stillness.

With the shirt still drying on my back, I walked in my most authoritative manner through the castle doorway to the Hall, dark polish, severe and homeless. Above a long dead fireplace an armorial panel displayed the arms of the Ist Duke and his families. Over the cornice hung the badge of the Northinterlands, the wild dog from Dogland. A bronze statue of the 2nd Duke as a boy looked like a souvenir. Moths had eaten the flags flown by the Northinterland Fencible Regiments at the Napoleonic Wars.

'Canna hilp yoo?' a woman asked before I could examine further. She stood behind the counter, arms bulging from a black chiffon blouse.

I said I was looking for the curator, that I was writing a travel book and would like to speak with him. She hesitated so I picked up a guide book from the counter. 'They're sairventy-fife pairnce itch,' she said. I put my hand into an empty pocket.

'You're meaning Mr Northinterlund, are ye nort?' she asked.

'Is he the curator?' I asked confused and worried, visions of the Duke marching out to meet me, and me wearing his breeches too.

'Aye,' she said. 'Ah'xpairct yull faind him aboot if you went through. Was it a student's tuckit you'd be wanting? That'll be two poonds plus sairventy-fife fer the geed book.'

'Uh, well never mind now. He must be a busy man today. I'll call on him at home, I think, later. He is the only curator, isn't he?'

'Och aye, he's th'only one ah knoo aboot.'

I almost ran along the foot of the north wall, coming up against a flight of steps, two men lugging a twenty-foot-wide rolled-up carpet over the threshold of an open door, the man in charge grumbling. Mr Northinterland, no doubt, his pipe snuffed out, his suede safari jacket belted tight, red beard like a blow torch burning the top off his blotched bald head.

Standing on the demolished pierway, a jabbled sea under scowling clouds, the dream came back like a wave against a rock. The more people I had to ask, the more likely he'd come to know I was looking for him. He'd caught me out again in one of his conundrums. I'd got the wrong Kildaggie.

Strokes of rain against my face, the tide turned scrolls along the sand. No human tracks. The hags of rock I'd dreamt were too far away with sea still spuming over them. No seals, only gulls worry and riddle at pickings. Once beyond the castle the tide ran in among the tree roots. Hares scuttered into fine grained burrows dug in braes of Stinking Willies. Along the scum tide-line Fairy Liquid bottles wiped clean of their lettering, clean as white dishes among the useless shanks of blue nylon rope, cork bobbers and plastic lemons. I threw myself down on the thick soft grass, felt I'd dreamt my whole life till that moment, waking to find myself washed up on a seaside meadow with junk chucked overboard. So I stood and walked another hundred yards, mood as bloddy as the weather. No use looking for Mallachie White in sea dreams.

As I shut my gate Marine Cormorant appeared from next door, walking like a horse on stairs. She had to pass me, nodding sharply.

'Och, there y'are!' she said, as if to a dog absent nights on end. 'An' Kit nex' dour sayin' y'muss b'daird an' berried a week gone she's naw set eyes on ye yet.'

'I could say the same of her,' I said to the wind, which slammed the door.

The Northinterland Estate Office slumbered in Sunday, no sign of Monday morning yet, no clacking typewriter, no telephone sprung to life as I stood listening on dun lino stairs, listening for Milky White's crêpe-soled walk along polished creaking floors in this place where he finds and slits open the letter from his mother, posted to a wooden panelled room. I took the stairs one at a time, brass rods gleaming, the wood polished and polished, coming upon a first-floor door of frosted glass, ENQUIRIES PLEASE KNOCK in gold letters. It rattled and a voice responded before my second knuckle landed. She was expecting someone, the business known and urgent.

'Helloo there,' she said, not at all surprised to see me, 'and what canna do for you?'

Square on, her padded shoulders were as wide as the desk.

'I'm looking for the curator of the museum,' I said, with glowing confidence in her. A hand-set radio on the table began to hiss, but she ignored it while I stared, expecting the next voice to come from there. It didn't, so the woman took me by surprise instead.

'Oh, aboot the job was it?'

'The job,' I repeated, neither question nor answer.

'Aye,' she said, 'the scheme, the cataloguing scheme.'

This time I answered promptly. 'Yes.'

'Weel, ah'xpairct Mr Wheet's up at the cassle or somewhere . . . '

His name, I assumed, at last. I was shaking as I confirmed it.

'Mr uhm who? . . . Did you say White?'

'Aye,' she said. 'Melvyn Wheet,' dialling a number and asking for Mr Northinterland, a name which dehydrated me. 'There's a young man,' she said, 'looking for the Wheet chappie.' Her persistent reply to his information was: 'Naw, aye, is thart so?' Mr Northinterland, it was clear, did not know where Mr White was, or where he lived. While she raised some other matter, I examined a survey map of the area, pinned in sections along the wall. Beside it, on a general notice board, was Lord Donald's Holiday Schedule. This week he was due back from Gran Canaria before departing for Cagliari for six weeks in November. Most of his winter seemed scheduled thus.

'Weel, there's naw luck there. Mr Northinterlund hasna seen hide no hair o'the marn.'

'But isn't Mr Northinterland the curator?' I asked.

'Aye, of the cassle he is, no the museum. The museum's closed doon, you see. Ah woon't be a tick . . . '.

She left me to the map again so I tried finding the museum without success. Half a minute later she returned with a large man who wore a brown suit and spotted tie, his eye lids drooped, his lips pure Eton hubris. He spoke Etonian, shaking hands like pumping a well, his thick black hair greying at forty.

'Ah hello there. Another stray? So, I gather you're tracking the elusive White – I'm Raif by the way, spelt with an "L", Trethowan. What's yours?'

'Cedric Lily.'

'Well, Cedric Lily, we do not know where he is. All I can tell you is that he gets his bread from Mrs Goskirkle. Saw him down there once. Bit of a mystery chap is Mr White, but then he's a free spirit, he's not employed by us. Which is no doubt why he doesn't tell us his whereabouts. Had a letter delivered here once, but that doesn't help.'

'I see. Well, thank you.' I tried to look as if I were leaving but Raif firmly blocked my way.

'What do you do at the moment Cedric, if you don't mind my asking?'

I said I'd taken a winter let to write a book.

'Oh jolly good. Perfect. Ideal.'

'Yes it is,' I said. 'Very quiet.'

'No,' he said, 'I meant for the cataloguing scheme, being three days a week. Plenty of time to write, yes?'

'Ideal,' I agreed.

'Any background Cedric? History degree?'

I said I was keen on history.

'Even better, hahaha. But you do know, do you, that to qualify for a Manpower Service Scheme you must have been unemployed for the last twelve months?'

'Yes,' I answered, without meaning.

'Splendid. Well, why not hop down to the bread shop. Best of British, Cedric.'

I chose a window seat in the Snackie Bar opposite the bread shop with a view of the High Street and many likely doors. The school dinner hour erupted quite suddenly, youthboys first, slamming the door or leaving it open, goldfish mouths as they leaned against the jukebox, boys who manage to find street corners in every room and hang there like drying clothes. I considered leaving but felt too tired and defeated. There was no hurry now. I was an unemployed man in search of his employer. I sipped tea and enjoyed my pastie and chips as two boys fed ten pence bit after bit into the Tiger Hell machine.

'SHIT . . . BASTARD! I'LL GAIRT THART MARTIAN BASTARD ONE DAY.'

The Tiger Hell repeated jingle-blips as green objects slipped out from behind planets to unleash pink rays.

' 'ERE FOCK IT. SEZ FREE GAW AN'ALL.' He kicked the machine and tilted it sideways off the carpet.

I stared through the window at the bickering rain as people started running or hugging doorways. The jukebox hissed and stuttered so the lads thumped it and made guitar sounds with their mouth, tongue and throats. Then the girls rushed in, wet-haired and fookin socked tuther skan. For ten minutes the door opened and slammed in fury, once in, fags out.

I kept a hole rubbed in the window scum and found I just had to examine every pedestrian, car driver and passenger in case Milky came down from wherever he was for a pastie or his daily loaf. It was only 12.30. I stared so hard my eyes watered and throat stretched. At one point of blurred and tricked vision I mistook the passing cars for seagulls picking scraps off the lintel. Then Milky always seemed to be among the red rubberfaced men who came out the Stag's Hotel with their dreg still warming the skin. He wouldn't lunch in the Snackie Bar. There was chip cleg over the floor, billowing fagsmoke, spilt vinegar dripping down chairlegs, dog-ends floating in ashtray Coke lakes and toast fights scattering shrapnel at every table.

One leather-gobbed boy named Earl told all the jokes and dealt the fags among acolytes only. Someone asked what he thought about Linda. 'Linda luscious,' he said, in an Asian accent, 'lush lush lush lush-*ious*,' handing his fag round for one drag each before the Paki jokes. Earl always opened his mouth and displayed masticated chips on his tongue if anyone else told a joke. Then the waitress tried clearing up and dropped a plate. After the uproar she said her mind just wasn't on the job today. Earl stood beside her and said his mind was always on the job, yum yum. He belched and said: 'Have ye haird the one aboot the Pakis in the Wuld Cup?'

Then suddenly they went. The machines died down, the Tiger Hell whimpering like a dog left in a car. The proprietress and Linda went round the tables loading the mess into buckets. The Chippie came to his Tiger Hell with a tube of florins. I watched the High Street clear of kids like fog in a sea wind and there, in a recent space like a boat missing all these days, bobbed Milky White, stepping carefully onto the pavement but not from Mrs Goskirkle's but from the other baker's, the white paper bag in his right hand, shaking his umbrella and looking skyward, brushing his trousers and opening the door of a white Mini. By the time I'd paid my bill and reached the door, Milky had driven by the co-op, the stationer and the ironmonger. From the doorway I saw him pass the old Kirk without accelerating, then round the corner from sight.

'Byeeeee,' the proprietress said as I pulled the door behind me and stepped into a brattle. 'CLOSE, AYE YER WEE GREEN BOGIE,' fat Chippie said to the Martian raider, so I said the same to the Wee White Bogie driving up the hill. My mind working perfectly now, I purchased a guide book of Kildaggie at the stationer's. On the back page was a photograph of the museum. It wasn't *in* the castle at all, but outside in the grounds, on the northern edge of the garden wall. A map showed access from the old coach road which ran along the coastline. Well, Milky hadn't been gone ten minutes. He'd probably driven down for his lunchtime roll, which meant he was at work on his cataloguing, interviewing candidates or just fretting about his antiquities. Yes, I imagined him in this pokey room, catching crumbs on the flattened white bag, kettle on a gas ring, grandfather clocks knocking out the heavy, hanging time. I ran along the sea path till I itched and sweated, soaked from the outside in drizzle as the sea whipped high. In sight of the castle I slowed, the rams backed up against the wall, the hares rushed into thickets. The museum track had muddied up, a beech copse one side, the old Factor's house and keeper's cottage to my left, abandoned like the hands' quarters and the outbiggins, slates caved in, battens rotting in the daylight. The museum stood at the far end of this track, facing south, its roof both slate and glass, one time summer house built by the 7th Duke, now grim and isolated, trees crouched over it, a gloom-grey Gothic pavilion where the Northinterlands hoarded keepsakes. I hammered on the huge double oak doors. 'MR WHITE! MR WHITE!' Feeble, useless shout, the leaden echo, deaf and dumb stone, windfall silence.

'MELVYN WHITE ... MILKY ... MILKY WHITE ... MALLACHIE WHITE ...

ACH YER WEE WHEET SORD MULLACHIE SCOATCH PUSS'N MUST . . . !'

My voice reared back in echo like a headless vision, sweeping through a locked room, the shrine of Milky's great work. I could tell just by the feel of the place that Milky hadn't been there for a long time. Nobody had, because at the foot of the steps was ample evidence of abandoned interest. My own footprints alone on a patch of builder's sand which anyone ascending these steps would have to cross. The grass grew up through vehicle tracks churned months ago, pale sodden fag packets, a whole pallet of new bricks beginning to age, McEwan's Export tins just starting to rust. Without a stick to beat a passage, the other door was inaccessible, but I crashed forward into the undergrowth towards a window and something shot out of the woods, flashing into sight behind the museum, crashing through the beeches and bracken. I listened to it running further and further into the woods, until it too must have stopped, listening to me.

By teatime the rain had cleared, so in dried clothes I set out for the museum once more, striking out through the woods the long way round, into where the deer had bolted. I followed the track that some heavy vehicle had flattened out until it was blocked by thickening spruce. A thin path along a nearby embankment emerged behind the museum. My footprints in the builder's sand might have come from the dream, so unlike my own after a downpour had perforated them. Working backwards, I obliterated them.

I turned in time to see a watcher pass behind the shutters on the second floor. Ahead of me the woman from the ticket office was a curious figure in black from head to foot, starting up the Home Farm drive, momentarily eclipsed by the statue, erected by the tenantry, of the 8th Earl. Fifty yards away, a white Mini drifted by the main gate towards Kildaggie. Milky White plain as Milky was in the driver's seat, his profile detaching itself and hanging for a second's scrutiny in better light: hard-edged as a medallion monarch, tight-lipped and wee twink-eyed, concrete-skinned, whistle-clean Mallachie Wheet. Two seconds and he'd gone.

My shoes pwanged over the tarmac as I ran flat out, just in time to see the brake lights redden, the orange indicator flash. He turned right at the sign: The Slug Sheds. A lane bordered on its southern edge by firs and a new white fence, the burn a faint rittling hundreds of feet below. North, the leens rose gently to the outmains of Home Farm, muckle John's Ayrshires coofed along the fence. That hill was a half-hour rise, The Slug Sheds being a cluster of cottages in a slug between hills, the shed lane going I knew not where, the other dead-ending in the forest above Home Farm. There was a phone box, and the nearest dwelling was a modern bungalow, where, on two strips of concrete for the wheels, Milky had parked his Mini and was, without doubt, inside. I felt no joy or satisfaction on my discovery, because it was a lonely place for one thing, and I knew why people choose to live in lonely places. The wind hissing through the hackle of whins, monstrous pylons strode from one hill to another. And I was soaked in sweat and needed a shave so the last thing I felt able to do was confront Milky White, standing there like scaff, blinking at the sitting-room curtains, waiting for Milky's eyes to burn a hole in them. But the bungalow looked deader in the harrows than his museum . . . so let the dead sleep a while longer.

Chapter Eight

Milky's bungalow at dark on a still evening. The blare of ewes, the melancholy curlew's wheeple, the far below sea a guessed-at sob, a glimp strip under a cock's-eye moon. A mile away the train runs through punctually and a dad wind drove in suddenly and sang in the pylon's humming wires.

A light glowed from Milky's porch, another dumbed by curtains from a side window. I walked by and noticed all the curtains drawn, kept walking for a hundred yards then turned back again, staring at each window as I passed, gaining the corner where a strip of trees formed a brake between the cottages and the bungalow. A door opened thirty yards away, each sound amplified in the cold night air, a damp sound of clothes rustling, peculiar to people going out in the evening dressed in their smarts. I daren't move because it was Milky's door and his ears were as sharp as mine, only I was puzzled because the sounds were too many for one person alone. Milky's company, the squark of leather jacket, the rubbing of legs in tight new jeans.

Whoever it was didn't speak, a growth of frozenness between them I could easily sense all in this instant, five seconds at the most, before I realized I must hide. The strip was only three plantings wide and twenty yards long, so I ran on tip toe at a low stone wall and vaulted into the corner of the nearest field, sending a dark-grey scrub of startled little bushes bleeting and hobbling away to safety. Ten yards away a car door opened and Milky spoke, whining, impatient.

'Why didn't you put the torch back in the glove compartment?'

The other person sighed and the car springs creaked. Milky walked back to the bungalow, soft shoed, clouting the backdoor key into its lock and switching on the kitchen light. I ducked low until the light went off. He locked the door and tested the torch on the road giving one sword-like cut across the trees. With great care the car was started, backed slowly and with much braking out onto the road and down the Slug Sheds Hill at twenty-five miles per hour. I ran to the top of the hill and watched its lights descend, flicker through the trees and disappear.

I don't expect anyone to understand why I'd to come to Kildaggie. In fact I felt I'd made a great mistake, made the more uncomfortable for having witnessed something take place between two people who had no idea of my presence. My last glimpse of the bungalow that night was as a tomb in which the living had already surrendered and invited mortality to move in with them for the next fifty years. A tomb in which the visible inhabitants had already taken life from each other and offered it to the lowest bidder. I knew the woman not just because the rubbings of her tight clothes and battle-sigh, but because I stood where she had stood beside the car, smelling her scent, conjuring her glumness from the silence and the petrol fumes. I even looked along the trees in case a burning slash from Milky's temper-torch might lift the confrontation. And still, the novel lived, taking me home like a guide book of doubt . . .

So late the following afternoon I revisited the bungalow, this time with the intention of an interview with Milky White, my reconnaissance completed and the writing up to date. In fact I wrote that last sentence in the woods on the way up, and this one on the lane outside the bungalow because the Mini has gone, there are no lights on or gaps in the curtain so I'd better walk round to the back-door . . .

I peered through the window and there was Milky White sitting at the kitchen table like a scene at Madame Tussaud's: The Contemplating Criminal as first seen by The Great Detective Lily after tracking him to his Mountain Hide-Out at the Slug Sheds. Glasseyed, he stared at me across the unlit room, rigid, his coffee mug and open book in front of him, wearing a cardigan we can easily get from Oxfam, only his came from the Menswear Department, brown with suedette front-piece. Red tie thickly knotted. He frowned, hands jerked and he came to life, standing up and knocking the table spilling coffee. He couldn't attend to me now, rushing to the sink to fetch a cloth, wiping the table, rinsing the cloth and hanging it on the tap. Like some peepshow, I couldn't take my eyes away and miss the next bit. I'd never seen Milky inside a house before. The light came on as if an attendant had come along and seen I'd put my penny in the slot. A key turned in the backdoor and the funniest bit was very realistic: this marmalade cat with no tail shot out the backdoor and then came to a standstill, scratching its ear standing up before setting off across the garden on business in a clumsy stamping motion like a trotting horse. Milky was standing an arm's length inside the backdoor, raising an arm – so this was the serious bit – which could have been a mime of a shield, the way he leaned backwards on one heel. No, perhaps he joked a mime, but I caught the expression in his eyes and face before he began to shake his head. Fear and disbelief, as if he'd been waiting to be tracked down, waiting for news of the judgment he knew would go against him. So here it was, and he couldn't believe that I had been chosen to bring it. I've never seen anyone so afraid of me before.

The penny ran out so we had time to prepare our reactions, only I forgot to show the same disbelief, the disbelief I'd rehearsed in the bathroom mirror. Here was the person I'd come to see in connection with a job. Ought I to have known him as Melvyn White? So I almost asked if he were Mr White. Instead, I backed away from him and smiled, a messenger of bad news. His tight lips stiffened, drawing in, eyes canopied in frown as if a great unfairness had taken place or he suspected I was from some detective agency his mum had hired to get those snap shots back he'd stolen, the inch-square ones of him on the beach with a bucket and spade, Milky only as high as his dad's wellington boot. And then we put another penny in. The Inspector of Primary Schools at Home. Milky with sideburns almost whiskers down to his jowls, his quick Victorian disguise a stern but recognizable transition. It was always there, even in the Family Portrait. But this stereotype disintegrated into The Meeting of Two Opposites. Human Milky, brushed against the door frame as he came forward and as he went to flick off the grime which might have thereby lodged in this transaction, he noticed real dandruff on his shoulder, no artist's powder this. From politeness I turned away and saw the cat farting over the dirt with its stump thumbs up, eyes screwed tight. I began laughing.

'Christ.' I hadn't meant to say Christ, I just assumed defence of the cat against Milky, 'What happened to the cat? Is it a Manx?'

Milky was upset, embarrassed by his cat too. 'No, no, not a Manx. He, uhm, it broke two years ago in an accident. The, uhm, vetinary surgeon amputated it. He's not well right now, having contracted constipation. I think he ate a hare, instead of a rabbit. An easy mistake I'm sure.'

A voice grown drier with the years, more neutral and word perfect, flattened by education into the sound of a long opening sentence to an essay. He twiddled a moustache which obviously wouldn't grow, a few coarse twists of lip hair like goat strands on barbed wire.

'But what on earth are *you* doing here?' he said and I was certain his surprise remained genuine. 'I mean, how did you know where I lived?' I said I was simply looking for the Museum Curator about the cataloguing job.

'I'd no idea it was you. Mr White's a fairly common name, isn't it? Anyway, I thought you worked at the British Museum.'

I'm sure I hadn't meant much by that remark but he received it as sarcasm and then the truth dawned on him so he said: 'But surely *you* don't live in these parts?' the way he used to say, 'but you won't get that for your birthday! Your old man can't afford it.'

'Well, I felt like a change from London,' I told him. 'Just . . . came here by chance. Heard there was a job going and was told the Estates Office had details and, well, they sort of put me onto you . . . '

'Ah,' Milky said, rubbing his chin. 'Would you care to drink a mug of instant coffee?'

In his kitchen he surrounded me with precision and cleanliness. It was difficult to imagine him surviving the dust of his museum vaults, harder still to think of him as an antiquarian. This kitchen was bare white, spotless as an operating theatre. How did people called Black, Brown or Green paint their kitchens or choose their cars? I've known a Tim Pink, Rupert Brown, Ginger Green, but they live in ordinary kitchens and drive cars of contrasting colours. I wanted to ask Milky if he could name the colour of his kitchen and car, if he could say his own name. I mean, I don't say my name unless absolutely necessary, nor would I point to a lily and say Lily. I'd avoid the possibility.

So we stood on his vinyl floor looking at the brand-new Polar-white fridge freezer matched to its easy-clean melamine units. Even the mixer taps were white, and the plastic auto-jug kettle, the adjustable browning-control toaster, the compact table-top dish-washer, the top loader, the pedal bin, the Dante Set table and chairs, those plastic mock rattan chairs, all deadly cold white domestic frost. Seated, waiting for the kettle to boil, the light turned grey through the picture window and turned grey over the Dornoch Firth. Milky rubbed his hands in the cold and said the storage heaters wouldn't come back on till five. I looked in vain for signs of another human presence, either within the kitchen or Milky's being.

'I was reading Dickens,' he said, showing off an immaculate copy of a Dickens novel.

'Have you read Charles Dickens yourself?' he asked.

He sounded on first-name terms. Charles . . .

I received a mug of cheap powder overheated coffee water, which I spat back into the mug, burnt tongue, burnt pride.

'I don't read Dickens,' I said, wishing I'd praised the view instead because I could see his body about to talk and guessed he was about to say: 'I suppose you read James Joyce,' snapping his Charlie shut like my mother with a handbag.

He fetched a small blue pack of saccharine tabs from his cardi-gan pocket and plipped three into his cup.

'Sweetex?' he asked. 'I won't read *them*,' he added, but I couldn't see the connection, not his connection. 'I like a writer with a sense of humour . . . '

'Joyce has a sense of humour,' I said.

'Oh yes,' he agreed. 'Irish humour, bog jokes. Dirty bog Irish jokes,' slurping at his coffee.

I reminded him that he used to like dirty jokes, as far as I remembered.

'I never did! How could you remember what I liked? We hardly ever knew each other.'

He sipped noisily, smacking his lips, so thin it sounded like the slacking of shallow water, but no scenic pond in his cold kitchen with its uncomfortable chairs, double glazing-trapped air, the same anticlimax I'd felt before when looking up fellow countrymen in far-flung places. Neither could I decide upon priorities in being there – my unemployment witness, the job, the past. Certain my motives were transparent, I felt unable to speak or act without manipulation. Hadn't he noticed my lack of curiosity? My refusal to defer before my potential employer?

'So, what exactly are *you* doing here?'

But he was tapping his fingers on the table top and looking at his knees. Four blips of melody alarm sounded under his cuff, commanding him to stand and open the back door.

'Watson! WATSON!' he shouted. 'Silly feline. Always goes off when it's his teatime, ha, just like my watch.'

I pondered this one in the chin-rubbing silence, calling your cat Watson, the butt of your intellectual superiority. And like a Victorian it had bowel trouble and I wondered which came first, Milky's assessment of himself or his cat. I did not repeat my question. I thought I saw exactly what he was doing there and couldn't face his version right then. It was a natural silence. My depression, his worry and distraction because someone was expected. The cat's teatime had simply reminded him to prepare for the visitor. I stuck to my seat now hoping he would continue to ignore me, warming my hands on the mug and staring at the fading light in this muddy brown liquid I'd hardly sipped, Milky watching the back door as if it might shut on his fingers.

'Uhm, look . . . Cedric,' he said at last and I knew I'd out-silenced him, 'this hrrm-hrrrrmmmm, may sound rather foolish but uhm, when my wife comes, if you're still here that is, I'd rather you didn't refer to me as, say, Milky, if the occasion arises. I'd just rather she didn't know about what was, well, a silly nickname I always objected to. Selina calls me Mel, but Melvyn is more appropriate under the circumstances . . . '

I should have guessed the atmosphere in the dark last night had been man and wife.

'Your wife?' I sounded far too shocked that he was married. In my world nobody married.

'Yes, of course,' he said. 'Aren't you married?'

'I'm not married . . . ' I broke off and threw my hands up at my inarticulacy, or the uphill climb.

As if, once more, he guessed I'd come with that judgment, he said: 'You have to live.'

I could have said I'd never found anyone who liked me. Or, as importantly, that events in the past had not helped my belief in human beings, but all communication was prevented by his raised finger demanding silence. His wife approached.

We listened to the shunting as she parked beside the house, the slamming of the driver's door and then footsteps. Melvyn shoved the coffee cups into the dishwasher, rinsed the sink and stood near the back door. As it opened I rose to my feet.

'Oh?' she asked. 'Who's this, Mel?'

'Ah, well, this is someone called Cedric Lily, who, uhm, hails from my former vicinity. He attended one of the uhm schools I temporarily attended.'

She understood this secret communication and visibly stubbed her welcome out, a greeting like spittle on her lips. 'Oh I see.' She placed her shopping bag in the corner and took her handbag and woolly hat with her into what I presumed must be their bedroom, leaving a trail of heavy-scented boredom and the sound of a slamming door. Her – call it ordinariness for the moment – swept through the air like a poison gas, the silence almost drizzling upon us, a thing I supposed came to everybody's house eventually.

'She works down the Chemist's shop,' Milky said unnecessarily.

She was less than plain in her round, powder-paled face with badly hidden scabs and new spots round her mouth, brown hair a perfect helmet of sprayed stuckness. Her silvered lips, large eyes lined like a drawing of felt-tip eyes, lashes mascaraed into a hedge. She bulged in clothing not from plumpness, but insistence on exact sizes. Her blue trouser suit with reinforced seamwork, feet convexed in white stocking-socks and wet-look black high heels. Perhaps she'd come with the bungalow and mass production. I'd seen those poverty-stricken Turks chucking bundles of those blue suits into the street from the second floor; men and women whose grandmothers once made Turkish carpets.

'Well,' I said standing up, the economic Osman strip light blinding us and glaring off the wipe-clean surfacing. 'I was about to say it's getting dark.' Milky still touched the light switch like he was showing off his Dan Dare Radar Set.

'Best be going,' and I couldn't even remember his real name. He clapped his hands and opened the back door.

'Ah, right then. Yes,' looking at his watch. 'There's a programme Selina likes to watch on the colour television. I have to get the set out and turn it on for her. Ha, I must say though, *EastEnders* doesn't turn me on, huhuh!'

'I'll find out about the job some other time,' I said. He looked at me like he knew this was only an excuse to barge in and nose about.

'I call it my bob-a-job scheme,' he said. 'It's only a Manpower Services thing. You are unemployed then?'

'In a manner of speaking,' I tried to sound sarcastic but failed and could have punched him in the gob, put dogshit in the washing machine, yeah and this one's fer Dennis yer mother's . . .

He asked me if I had experience. 'I don't know what you've done, do I? You failed your A-levels, I know that. This doesn't always matter for the inferior posts . . . '

'Experience of what?' I asked.

'Cataloguing, of course. Or computer management, historical research . . . didn't you even do the filing at that builder's merchants you worked in, last time we met?'

'I've taught English in Rome, Naples and Bari, literature A-Level in Uganda, which doesn't help at all of course. No Dickens. No computers. Still, if you get any Centurians in formaldehyde come to life on you, you could always let me have a go at them with a few nouns and the simple present and I'll have them reading Dickens in no time.' I'd meant to insult him and would have if he hadn't clapped his hands together in delight and scared Watson back down the garden, laughing like a road drill because he thought I'd made a joke for him.

'Centurians in formaldehyde, ha ha ha, yes, good one that. Sounds like Basilicas in . . . in . . . '

It eluded him through several leg slaps and wracked brains until his eyes, still in their slits, prised a slit further with satisfaction.

'I've got one,' he snapped as if he'd hooked, or wanted us to believe he'd hooked, a fish. 'Doxa-logies!'

In case Selina heard him laugh he shoved his fist in his mouth while I stared at him in disbelief. I knew the word, remembered it from Sunday School. Another boy called Melvyn, known as Bacon Ears, had shouted it out when Miss Langley asked us which Book in the Bible told the story of David and Saul. It must have been the sound, the way he squeaked it out and added Miss Langley's Christian name which made us piss ourselves. 'Doxa-logies, Nina.' All of us, that is, except Milky White and Nina. 'That's not funny,' Milky had said with real contempt, 'I don't see what you find so funny about that. Bacon Ears is a gib loof twit . . . ' He was jealous, that's all, because it was the species of word he made jokes about himself. And now he was saying how funny it had all been, old Bacon Ears and Doxa-logies, old Nina Langley licking her lips in dismay and shouting 'Boys, please boys,' as we chanted 'Doxa-logies, Nina' and nearly threw up sniggering. Miss Langley became Mrs White slamming the bedroom door, coming down the passage, Milky coughing and blushing, hurrying himself now: 'Anyway, look Sedge, it's not up to me entirely. Uhm, you see, I have to, er, bring Lord Donald in on it of course, seeing as it's his museum. All the exhibits were collected by his ancestors.'

When he uttered Lord Donald's name he straightened himself and his tie, so I tweaked the green cord breeches and thought: you silly bastard. Selina came into the kitchen and filled the kettle. She'd changed into pink fluffy slippers which had floppy ears, two eyes and a black cob of something for a nose. The door closed on me as Melvyn stuttered about our paths crossing, no doubt, due to the smallness of the world. I thanked him for the coffee and turned my back on his strip of face in the door crack.

In the forest I sat on a toppled trunk and attempted self-persuasion. Stay in Scotland. See it through. Around me were felled trees like piles of antlers in the moonlight, sneddings strewn around the stumps. I'd known many people marry from fear of living on with their own thoughts and memories. Marry, and all thought is scrambled like an illegal broadcast. The cemetery of life, like up here in the Slug Sheds. What place could I expect in that life? What possible question could I ask?

This was my usual role after all: a threat to ordered lives; the destructive force, untapped, unshared. It meant you drifted on, another job in another country, more couples ask you round then drop you for no reason you can identify. I frighten people. They think I won't accept happiness. They feel I expect them to question what they've accepted. What I failed to understand was how one person could live with another. Why anyone should wish to spend more than a day or two in another's company, intimacy, world. Some feeling they profess to have for each other? A deep lie which concretizes on the pillow. People have said I kept my hands in pockets when it was normal to gesticulate, that I averted my eyes when speaking. I've known waitresses refuse to serve me for not smiling. I've known people turn the light off when they see me coming, pretending they're out, hiding behind the door on their knees. So I expected, understood Milky's expression, behaviour, language. Why go again? Milky would remember me looking through his window for years yet. It was time to deceive myself again using words like intention for pointlessness, solitude for loneliness. I didn't need anyone. Milky White was a novella after all, an 85 page dead-ender, a triumph of solipsism, a tour de force in failure. It remained for me to shut shop, sell off the remainder, and leave the reader with a thick ear.

I had to admit they made a perfect couple, Milky and Semolina. My laugh echoed in the shadows. A hornie owl skirled and made off with queeking shrew. I set off slowly along the track.

The track widened and the trees thinned and then I was overlooking the farm, the castle, the sea with the wind coming off it. Reaching the cottage gate I could not advance and face the next move yet, so I stood and watched the clouds race by, the wind shaking things. The clothes line danced like a skipping rope on the grass slope out front, wind vanes rattled, television aerials hooted, plastic sheets over the hay bigs rapped like banknotes flicked and tested – all set then for the ending. Only I possessed none of this force on display around me. In comparison I was actually nothing – I had to think this, of course, the idea that you are nothing without a voice recognized by listeners. But, I'll publish this novella and everything will change.

I didn't even know if I had enough money for the coach fare to London, but this desire to be gone conflicted with a rising hatred of Milky for having wasted my time – yet without him this text would not exist. I didn't care. I simply needed an ending so I acted one out which I reproduce here.

My whole being was in an impotent rage. I begged to be torn apart and flung in the sea, crushed by darkness, scared out of my wits by the clawing branches and hissing winds. I almost kicked the front door open, threw clothes everywhere and changed into my thick roll neck, kept the Duke's breeches on, made a thermos of tea and packed it along with a torch into a knapsack, slammed the door shut and set off, marching down the blinded track with the wind still gathering, spitters of rain in each blirt and driven clud. The blakeys on my walking shoes sparked on the castle drive. I saw a light in the southern tower, a car parked below Mr Northinterland's door. The cobbles were hushed and ghostly so I whistled, a joskin, a right hoolet inclined to begunking at the back gate. High walls moved in the dark; huge trees leaned out the sky; and far beyond the nearest rocks the sea boomed like its jaws were running through a catacomb. I reached the sea wall and the sound flattened out, stones shoggling underfoot as I ran towards the sand, the gentle bay at the old pierhead expecting sensation to rise and live and shake free from the feeble beat of Milky and Selina's world; where sound was an electric hum and feeling came from running a finger over the spotless worktop. So, drawn towards the drag and dog of the long, low tide, I (avoiding words like doomed and soul) tested 'surrender of body and mind'. I was cantering over the rippled sand the length of the skellie, through sleech and lake and kelp towards the vast sea space. Shouting came naturally, the sea called back from its swill at ground ebb and its spunedrift outby. I threw stones and stampeded. I could hear the critics yammering like gulls at my formidable talent. A scene like this would look good on a wide screen. I'll write an African novel next, whoooooeeeeee aiiii-yeeeeee. And then the gulls were like readers skipping and snarling, cheated of a mystery or six-page affair (no way am I screwing Selina in Kildaggie woods or having the Duchess put her hand down the Duke's breeches) or confessions of a murderer. Clouds spun, wind punched and sailed in billowing breeches until, being a smoker, I dropped and gluttered on the link's edge like a flung I don't know what – bobber or Head & Shoulders bottle – as the moon pulled . . .

This was exciting, panting on the tide line at the end of my first novella, knapsack thrown carelessly into the salt-fail, sleeves rolled, face up to the deep sky and waxing moon. The other truth was that I'd thrown myself like spittle from my own mouth against the wind and been thrown back, and it was over, choked down by a sob, the next hundred pages out there somewhere in the dark. From behind me a scuffing in whins, the swing of a hinge, the fall of a boot. I grabbed for the torch. Had someone watched me dance? The beam swept uselessly. I knew why Milky had made such a fuss about the torch. In Africa you didn't bother, you just saw by the moon like everyone else, stumbling amid sandle-fall and hoping you do not say good evening to a robber with a ready panga. There was nobody there, only rams and hares and the wind's fingers fiddling. But I gripped the torch as if it were a gun of light, safety catch off, ready to scare the living day-nights with a spark of day. I suppose the fact that I'd taken it with me at all indicated the place I deserved in the world. Those few months in London had done this. Well, I could be back there by 6 am the day after next, having breakfast in the cafe opposite the VSO. Perhaps within a fortnight I'd be in Tanzania. Chapter Nine?

Within sight of Middle Cottage I could tell someone had been. The gate was swinging loose in the wind and banging on the post. I don't know why I starting running, but, yes, there was a note in the letterbox.

Dear Cedric, I am sorry if you think I appeared remiss by failing to invite you to remain for a light supper, but there were several pressing items on mine and Selina's agenda.

However, please accept our invitation for tomorrow evening at 7 o' clock. Melvyn White MA.

I threw it in the Rayburn and watched it flare.

THE END

Cedric Lily, Kildaggie, Scotland.
September 1987

Chapter Nine

Daz's nature turned the most, but Skinny went the weirdest in my opinion. As a boy, Daz was stocky, snub-nosed with a blond curly fleece, thriving on speed and perseverance. He gloated in victory but shrugged defeat off carelessly. Until we went to Little Nineveh he was my best friend. Loyal, he defended me and we shared the spoils and did most things together except bike rides. Daz had the ability to raise your spirits and keep morale by saying: 'Nah, doan worry abowd it.' He was rough but never cruel, always put his fish back alive and never threw stones at cats, only lumps of dirt. He had a cat of his own called Smokey Joe. At times we were insepa-rable and I relied on his strength and optimism, he on my skill and ideas.

The well-being of our friendship was marked by certain rituals carried out with inobtrusive importance, the meaning of which went deep in us both. The highest ritual was the showing me over his house, number forty-three. This took place when his parents were out and his sister couldn't be bothered to keep her eye on us. From one room to another – there were only four – we viewed the contents: every drawer and cupboardful, every box on the wardrobe, every bit and bob in the jars and envelopes. Daz showed me his family secrets just so we could laugh together about how foolish, strange and horrible grown-ups were. You see, there was his father's watchmaker's eyeglass, his false teeth and eye-patch, his eye-bath and denture tablets (Daz once sucked one and puked up in the sink). His mother's girdles and false nails. His sister's first tooth in tissue paper with its curled root like we'd found in sheep skulls. And a tin of smoker's tooth-powder. At such objects we'd piss ourselves and prance about. This was an intimate and mysterious ritual, the showing me over the house.

Then, Yvonne's murder, after which I only went once more into Daz's house. This time I was shown things which restored his father's image. Daz's way of telling me he'd transferred his affections to his father. I was shown but not allowed to touch his father's snooker cue, which had never interested him before, its master no longer the twit with runny glass eyes and plastic teeth but part of the greater world, one where Daz was going and where you carried a long, thin wooden case and played snooker for the British Legion in their clubhouse next to Seeboard. He'd won a shield to prove it, Daz's dad.

BRITISH LEGION. EAST SUSSEX LEAGUE WINNERS 1968.

'Smart that,' Daz said, rubbing my fingerprints off it with his cuff. ' 'E's gonna take me up there one day.'

The change in him was so sudden. His loyalty and strength turning to cynicism, bullying and thoughtless acts, the insensitive youth emerging fully haired, worshipping speed and domination with a sneer. His voice broke like a bottle against a wall, shards of cut voice everywhere, slitting whispers and gouging growls. His movements vulgarized. He was no longer stocky cute but rape-man coming, the youngest smoker down the bike sheds, the first in our class to get suspended. We stopped calling him Daz and called him Ashdown. We didn't want him fishing with us either, the way he ripped out fence posts and javelled them at cats and shoved bangers down fish's throats, setting light, watching it swim off and blow to bits shouting 'Fuckin' brill, smart, smart!' Then the Ashdowns moved to Paddock Wood. Daz's sister had Basil Latter's bun in her oven and she was only sixteen. Basil was off in the Transport Corps, Germany.

Me and Skinny watched them load the lorry. I'd seen their stuff hundreds of times and felt embarrassed to see it carried by men into the street and dumped upside down or sideways into the lorry. Of course the teeth and shoeboxes and girdles weren't visible, but we all remembered what came out of Milky White's lorry. Poor old Daz and his tatty furniture. They didn't bother packing the telly. Mr Ashdown wheelbarrowed it down the pond and tipped it in the bushes. Upset a lot of us that did. Told Skinny's dad he couldn't give a tinker's, the telly was knackered and wouldn't survive the road. Time came and Daz wore his best gear, skinhead stuff, chewing about six sticks of Juicy Fruit. Me and Skinny shrugged beside the car. 'See yer then, Daz,' we said. He said: 'Fuckin' glad'm ge'n ouda this dump at last, oi c'n tellyer.'

'Whoiy'zat then, Ashdown?' Skinny asked.

He came back two years later to answer the question. One hot July afternoon, a screech of wide tyres outside Skinny's house announced his presence in a souped-up, rally-striped Go-Fast Anglia. I came out and he was sitting on its roof, feet on the bonnet, talking down at Skinny. When he saw me he flicked his dog-end over Mrs Taylor's fence into her best chrysanths.

'Alroight then, Sedge? 'Ow's it gooin' Skinny me ol' moosh?'

His girlfriend sat in the car smoking and gawking out the window, bored and hot. At seventeen Daz had a beer gut, twelve hole lace-ups, and a white T-shirt, which said UP THE GUNNERS. 'Fuckin' dump still then, this ol' place? 'In it, Teen? Whatcha fink, Teen? Nah, she ain' tawkin' the grumpy ol' cow. Di'n wanna come, did she? See the ol' pond's still there then. Ain' filled it in yet then, Skin? Jesus!' So he asked me what I was doing instead. A-Levels, I told him.

'Cor, brainy all of a sudden incha, moosh?'

I never heard why Paddock Wood was so great. I left him cursing the village, Tina fanning herself behind the baking windscreen with its DAZ 'N TINA green strip, Skinny wiping his forehead with a handkerchief and looking up and down Barratt's Road.

The schoolboy Skinny wore his satchel slung diagonally across his blazer in the longest hole so it bumped his legs and tripped him up. His cap was either skew-whiff or back-the-front, a habit I reckon he picked up from Partridge. Anyway, he looked the clot he was taken for, what with giglamps and thick, hedgy curls. He was teased but not bullied, and nobody actually disliked him, his ineptitude always comic. Only his incomprehension kept him introverted.

He accepted his fate early on: that life continued in your father's footsteps. Village tradition, this was. Our fathers came home at teatime moaning about their jobs. Village tradition meant living at home after leaving school, working up the woodyard, getting a moped on HP, learning to drive, getting engaged to your first bird and going on the council list. Fatherhood sort of began about then.

Skinny had to put up with his dad coming in from work each day covered head to foot in pale-grey grime from the gypsum pits. Skinny's mum was incontinent – I only knew this later, so I suppose Skinny didn't dare wonder at the way things were with any sense of regret. If he had I saw no evidence, so I suppose it entered his incomprehensible file. We all laughed at Skinny's mum and even said 'Cor, your fuckin' mum, Skin,' to his face. 'Wha's wrong wiv 'er?' he'd ask. Well, she always wore a turban scarf, housecoat and slippers, even up the shops. Bare legs winter or summer, stockings rolled down on Sundays, a fag perpetually stuck to her bright-pink cake of a bottom lip, she stooped and you couldn't understand a bloody word she said the way her voice meowed some word until she coughed and couldn't stop coughing. The rest of the sentence came in hand signals. Skinny's sister Joyce was four years older than him and had a reading age of eight. Her entire school career was in remedials. Skinny's mother couldn't read or write. They never went on holiday.

I don't know though about his incomprehensible file. There were aspects of his family life he saw as comic publically. He may simply have kept his human assessments to himself. Their cat had one eye, their budgie's feathers fell out and it spent its last week looking like a chicken leg on a perch. He said he wrote to *Blue Peter* about it but never got a badge. He fetched the cage out every night so we could watch it while we played football but his mum'd run up the road to fetch it in, nearly dying herself from coughing and shouting, sounding like a dog who couldn't bark. We had a dog like that, a Basenji. Couldn't bark, just gargled in its throat. The budgie at least died singing. Joey, Skinny said its name was.

Skinny saw jokes like this and came through it all, till Little Nineveh that is. Even though he didn't see anything there and wasn't even scared, thought he was making it up as a laugh. He ran off before he had a chance to know that *we* were scared. But afterwards, weeks, a year, longer, it terrified him. Our account of it, that is, with all his reconstruction. In the worst kind of way it bewildered him, then so did everything after that. He was always saying: 'Cor, fuck me, Sedge, whassat all about when it's a' 'ome, ay?' After the murder he started getting headaches. By Christmas he was seeing doctors at the Kent & Sussex for a nervous rash. Soon they dropped him to the B stream and chucked him out of the school orchestra, where he'd been given the violin because he wore spectacles and must have looked more musical than the triangle and tambourine players. An inexplicable skill in fractions regained Skinny's place in 3A the next year.

My own school ways were football and pranks until the fifth year. Daz's were *Motor Cycle News* and smoking. Skinny's was doing 'inventions' with his peculiar friends. Everyone thought he'd gone weird in the fifth year.

'That silly cunt Skinny's a nutcase, i'n 'e?' we said often enough, 'You should see what eez done to eez 'ands.'

I date it from the day he showed me a comic called *Dead Worlds*, which made him fiendishly ecstatic. I thought it wasn't bad but I didn't want to eat human flesh over it like he did. The next day he showed me another one, *Creepy Tales*. Soon he was telling me what the Germans did to spies, what the Japs did to POWs, what Nazis did to Jews. Did I know that chickens run round in circles if you cut their heads off? Did I know there were men who bit the heads off newly-born puppies for a bet? There was this film he wanted to see about a scientist who pulled a man's intestines out and stretched them like rope for twenty miles along the ground so he could measure them. Did I know anyone who had a hamster? 'Cause he heard that if you give them meat they eat themselves, so he wanted to try it, see how fat it got before it died. Easy – get some meat from his ol' woman's fridge.

The fifth year began with something going on between Skinny and his cronies. They chucked inventing and took to writing stories about ghouls, necrophilia, horror chambers, flooded dungeons, werewolves, bodysnatchers and cannibalism. Skinny's large, spidery handwriting filled whole exercise books with the stuff; words and phrases underlined at random with double-ruled, red biro. They called themselves the Nasty Party. Their anthem was cackling, fiendish cackling. Nobby Clarke, a fat kid with a donkey laugh and round spectacles. Gnashers Langford, flat-topped head, huge square teeth and massive lips like inner tubes which smacked and slithered. Pip Winter, dark-haired, dry, scaley skin like a snake's due to some oil deficiency. Even fellow members called him Lurgy. In some light he was green. In class he was yellow or brown. And lastly there was Chex who suddenly changed from the nervous, blubber-skinned feeble giant with the shakes and the longest face in the school, into a slow pounding monster of sado-masochism.

One afternoon when we had a free period in the Rural Science hut, I came upon the Nasties cackling behind the greenhouses. Skinny was kneeling on the ground in their midst, his outspread hands palm down on the turf border, as large a gap between his fingers as he could strain, while the others waited with their penknives out, blades open. Skinny gave word that he was ready and Gnashers took up position for the first turn, standing above Skinny's right hand taking aim with the penknife, Lurgy standing by with a tin of plasters. Gnashers opened his fingers and the blade dropped. Skinny screamed and danced up and down hand cupped up his wing, the expression on his red face ecstatic, fanatical, pure enjoyment. The other Nasties cawed like crows and rubbed their hands, circling to get a look. 'Blood-blood-blood,' they chanted. 'Less 'ave a look, YEEESSSS, a slit, YYYYEEEEAAAWWWWW, BLOOD . . . '

Skinny passed his O-Level maths and found a job that summer: office boy at the Land Registry in Tunbridge Wells. I hardly saw him all summer, but then he was the last person I thought I'd see in college come September. Every Wednesday the Land Registry sent him on day-release for Business Studies. In the mornings we waited at the same bus stop in any case. At first he followed me upstairs to the back seats, each Wednesday bringing along his old school briefcase with its dead-biro engraving of some befanged Draculitic hero gouged into the leather. I was already in the habit of speaking with another boy I'd struck up a bus journey friendship with: Adrian Staples. He'd left the great Skinner's School to take his A-Levels at college. He told me about Plato's *Republic* and Galileo. I read Faust and Seneca's *Oedipus* so I could discuss it with him. Skinny continued to sit with me from loyalty at first, silent the whole hour there and the whole hour back, blowing on the window and doodling patterns in the condensation of those cold October journies. Then Jeremy Feakins got a job in Tunbridge Wells too, and Skinny sat with him downstairs, where they read and discussed horror comics. Neither of them smoked. In the end I was on nodding and 'watcha' terms only with Skinny, usually at bus stops.

The summer that Daz turned up in his Anglia, Skinny's mum had a colostomy bag and his dad a hernia. Joyce Wickham gave birth to Beverly Belle and made Skinny an uncle.

Which brings me to the very last visit I paid to Barratt's Road. I was home from Italy, two days before I flew to Africa. My parents were on holiday, Skinny's dad told me, so I let myself into an empty house. Young Skin was twenty-five now, but Mrs Wickham had died and Mr Wickham purchased their council house in his grief, perhaps for Skinny when he married – you can be on the list donkey's years now. He'd done it up nice. Yes, I'd said, collared because I'd got off the bus and walked down the back path past Skinny's house. Pink facia bricks. Georgian hardwood front door. Come and see inside the extension, Cedric. Then he told me all about his wife dying and how he'd had to demolish the old garden shed we all remembered, to make way for progress.

That evening out of habit I went into my parents' bedroom and looked out the window. I could see as far as the two trees up, the pond down. In the road below, Skinny was getting into a car, a Driving School board on top. Milky White's dad got in beside Skinny.

LEARN TO DRIVE THE WHITE WAY

The car lurched forward like a rabbit sniffing. Skinny tried again and the rabbit escaped, rocking up the road on invisible waves.

Three years later I was on school business in the Ugandan capital and stayed overnight with a Red Cross worker from Marden in Kent. Each week his mother dispatched him the *Kent & Sussex Courier* and it came by diplomatic bag. One evening my host was called away and so I took a pile of *Couriers* and flicked through the Village News sections, coming across a headline on an inside page:

RETURN OF THE BARRATT'S ROAD SLASHER

For the second time in a month, tyres had been slashed by night down Barratt's Road. I turned up seven such articles on the Slasher, who struck randomly over a period of fourteen months. One morning Skinny's dad had found all four tyres slashed on his work van and Skinny's moped tyres had been ribboned and disembowelled. Dennis Packham's dad finally caught the Slasher.

MYSTERY SLASHER WAS DEPRESSED DRIVING INSTRUCTOR

Milky White's dad was fined, ordered to pay damages and was under psychiatric treatment, but it didn't say what he was depressed about.

Chapter Ten

Suppose I didn't go to Tanzania or London? Supposing I lie on my back and stare at the bedroom ceiling, unable to move for the pain? The thing was I knew Marine Cormorant would inspect and scrutinize the cottage before I left it, so I began putting everything back where I found it prior to cleaning up. She'd gloat as it was, so I couldn't give her the satisfaction of calling me a slob too. I had to return the carpet to the bedroom first so I lifted the sofa at one corner and attempted to yank it out from underneath. My back was unsupported and twisted. My lower muscles spasmed and I fell like a rag doll. It had happened before. I'm used to it. Three days in bed, hot baths, pain killers and I mend. Then, I won't lift anything heavier than a cup of tea for a week.

I slept the first night and half the next day on two sleeping pills and half a dozen painkillers from my emergency ration. It took me half an hour to get onto my knees, stand up and crawl downstairs to make tea, yelling from pain every yard and shaking like a drunk, trussed in an old sheet lashed tight, clutching the analgesics.

It's the third day and I'm able to leave the bedroom at almost normal procedural speed, sliding downstairs on my arse without too much discomfort. I've an emergency quarter ounce of tobacco and I sit still and upright in the armchair no longer able to contain the novella at the Plimsoll line. Chainsmoke. Coffee boiling on the hob. I've just reached into my jacket pocket for my field notebook, expecting to feel two folded ten-pound notes the size of a book of stamps which I keep in a 'secret' pocket under the flap. They're gone. My jacket has been on the chair three days. Apart from some loose change it's all I have – the coach fare to London. A painful search of the entire cottage reveals nothing. My loose change amounts to a week's food. I look at the signing date on the Declaration of Unemployment slip and count the days on my fingers. Today . . .

Yesterday I struggled up and typed a letter to the DHSS in Wick, each word accompanied by a kick in the back. I wrote about my inability to acquire a witness, not knowing anybody in Kildaggie, unhappy that my landlady should discover my circumstances, suggesting they accept my own unwitnessed signature as adequate. Then I rewound the sheet so tight I could hardly breathe, buttoned my oilskin over it and took a test walk down the garden path, swaying like a hung carcass, yelping each step, but confident of reaching the post box at the end of the track. Halfway there I almost threw up with pain, but I caught the last collection.

That evening I sat by the window watching the rain swing from drizzle to downpour, fighting exhaustion under the assumption that Milky White would call, thinking I'd missed his supper through illness, too arrogant to think otherwise. I tied a pillow to my back but the urge to lie down was too great. Hundreds of insects dashed themselves against the window, running with the rain in sheets down the glass.

The dream is well placed, very short, another series of tableaux. This time he's in his museum. I can see him through a gap in the great heavy doors throwing exhibits onto a fire in the middle of a cold, dusty floor, stirring the flames with a stick, which, unlike his sacrifices, catches fire and he stamps on it like it's a snake as I hammer and hammer on the door for him to stop.

Mid afternoon of the fifth day a letter from Wick arrived containing a blank duplicate of my unwitnessed slip and a small note: Try the postman for a witness. The alternative is to attend this office every fortnight for which this dept. offers no travelling expenses.

I counted my money again. Just over six pounds. A loaf of bread and enough onion soup on the Rayburn to keep me alive three or four days. I hesitated at the front door and finally slammed it behind me with decision, setting off up the track through the forest towards Milky's bungalow.

The car was gone but Milky was taking in his washing. He'd slung a blue shirt and a pair of cords across his arm, both encrusted with dry scabs of congealed soap powder which he was picking at. When he saw me he tried to cover up but didn't know what to say so went on picking. I told him I was sorry I'd not turned up for supper but it was like talking to a child sulking over a mud fight.

'I've been an invalid,' I said. 'This is the first chance I've had to call.'

Milky brushed and picked. I really wanted that giro so I smiled encouragement. 'I don't know what happened to these,' he said. 'Washing-machines are so sophisticated these days, all those pro-grammes. Selina usually does it. I don't think you're supposed to put the powder on the clothes though.'

I tried again. 'My back went.'

He held a finger in the air, the way some men do to herald a fart when their bowels move. 'Ah, I thought you went back. But your back went, ha ha. Sorry, Watson, was it serious?'

Two things there, but I expect you picked them up. I must move on . . . People say I'm too impatient, that I expect too much of them, that their minds aren't working all day even if mine is. They're right but knowing this didn't help me under-react with Milky, picking at his soap scabs with narrow, disbelieving eyes. Just one sign, please, of the intellect you must have acquired, the serious mind essential to one who had to drag himself away from Barratt's Road. What did I see instead? A pathetic husband, the sort one or two of my aunts had kicked out over the years, a man who faced the world with feeble, childish jokes. In such a presence I physically weak-ened. I could have curled up on the ground and gone to sleep, only my mind kept alive, endangering self-hatred for having expected anything from anyone, let alone him, a disappointment so intense it was almost a religious experience. In his eyes I had no place. He kept the knowledge of our equality to himself, denying me the pleasure of his authority. This way we continued to invalidate each other.

He began to talk in parody, calling tea 'a beverage', arching eyebrows high with each utterance, his voice taking a gradual, then heightened artificiality. He was testing the cold water, waiting to see if I would follow and act the scene with him. I knew what he was doing because I'd come across it so many times before. In Africa I met an English traveller and invited him to stay with me at Mbugazali for a few days. In all that time he hardly ever used his natural voice, imitating stage Irish and making a joke of everything he said. He was so afraid of communicating with me that he would rather demonstrate his total inability to imitate a half dozen accents than ask me, face to face, if he could listen to my radio or make tea or if I could fix him up with a schoolgirl. Desmond had been much the same. Anything serious to discuss, money or a slice of bread, he could only raise the matter after ten minutes of comic overture in a comic voice. Micky Mouse asked me for a quid. Donald Duck borrowed my sugar and one night Bogart playing Philip Marlowe Private Eye came and asked if I could spare him a rubber jiffy, like some cop musta pumped some lead through his, wise guy. Milky started the same business to avoid raising any matter, only his voice impersonated the Victorian gentleman, or Sherlock Holmes or some fatuous country squire. By implication there was an old chap or Watson at the end of each sentence, depending on its style or subject.

'Would you care to partake of some beverage . . . ?'

I said I hoped Selina hadn't cooked anything special for supper.

'I hoped that too, what?' he said, mumbling. 'Just scrambled egg, Watson.'

He looked for somewhere to put the clothes. 'I was asked to iron these. Servants all orf playing golf – took the iron. Ha. We go to Wick every Friday evening, you see. Like to light the candle both ends. For the weekend.'

'Is it Friday then?' I asked.

He was astonished. 'Good Lord, do you really not know which day it is?'

'No, I don't. I never know the day or time anyway.'

'Consult my chronometer, Watson. A simple solution. Hark.

Fifteen zero three and twenty seconds. Fantastic watches these. Hark again!'

My fist touched the Declaration of Unemployment slip in my pocket and I changed the subject. 'You go to Wick, don't you? I may have to go to Wick.' Milky said he'd lived there for several years. In fact they'd moved there after marriage. Selina had a sister there. Wick, he said, was on top of the British candle. 'And you're its blue flame, are you?' I asked. No response. I left the Declaration slip in my pocket, deciding to visit Wick myself. We were still standing.

'Take a pew, take a pew,' he said.

As he made the tea in silence I couldn't think of anything to break it. Having shaken off all that inarticulate ignorance of Barratt's Road, we found our new worlds of Museum Curator and Novella-ist more stifling than the old, more untrusting one. Afraid to reveal what knowledge we'd gained, we didn't even wonder if our paths had crossed. Milky stood by his kettle racking his memory for some neutral incident from the past, something inoffensive to chuckle over, something we did as twelve-year-olds before we'd read all those books. For his sake my mind blanked out the past. Our old, dark ways had been all instinct and suspicion. Insight raised self-consciousness and our lives were guesswork now we'd broken with tradition and rejected the village and our family; left to codes of our own, illuminated minds which made us lonely, proud and bitter. Injured by uncertainty, we'd emulated an ideal of the larger English tradition which had no use for us. We were working class, and what we'd rejected would never take us back, yet we remained unrecognized by that which had seduced us. Our gains were useless to us. Any slight compassion in the system, any exception made for talent (the plausible promises we both received) had been snatched back by the same hand, no illumination after all. The past darker than it might otherwise have been. The future invisible and feared. Any promise was a bulb which blew as soon as you threw the switch. And Milky bloody White was just as responsible. I felt he'd led me there, that none of it would have happened if he'd stayed away from Little Nineveh, if he'd made a greater success . . .

So here we sat in his unlit kitchen saving on the light bill, chinking tea cups made of yellow glass, unable to offer each other a single word of comfort learnt from reading all those great books; which leaves an inescapable position. And an inescapable question: is it as inescapable for Milky White?

Finally, he spoke first. 'Very different up here from the Garden of England, you know. Aye, naw cheery blowsome on Wealden tree.'

I said yes, the weather was up and down too and he said: 'Hah! You may repeat that twice, I say. The wind gets up and the rain comes down.'

'Do you go back much?' I asked.

'To where?'

'Barratt's Road,' I said.

'Now and then. Why?'

'I wondered if they'd filled the pond in yet.'

I smiled at my weak tea and the milk flecks spinning in the cup. The tongs in the sugar lump bowl were a souvenir of Inverness.

'I'd offer you a digestive biscuit, but the digestive tin remains a repository of crumbs at present. Selina was supposed to stock up yesterday but failed.'

Cold and hungry I wished I knew what deadening emotion rooted me to the chair.

'How did you get this bungalow?' I asked.

He said it came with the job, that the Estate Office let it to him for a nominal rent.

'Oh, are you employed by the Estate Office then?'

'Well, yes. They run everything up here.'

I knew it was a lie. They'd told me themselves that Milky was not their employee.

'I'm still interested in the job.'

I had no intention of applying, but I could see his revulsion at the idea. Shoulders stiffened, breathing suspended. If I'd told him I would leave for London the moment I had the fare I know he would have paid it. What he wouldn't do was sign my Declaration slip.

'There's plenty of time to discuss it,' he said, then asked me how much rent I paid.

'Twenty-five pounds per week,' I said. 'How much do you pay?' and he bluffed old Watson this time.

'Ah, well, hmm, ours is nominal too. But, we had to spend a tidy sum to make it nice though,' waving a hand over the gadgets, longing to pat something on the head or show off its funny drawing. Then his hand patted the wallet in his back pocket.

'Had foul neighbours in Wick, oh yes. Hah. Got on my Wick too. At least it's quiet here. No one swearing through the walls or coming home drunk at two in the morning.'

It was a relief to be out of that kitchen. Milky suggested the stroll. Again I mentioned the museum as a way into his thinking but even in his mind the museum was locked. He said he didn't spend much time there. No point. The cataloguing was a mess, there were no records, the whole place needed renovating and he couldn't do anything until he had some proper help. When he said that he looked away, reminding me that Lord Donald owned it. 'You place me in an awkward position,' he said, 'I can't promise you anything. Besides, you have to get the forms from Wick, send them back, they send them to me and I shortlist the candidates for interview. Many highly qualified graduates have applied and uhm, well, it doesn't come off till November anyway.'

We descended the lane hands in pockets, leaning backwards a little and taking short slow steps. Milky's choice of a walk was to reach the shank of the hill then walk up again. But the wind was dropping as we made the hiddle, relaxing, though nothing said. Milky was more uncomfortable with this than me. School was the only thing he dared bring up.

'Cor, do you remember old Hoppity making us do road run?'

His effort to link us in retrospect was desperate. Different years, we'd never done Games with his class, never run together. Then he began to mimic the masters, easy targets, old fools the lot of them, only Milky hadn't thought so at the time. And did I remember old Pratt and Tapp, and Palmer who couldn't even spell his own name; and what about that twerp who tipped a bottle of red ink in the swimming pool? Cor, what was his name? He only remembered the odd boys, boys with impediments or real ugliness, poverty, stupidity, handicaps.

'What about Gary Starling?' I asked.

No, he didn't recall. Gary Starling, I reminded him, beat up Milky's best friend Worm'ole behind the coaches. A wild boy with slit-eyed charm, fond of smoking and shoplifting, expelled from 3B for duffing up the caretaker. No, Milky didn't know about this, but how about his impression of the caretaker. 'Oy. Boy. Gid-orf the grass. Gid-orf the grass.'

'Yeah,' I even laughed, 'ol' Barney was a bastard. We used to call him "murderer". Remember that then? Old Barney knocking someone over in Cranbrook?'

'They let him off though,' Milky said.

There was time to come to Partridge, once my case against Milky was prepared. My accusation needed careful formulation. At times like this he was more prepared with his defence and intellectual alibis. Besides, I wasn't close enough to the true real questions, questions which had to act as forces when put to him. Nor must he anticipate the inevitability of them. This afternoon I think he expected me to mention Little Nineveh. He thought I was close, but he didn't tremble, just turned his back on me full of arrogance, tapping fingers in his macintosh pocket waiting for the chance to change the subject. Next moment he was watching a flight of homing pigeons which I'd seen cowman John release out back, rooketty doos which circled and figurated along the Home Farm perimeter till one straggled off and upset the others. Milky followed them with intense concentration, counting their wing beats or timing their circles with barely perceptible nods of his head. I knew he could feel me watching him. The idea that my presence in Kildaggie was not coincidence must by now have crossed his mind. He had no choice but to wait, turn and face me. Truce.

He was miming something. Television camera. Zooming in on the pigeons. No, they were ducks, yes, ducks passing overhead. I knew the game, so he ruralized his accent.

'T'other die oi went an' troid a spart o' roach fushin'. Aye, he were crusp blue sky but here's a go, the parnd were frozen o'er.'

It was a poor impression. Jack Hargreaves sounded nothing like it but I played along and said: *Out Of Town.*

'Yep,' he said. 'Friday nights after *Scene South East.*'

We'd all watched *Out Of Town* as kids for those few times he went fishing while the tea table was cleared and our mothers got ready for the Bingo up the Victoria Hall. Mrs White didn't do the

Bingo. I imagined her ironing. Milky sang the theme tune in a low wailing rumble.

'Say wwwwHAT yer-willlll . . . '

He was desperate for me to join in so I did, on the second line.

'The countryside is still . . . '

But Milky sang his own silly version as if he'd fooled me, shown he could trap me too, that he was still an unpredictable individual:

'The country's up the 'ill . . . '

Now we sang together and my God I've never come that close to wanting to kill myself. If he'd handed me a loaded gun there and then I'd have stuck it right in my head and pulled the trigger, laughing and singing in Milky's face that moronic song: which he thought clutched at my sleeves and said doesn't it mean anything to you that Friday nights when we were boys we used to sit and watch this silly old fool go fishing or harness a shire horse to a plough? NO. I couldn't tell what was happening to me, nor could I remember ever having a decent feeling, one in which I didn't reject a given meaning, object something, subject someone, question rights and assert them simultaneously, deny there was any such state as success, and so on. I wanted existence, all existences, to end there and then with mine. One more second of life was unthinkable, but it passed and I screamed that song like a pain, Milky stringing it out like his last few seconds, the condemned Princess whose executioner agreed to her dying at the end of a song so she sang and sang . . .

' . . . The only place where I could settle dowwwwnnnn

Trou-BALLS there-AH

So much rare-AAHH

OOOUUUUTTT OF TOWN . . . '

What might have been done or said if Milky hadn't spotted Selina still interests me because Milky's voice was petering out from forgotten words and his face, stripped of all disguise, was that twelve-year-old who'd beaten up Dennis at the marbles hole. I sang what I remembered about the sun being like a bright-yellow duster polishing the blue, blue sky and then Milky pointed down the hill.

'Ah, here comes Selina,' like he might have said 'here comes my dad.'

Through gaps in the trees half a mile away, Selina's white Mini turned into the Slug Sheds road, obscured by trees once more, half a minute from view. Milky clicked his fingers and teethed the insides of his cheeks. 'Er look,' he said, click-click-click, 'I shouldn't really be down here with you. I mean I promised Selina I'd get things ready . . . The point is, you see, Watson, we-er wouldn't want Mrs Hudson in a stew. What! Don't want her to sort of surmise I asked you up here behind the good lady's back, by Jove . . . ' He clapped his hands, thirty seconds nearly up. 'Uhm, Sedge, you couldn't just leap o'er that wall and conceal yourself until we've driven orf, could you? Wouldn't ask if it wasn't urgent . . . '

'Weren't urgent,' I corrected.

I could hear the Mini now, a grinding gear change as the hill steepened, one bend from sight. If Milky hadn't asked me to I would have said 'Sorry, Holmes, but I'd rather not meet the young lady in my present state,' and bunked over the wall in any case. Milky ran on a few yards and I heard the car stop.

'What are you doing?' Selina said.

'I only nipped out for five minutes in the fresh air,' Milky said.

'Who were you with, Mel?'

'What d'you mean: who was I with?'

'Oh, come on, I know I saw you with that Cedric person. I thought you said you didn't want him hanging round and bringing embarrassment to us all . . . '.

'For pity's sake, Selina! Open this door and let me in.'

A great day for the rejected. Saved from humanity. Astonishing self-affirmation. So I stood and showed myself, three yards from Selina's big mouth.

'Oh my Gorrdd, Melvyn, what on earth is going on?'

'Fer Christ's sake, Selina, open the door will you!'

Who knows if she opened it for Christ's sake or not. Milky threw himself in and wound up the window up so fast he could have sliced an apple with it. Selina wouldn't lurch forward until he fastened his seat belt, then the Mini hung a moment on the clutch and struggled away, better driving than Skinny's. Had she learned the WHITE WAY too?

Chapter Eleven

I haven't been honest with you. Call it self-deception. I have enough money to leave but the fact is I've no intention of leaving because my way forward is clear. Some money *is* missing, and this creates the illusion of passivity. The real point of no return is the journey to Wick.

So I can still wake at dawn in good humour and walk through the monkey puzzle, to the station. A 6 am shower like net curtains in the sunlight. Black rabbits paused at their grubbings to watch me pass. Content, underway, resolving like a crossword.

Kildaggie station was two miles the other side of town, its ticket office boarded up, the grille window punctured. On the wooden shelves was an old enamel kettle standing in an inch of dust. An old diesel train coasted in, wooden interiors, sliding doors with brass fittings. I marvelled as the landscape changed every few minutes from seas and coves to salmon valleys, then desolate windspun peat bogs skailed and banked, then bents, and dog hillocks, flows, runs and lochsides until in hail of Wick we gentled by the toun ends of farms under bright white skies and clouds as big as London. As Wick appeared I craned forward on my seat and tried to see into every window of the buildings. Wick is hewed from sombre stone constantly showered upon. The wind was cold and picked all day. The Benefit Office was the last one north but looked like all Benefit Offices. Fag-ends down below the filter. A few scaffs on the cadge. A scuddie couple slagging each other. This babby with a tattoo on one plump arm crawling round the floor pepping dog-ends. The woman I saw at the hatch said next time ask the postman. She gave me the Manpower Services forms and I filled them in at the cafe overlooking Woolworths.

I followed the harbour road up onto the bluff, past half houses with dark-red doors. Glencoe. Drumcairn. Louisville. Black slate chapels, a yellow banner LET THERE BE LIGHT. The old men were huddled in a shelter on the bluff.

In a shin of sunlight on the slope into town a dog lay in the middle of the street licking its lipstick cock as a lorry drove round it.

At the station I sat on a bench with a takeaway tea. When I looked up at the station clock there was Mallachie White making his way down to the end of the platform. The way his back burned I knew he'd seen me, hurrying like you do when someone's chucking things aimlessly at the back of your head. There was half an hour till the train so I left the station and walked slowly down to the bridge where the tide ran in, green water full of skitter.

Back on the platform a few passengers boarded down the front with Milky so I had the carriage at the back to myself. The moment the train pulled away the skies were all change, this constant pitching of Scottish weather like a whole Kent autumn speeded up into a single hour. Bright low sun and slam-door gusts, dark sweeping clouds like coal sclits, windows blind with spate over the bogs. At each change I rose and walked through to the next carriage. This game is called Weather Roulette. Eventually, I would come upon Milky – that is unless we reached Kildaggie first.

I had to wait longest in the third carriage, during which the train stood at Georgemas Junction, where shafts of late sunlight scarrowed tripods under the clouds. In the fourth carriage two Dutch girls were thumbing over souvenirs of Orkney. Milky must be close, there was a toilet in the corridor and he'd think of that. Or would he save his slash till the Slug Sheds and hygiene? The miles galloped flatly by, flatly by . . . The fifth carriage – call it the third now – was First Class. The second to last was a smoker with another toilet so I sat and choked more on this woman's cigarette than my own. Back trouble had made me a real shag smoker again. We pulled up at Altanbreac for a study of desolation. The Dutch girls alighted, walking into nowhere across a track over the moss between peat stacks. Winds buckled in and strummed through the train. Purple light and bruising air, but the track joins a lane in the distance, where a building stands alone in bog on four sides horizon. It might be a castle, hall, monastery, its tower perforated and showing sky behind. The dare is to go and never come back and see how long it is before anyone comes asking for you. The seventh carriage had a family of four rustling plastic packets, sandwiches and cheese puffs. I've counted wrongly as this is the first, in my calculation, and Milky isn't here. A spitter from a heavy spud of cloud and I stand and make my way into the eighth and last carriage. Milky sits reading at the front. Growing late, a staunched sun sets in a yellow sky. At the bottom of a field I catch sight of an abandoned Commer van, faded red letters on its side. CONFECTIONER. It's half submerged in the black bog rush of an alkaline pool. I whistle a Fanfare for the Commer van but Milky can't hear the allusion over rails. Twenty minutes pass.

Still several seats behind the edge of Milky's elbow and a tiny piece of the top of his head when we neared the coast, ten miles north of Kildaggie. A real black weet on its way down so I walked over thinking of the lift I'd better get from the station. He was reading the *Museums Journal*, an article headed LIGHT IN MUSEUMS. (I'm not selling this light/dark metaphor; it's not a final discount or a new favourite with post-structural resistors, it just happens to be an article in the *Museums Journal* same way as the yellow banner hangs from the Baptist Chapel in Wick.) So I glanced down his article before Milky sensed my presence. A new generation of low voltage luminaires. Micro Profile spotlight with integral transformers. Then the Dornoch Firth appeared at Milky's elbow and he put the journal down and leaned forward to peer out the window only to catch sight of my reflection, swinging his head round to see who it really was.

'I thought I recognized you,' I said first.

'Cedric! Oh, what are you doing here?'

'I've been to Wick.' I sat down opposite him then asked if he minded. He shrugged and said 'Free country.'

'So, swotting up the job?' I asked, nodding at his journal. You'd think it was a secret document the way he opened his executive case and slipped the journal inside through a one-inch slit. I said I'd got those MSC forms about the museum job and that I'd filled them in. All I had to do was send them back and the MSC would send them on to him. I am used to making people look uncomfortable, but Milky had courage. Let me offer an example of this courage.

Me, Daz and Skinny were hunting him along the path behind the church on our way home off the school coach. Milky was almost noble that day because he'd actually been caught doing what we charged him with. Lurgy and this short-arse red face called Wheelbarrer'd gone into the Maths room during break to look for something they'd dropped, so they said. You weren't supposed to be in school during break without permission, so they crept along the corridor and sneaked the Maths room door open. Lucky they did too, for there were Milky and Wormhole caught in the act, snogging, school ruler flattened as a stopper between their lips. Snogging with a ruler was the new and secret craze which swept through the second and third years. We all did it, but made sure we weren't caught. Snoggers were humiliated in public with cries of 'Bum-chums!' for as long as it took until new victims or other crimes were discovered.

So that afternoon me and Daz and Skinny followed Milky home, chanting: 'Worm'ole's bum-chum. Worm'ole's BUM-CHUM . . . '

Daz lead the chant, even marched out front. But Worm'ole's bum-chum turned on us.

'Don't you know that Daz is the same as OMO, except it comes in different packets.' This was clever. All I could say was 'Fuck off bum-chum,' much to my shame. Milky said: 'Cuff off yourself, Fairy Liquid. Jump in the tub with OMO and ole four-eyed pansy Flash.'

We let him go. The anger, the muscles on his tongue. We shouted once or twice, but only to ourselves.

'I had lunch with the Director of Caithness Museums Trust today,' he said in a herald of revelation, 'and I'm afraid you're ineligible for the scheme after all. He advised me to consider degree holders only. We've always found degree holders more able to work effectively without supervision.'

'Oh really? Well I managed to teach English without supervision.'

'Well, I don't know what kind of schools employ teachers without qualifications, but they can't be professional establishments.'

'I lied. I said I had a degree, and if they wanted to see it I showed them a forged one. Still, if that's how you feel I could always find a job at the Chemist's.'

'That was uncalled for. Selina obtained a BA degree in Museum Studies too, I'll have you know. My word, if I caught an employee or even knew of anyone obtaining a salary by deception I'd make sure they never worked again . . . ' He'd half risen off his seat, white fists, neck red under the collar.

'Good God,' I said. 'You're like my old man, you are. He tried to turn me into the police once. I suppose you'd do the same. Pity you weren't on the Neighbourhood Watch when your old man was slashing tyres down Barratt's Road.'

He stood and put his macintosh on now the train approached Kildaggie and slowed. I stood aside into the aisle. 'You've lost a button,' I said and picked it up for him. We stood at the same door waiting for the train to stop. Rain pished out with great clack on the roof and platform. I only wore my tweed jacket (left the Duke's breeches at home seeing as I went to sign on) so I sheltered under the corrugated iron as Milky ran across the forecourt to where Selina sat in the Mini with the engine running and the headlights on high beam. Me and Milky had been the only passengers for Kildaggie. The train left and it was pitch black in the station. Milky knew I had over two miles to walk in this monsoon, which seemed set for the night, no wind, ten raindrops to the pint. He couldn't leave me there, so he came hopping and shouting in a panic over the lakes, waving and making thumbs. Selina could have driven him up or beeped and flashed, but she'd got him soaked on purpose.

'Quick, we'll give you a lift. Come on.'

Selina had the radio on loud, which made talking impossible. She didn't even look at me as I fumbled for the seat tilt and crawled, hair dripping, into the back. The windows steamed with all three of us breathing and steaming, the heater on, all listening to *Out and About* on our way up the Slug Sheds Hill. *At the Bayview Hotel on Friday a dance with guest group Sanity Claus. On Saturday Skin and Bone are playing at the Grange Bar, Lairg . . .* This was too much. 'My God,' I said, 'Skin and Bone!' No response. The rain beat down, the wipers squeeged too slow for the downpour. Then half way up the hill Selina stalled on a down change and couldn't start again. She refused to bump it backwards, so me and Milky had to get out and push her round so she faced downwards. This time we were truly soaked as Milky and Selina bickered, the rain drumming out much of what they said. She said there was something wrong with the engine and it was his fault for going somewhere or other. He said rubbish, she just never remembered to have the oil checked. She said it was alright before. So she bumped it first go and we piled in. They bickered about where to turn round. Selina went most of the way down again to execute a six-point turn in the picnic layby. Milky said a flaming monkey could have done a three-point turn anywhere on this road. Selina said we weren't all flaming monkeys, so there.

'Go up in third for the love of Mike this time,' Milky said.

We reached their bungalow and I wondered where I might be dropped off. Selina said she wasn't driving any further, certainly not up some muddy farm track. She was getting out. Melvyn could drive me home. He said he wasn't going anywhere without drying off, so I'd better come in and dry off too.

I took my shoes off in the kitchen and stood dripping on the line while Milky went to the airing cupboard to fetch a towel. Selina came in from parking the car, sweeping past me like a net full of fresh eels in her black shiny wet leather jacket, leaving a trail of pools behind her. I heard the bedroom door slam and instinctively moved nearer to listen.

'Alright Melvyn, what's he doing on the train with you?' She was shouting and Milky tried to shush her.

'Don't you shush me. I want an answer. Did you arrange this?'

He mumbled something. She lowered her voice. I moved back to the doormat, trying to imagine the two of them in love, Milky snogging Semolina with a ruler like it's a contraceptive. Then Milky arrived with a towel while Selina ran a bath. He'd changed his wet clothes and put a dressing gown over dry ones. I shied away from this intimacy. It saddened me, his hoping I'd stay for coffee and biscuits.

'Selina!' he shouted through the bathroom door. 'Where on earth are the chocky digies?'

'Oh for God's sake Mel, they're in the chocky digies tin where they always are. Where else would they be?'

'I can't lo-cate the chocky digies tin, Selina.'

Selina began to sing. 'There's a hole in my bu-ckit, dear Melvyn, dear Melvyn, there's a hole in my bucket . . . '

'Oh very funny Selina.'

We found Watson in the front room curled up on the sofa. Milky kicked him off, said he stunk the place out. He was Selina's anyway, he said, as he kicked him out the backdoor. Their front room was Peach Melba, fresh and over-lit. Prints of striped deckchairs in aluminium frames, the remnants of university reading lists on the bookshelves. One slim volume caught my eye. *How To Exhibit A Bullfrog*. This was my title at last. Perhaps activate it and have *Exhibiting the Bullfrog*. One of Selina's, Milky said, but his own name was inside, on a frigging book plate showing some Tolkien-like dwarf with a book under its arm. Pride of place was the complete set of red-spined Dickens and the Booker Prize winners for the last ten years. On the bottom shelf was a pile of board games 'as seen on TV'. Sitting there was like a seance, only we seemed to be waiting for the spirit of Selina, both of us watching the door, listening for each sqwark of her bum on the bath tub. Then Milky said it would probably cease raining shortly, so I tried to swallow my coffee without tasting it while Milky thumbs through his record collection. Seven Pop Wonders of the Classical World. The Blue Danube and Milky's slippered foot relaxed into baton-swinging.

'No Mahler on this?' I asked; not that I insist on Mahler. I was waving a red rag as the opening bars of Grieg's Piano Concerto gave Milky an opportunity to impersonate a mad spider playing the piano.

'Don't you admire this rousing tune, Watson? Great composers know the joys and miseries of life.'

Selina came in. 'Yes, Mel, we know all about the miseries of life. Now turn it off, there's a programme on Scottish glass blowing we want to watch, remember?'

Milky gave up the armchair and reclined, still joggling his slippers, on a big blue beanbag left over from his student days.

Selina thawed after the programme, suggesting Milky put the record player back on while she cooked his favourite: scrambled egg. Milky asked if I'd like some. I said yes but neither of them indicated I'd get some. We listened to another classical sampler, *Unwinding Strings – Serenades for Sunset*. The first track Milky said was pure beauty, even Tchaikovsky himself was fond of the *Serenade for Strings*. He settled back to read the sleeve notes and conduct with his slippers, so I picked a few books off the shelf. Milky had written in the fly leaf of all the Booker winners, all hardbacks. Things like: To Selina love Melvyn Oct 19—. A Book is LIKE A FRIEND. Or, Reading Opens the Door to A CLOSED MIND. In one I found: LIFE IS A CLOSED BOOK. In the following year's winner I read: I WOULD BE PROUD TO HAVE WRITTEN THIS. The novel was the usual Booker pseudo-writing. Slight but 600 pages.

'Oh Christ,' I said, putting it back, 'what rubbish.'

'How can you say that?' Milky was astonished. 'How can you say that about a novel which wins the most prestigious literary award of the year?'

Selina carried in two plates of scrambled egg, one for me, one for Milky, who chewed his absently like a goat while Selina picked at a lettuce leaf, painting the nails on her left hand and playing patience with a pack of miniature cards. 'Who's been moving the books about?' she asked, straightening the authors' jackets as if they were dolls.

'Me,' I said.

'Mr Lily doesn't believe in the authority of the Booker Prize, Selina,' Milky said. But she must have listened to my earlier comments.

'I don't need you to tell me that. He's just jealous of success . . .'

Milky stepped in and said: 'Why don't we play something?'

'Because I'm going to bed soon, that's why,' Selina said, screwing the cap on the nail varnish and holding her nails up under the lightbulb. Ten bleeding hearts.

'I hate playing games,' I said. When I was thirteen I was given a mini-size board game called Whoops, marketed by a Waddingtons imprint. Half price down the toyshop, Whoops fascinated me because of its pointlessness. Then I saw in some comic about a boy who invented a game and sent it to Waddingtons who paid him a huge fee and marketed the game. So I decided to do likewise. The result was Village Life. A map of our village formed the board, with all the main roads and important lanes turned into squares like Whoops. Progress and forfeit by means of various adventures at real landmarks, all incidents taken from real life. At LITTLE NINEVEH, for instance, there was STRANGLED BY VILLAGE IDIOT. BACK 10 SQUARES AND MISS A TURN. Barratt's Road had KNOCK TEN CONKERS FROM TREE. ADVANCE TWO SQUARES. I'd drawn the pond showing its various inhabitants. HOOK LOST ON SUNKEN MOTORBIKE, MISS A GO. Four small boys were the players. Green, Brown, Ginger and White. YOUR DAD COMPLAINS TO COUNCIL ABOUT DANGEROUS POND. BACK 5 SQUARES. MUMMY'S BOY COLLECTS MOST MONEY FOR GUIDE DOG WEEK . . . BEST FRIEND DUFFED BY NEW BOY . . . Waddingtons sent it back with a standard, impersonal rejection slip: 'Thank you for your enquiry. If you are interested in any of our products you might like to receive our catalogue . . .'

Several years later I saw my game in Woolworths. They'd given it the fictitious title Hawkhurst Gang. It was a much sanitised version of my original idea, but to me it was identifiable. The FIVE CONKERS instead of ten and the TWO TREES and our POND were probably enough to go to court on, but in the meantime I'd thrown mine away. There was no murder down LITTLE NINEVEH. There was no LITTLE NINEVEH.

Milky fetched his guitar and Selina's flute case. We finished the delightful evening singing folk songs. Milky called them folk songs anyway. I knew a few simple chords so Milky dusted off his old six string for me and I tuned it up while he twiddled with his twelve steel strings and Selina complained that she couldn't play her flute properly now she'd grown nails. But we opened with 'Hey Mr

Tambourine Man', then that old song-book simple 'Una Paloma Blanca'. I couldn't sing to save my life and neither could Milky Presley. Semolina de Los Angeles Gallway sounded like Billy Graham. I was busy composing sentences in my head about the whole day. I mean, there I was at their inner sanctum and I'd forgotten my camera. So during a pause to catch our breath I asked how they'd met. Both had done Museum Studies the same year. Milky was quick to point out that only he had done the MA. Selina had worked for Waddingtons so they'd got their games at staff discount. She'd not heard of Hawkhurst Gang, even though she'd been in archives and records. I briefly mentioned why I'd asked. 'Don't talk rubbish. That sort of thing never happened. All games were either commissioned or we bought all the good ideas for development on site. You really have got some weird ideas about your talent.' This subject led to bickering about the museum in Kildaggie, which Selina said was full of rubbish because all the real antiques were in the castle.

'Works of art', Milky corrected her, 'are not antiques.'

'You don't have to tell me that,' Selina said. She was supposed to be Milky's personal assistant once the museum opened, as well as for the cataloguing scheme and the overall design for the refurbishment.

'But you can't get anyone to do anything properly up here,' she said, looking specially at me. 'Everyone in northeast Scotland's applied for this thing and they're all idiots. Honest to God, not a single graduate. I mean, top of the list there's the taxi driver and his wife from Helmsdale and those ghastly spinsters from the Charity Shop. Then there's that fat woman who sells tickets in the castle and . . . who else? Oh yes, for God's sake, the bloody Indian cleaner's wife at the school. The whole thing's a joke.'

'And me,' I said. 'I've applied.'

'You never told me!' she shouted at Milky.

'I don't want to talk about it now,' he said. 'There's nothing to talk about anyway, Selina, so let's just change the subject till there is, alright?'

'No, it is not alright. That's just like you. Can't face the truth. The whole thing's a house of cards and you know it, Mel.'

Mel strummed 'My Sweet Lord' over and over, waiting for one

of us to come in. Both of them had red faces. One of them had guffed. Selina sighed hard and emptied spit from her flute. Milky stopped strumming and opened a window, pretending to see if the rain had cleared. It had.

'Shall we do this one then, or not?' he said.

'Do what one?' she was still angry.

' "My Sweet Lord", of course.'

'If we must. But I'm going to bed after this.'

My Sweet Lord, we sang. I really Wanna See Yer Lord. Oh It Takes s'long I know. Hari Hari. Krishna Krishna.

Milky said: 'My word, Watson, that was fun, eh? Nothing like a good choir to sweep the ol' spewbocs away, ha.'

He walked me to the end of the lane and actually asked me how I filled my time in Kildaggie. I told him I was writing a novel, of course. Oh yes, he remembered me saying something about that. So which writers did I aspire to, then? He didn't follow me when I said I'd turned from the English novelists to contemporary American South and Europeans like Bachmann. When he said that surely there were more good English writers published these days than ever before, I could have wept. I said this was not my impression, nor my point. They were not one of us, however much he believed in equality. Ah, but that is also the point, he said. I said I didn't feel like arguing this point, I simply reminded him that we ought to be part of a linguistic revolution, only education had driven us into hierarchy. Milky said he believed in economic equality, reward for achievement, and asked me how I could deny that education had been the great liberator which jolly well set us free of background. Being free of background was, you prick, was just the non-state they want you in. Jesus Christ. Had the creep never questioned in whose interest books were published and prizes offered? Not on his fuckin mother's nelly he hadn't. Nah, you're juss jealous cause you ain never had nuffin published. Jealous? Of fuckin what, yer cory! Jealous of not writing that standard the tour-de-force? That big witty triumph? Well but ol'Milksop wouldn't have minded being skilful enough to write your so-called standard skilful novel, oh no, not Milky the aspiring novelty who likes to keep up wiv the celebs in the littery weld. Zis 'ow yer pass yer toime, I assed. Big confession Milky. Shouldna laughed I spose should I, cause what

I'm doin' ain so friggin swish. Oh an' yer should've 'eard im on the duty ov the novelty writer, like egg 'nspoon race on ice. Samuel Johnson says, he says, the first duty of the novelist is to entertain and if thereby he instructs so much the better. Well, a slap-up notion from Sam there, but what's ole Mallachie White write what's so entertaining? And so on . . .

Because we must leave this paragraph now. You see the problem, I think. That got me nowhere, did it? It's just that sometimes I'm ashamed of what I've said. *What* linguistic revolution? Neither is there a single example of the politically radical in that paragraph. The problem is I can't discuss the failure of the English novel because at the point where I should engage with logic I become inarticulate. Logic requires middle-class language. I can't question middle-class values with the language at my disposal. Worse, I can't maintain any meaningful linguistic contact with the middle classes. I fear that my readers are likely to be middle class; this leaves me unco-operative and you can't bridge the critical distance I've adopted in order to write, an act which is itself a counteraction neutralizing my belief. Like becoming a martyr to prove the non-existence of God, the argument being that if he exists he'll save me. The question then becomes: but he may exist and if he does he therefore knows my intention and sees no point revealing himself either before or after the act. Also, I fail as polemicist because I'm not one, nor do I have a Department of English HGV enabling me to drive theories. As a pedestrian, I am merely driven by them.

The same distance then between me and Milky. He told me he *wants* to 'communicate' with you. This leaves me an excommunicate. The way Milky puts it is that he feels something 'inside' desiring to engage with something 'outside'. He adds that this insistence is without negative psychological impetus. Who narrates? I ask him. He supposed that he did. Who are your characters, what voice, what language? Not himself, he says, oh no. But to be honest, he said, looking at his shoes and tapping them on the wet lane, which annoyed me with their slap slap on a bare arse noise, hands deep in macintosh pockets so it stuck out like wing stumps on a flightless bird, to be honest he has slight problems with characters. They come out like, well, Woodentops. Doesn't he write about people he knows? He doesn't think you should ever do that. Thinks it's wrong. Betrayal of trust, spying and so on. Unless they say: here's a good yarn old chap. Perhaps you'd like to make a story of it. Dashed if I'd know where to begin myself. Truth is, hanged if I can make head or tale of it, actually. Not that I haven't put pen to paper myself in spare moments. Just haven't the knack, old man . . . So where do your Woodentops come from? Imagination. Milky imagines them. To avoid the self.

This led us over ancient burial sites, this question of imaginative fiction. Among other opinions he said he'd never read a decent woman writer or considered looking at an American novel. *War and Peace* is the greatest book ever written in any language . . . In other words, my continuing argument with Milky becomes an irrelevant disgrace to any discussion of the contemporary novel, the doyens (yes he said doyens) of which reside in England, London to be exact, the literary capital of the world. American fiction, Milky believes, is sickness made into language. He likes the deep and intellectual, does Milky. Dons and novelists I suppose he means, having affairs of the brain on Hampstead Heaff. No, he likes humour, he says. Some of them write jolly funny stuff. Very satirical it is. Me an' all, I say, wishing he'd stop plashing his crepe soles on the wet. Still got his drum kit? In fact, I said, I'm so fond of humour that I'll probably write this conversation down the moment I get in, then end Chapter Eleven with it. What dyer think?

I don't see the point, he says. He stops tapping anyway. Why do you have to say a thing like that? I don't understand *you*.

It emphasizes our difference, I said. As writers from the same street. Hoity bloody git says that he doesn't see that anything we've said has any relevance to our background. You're just trying to be clever. You're just writing to be taken notice of like anyone else.

Milky's trouble is he sleeps at night. Nothing keeps him awake. Can't hear nothing through the double glazing anyway. Probably has his best ideas asleep or reading *War and Peace*. Fond of humour, he didn't like me laughing. His face is hardened by moonlight. Alright, I tell him. Truce. I'll read you something I've written if you like. But he just shrugs and I say goodnight.

The wind's dropped, some stars are out, the moon's risen huge, glazing hard scugs across the lane and sodden land which papped from the day's rain still running off into the lane. Milky tiptoes home after saying his own goodnight, all trace of the Victorian patriarch drained.

'Why not call in on me sometime?' I called after him, aware of speech marks again like the truce had ended, moon on his face again like a rabbit in a headlamp. 'Show me some of your stories,' I added.

'Thanks,' he said, 'but I've never shown them to anyone.'

Sitting on the wall I watched him go, Mr Author-dox still bound to do the right thing after all his lies about graduates and God knows what else, all the way back to Bluebird/Partridge and beyond or since. Ordinary encounters, let alone belief-encounters with people, always leave me trembling and exhausted. Worn down by their lies I can tremble for hours. Their whole being sticks to me like gum and I can never sleep, going over and over everything said and felt at the time, stretching and exaggerating meanings until they're back to the way they started, like the way you flex an elastic band before securing an object. Being with people is a battle, an exposure to forces which reduce contact to dependence.

Clouds on their way out to sea dimmed the moonlight as they passed. I slipped off the wall as soon as Milky was out of sight and ran on my toes after him. I guessed the effect I had on each of them individually but wanted to see how as a couple they behaved with this effect. It seemed a good time for subjective interchange too, uncomfortable as centre of the narrative. Cedric jumped the wall into the sheep grazing and made his way round the back of Milky's bungalow, crouching on wet knees behind the low wall which marked the foot of their garden. From here he watched Milky enter the kitchen door. Selina was at the larder dipping a spoon into a jampot and licking it clean each time. She didn't even look at Milky as he went through, shouting after him when he reached the passage after letting him think he'd got away. 'I don't ever want to see that person in here again, Melvyn White.' The light went off a minute later then came on in the bathroom. Cedric crept up below the window. Soapy water and toothpaste spit came down the drainpipe. Watson came upon him unexpectedly and bobbed over the wall. At the bedroom window he heard nothing. No lights, they didn't read themselves to sleep. Then just as Cedric was about to retreat the way he'd come, he heard Selina's hard voice through the ventilator say: 'You moron.'

That was all she said, no response, not a sound of any kind. She may not even have been talking to Milky. Cedric had the horrible feeling she'd said it to me.

Chapter Twelve

She sat on the seat by the sea wall while the black spaniel ran along the beach. She couldn't see me, this girl who lived at Burnside Cottage and walked her spaniel along the beach every day after school. I was in the Kirkyaird looking through the lair stanes across the paddock where some heifers lumbered between us, cudding or tigging for the flies. From this far her jacket looked red velvet, her black skirt made her look older, sadder, more alone than anyone I saw. All the other girls in Kildaggie sauntered in keckling groups along the High Street, mobbing in the carpark or ganged up in a sharrie outside the green tin Nissen hut where they clubbed for smoking and table tennis. They were never alone and hardly ever walked near the beach except along the concrete promenade. I never saw them sit and gaze intently out to sea like this girl. Couldn't imagine her chewing gum with a fag on the go, sneering squits of smoke at midges.

After a while she stood, walked along to where the burn chuckled down the beach stanes into the sea and out of my sight. She might have continued over the stepping stones, round the point, onto the path which leads to the castle. Otherwise she'd take the path to the old mill, over the footbridge and into the lane which emerges where I'm standing outside the kirkyaird.

I waited for the spaniel which had run ahead, but she called it back and hooked it onto a lead. Hands shoved in both pockets I leaned against the wall in abstract expression and she passed me as if I were one of the lair stanes. Her velvet jacket was a nylon anorak but her black skirt moved like a curtain drawn over an evening window. No, really – though the manner in which it's drawn is probably irrelevant. Her face was hidden, tilted down behind brown hair, all but a tiny angle of the chin which was caught in an expression I felt rather than saw of what might have been regret, boredom or churlishness. Not much to go on, Watson, but she was walking at 2.25 mph for the next thirty yards, during which time I tried to catch her smell: soap, sandlewood perhaps. Now, tell the readers her age. Sixteen, maybe seventeen. Then, I tried to put her from my mind.

By evening the wind had subsided and the weather vanes were perfectly still so the Rayburn failed to draw and the kitchen filled with smoke. A blear cock's eye harvest moon like a hole burning through paper, lampshade clouds over the sea. I took the sea path to the burn, jumped the garth and followed the girl's path by the Kirk to Burnside Cottage. I hadn't actually meant to. She hadn't been in my mind when I'd set out but now I couldn't accomplish anything till I'd seen into Burnside Cottage. I stood outside wondering which her room was, but the only light came from the porch, moths killing themselves against it. So next I took the Slug Sheds Road home and passed Milky's bungalow. The car was gone and they'd forgotten to leave the porchlight blazing.

Next day she appeared as usual with the spaniel, crossing the road in front of me, cutting by the Post Office to the promenade. I followed and stopped at the sea wall railings to watch her go. It's time to think why I'm doing this, though watching her makes it obvious. Literary talk with Milky the author-dox(onian) had raised the question of futility. Thing is I feel inclined to abandon you. Loneliness sees only the desolate and unconsolable. You can write to me years after today and say you enjoyed my problem, that it was pleasant to read of my failure and identify the narrative flaw (pronounced flow in Scoatland-Scortland) before I admitted it, but she, this other lonely creature, is here, walking as I do, slow, eyes down, no one to tell why, along an empty beach . . .

A hundred yards away across the roll of sea ware, treading out fogs of midges as she goes, the tide turning at a whisper, gull scuffs in thin strips of wet sand. I looked for spaniel paw prints and made a footprint beside one of hers, heels dug in like mine. When I looked up she'd rounded the point but I could see the spaniel playing so guessed she sat where she always sat. Drawing nearer I heard the spaniel gurlie as it chased a scent, then a flap of brown hair showed just above the bend in the wall. She couldn't see me but she might have heard. The spaniel, chewing a stick, raised an eye, alerted, wagging its stump. I noticed something in the girl's hand before I saw her head. She was looking at something but she sensed my presence, looked at the dog, stood up shoving whatever it was into her pocket and shouted at the dog to move off with her. 'Archie' it might have been. Again all I saw of her was a tiny edge of skin, this time under her right eye level with her ear. As she hurried away I sat on the bench, feeling it with my hand, not expecting to find it cold. She was like a bird on a window ledge, darting off to a safe distance, slowing when reaching it and following the dog with its stick as if nothing had occurred. I looked for some sign that she'd existed but saw nothing of her, only yellow grass at my feet. So I continue with written language from me to you, adding a retainer, an incentive image to lure you back: the skim and trail of her skirt over the leens elsewhere, the memory of her tightened jacket as two hands in her pockets drew it close, one of them clutching something.

Milky and Selina were washing the car without speaking; she was on the driver's side. When she saw me coming Selina said she was going in to press his suit and get ready.

'Going out?' I asked Milky.

'As a matter of fact we've been invited to the castle by Lord Donald.'

I didn't look impressed because I wasn't. I was in the Laird's green breeks that day and craved action. Lord Donald on the bagpipes with Milky and Semolina singing 'Twa Corbies' promised it.

'About the museum?' I asked.

'No, no. Actually it's a social occasion, the annual History Society Evening Buffet. Lord Donald has kindly consented to host it himself this year, and Lord Northpole is going to read a short monograph on Pictish gold panning at Dinkiligg.'

Semolina was at the window, old bagging at her husband. 'Hurry up, for goodness sakes, Melvyn. We still have to bathe yet, remember?'

'Ah, haha, the good lady Watson summons me yonder. Must get on, in,' Milky said as Semolina Watson slammed the window shut and I continued on my way, kicking stones and grinning between the ears, the game afoot.

I covered the arrivals from deep within the woods so I've no details on the pride and modesty angle, but when the twenty cars were assembled before the castle I continued my surveillance from a pitch-dark hollow nearer by. From here the cars glazed under security spots like trade-ins at Bob's Autos. Mrs and Mr Melvyn White's Mini squatting like an oil can beside a Range Rover. An Austin A40 playing flea in the ear of a Rolls Corniche, number plate DNSR 1. Like a drive-in movie or *son et lumière*, the second floor stood out in cinemascope, guests moving across the long screen between shutterless windows, looking up at the family portraits, pausing beside needlework chairs done by the Countess of Carlisle. I settled down for the big picture on my stomach, cushioned by leafmould and soft brittle twigs, wiping the lenses of my powerful binoculars, training them on the long Regency windows. I felt lucky. Time was running thin on this case anyway so I had to be. Either Milky White gave in and I got the novel, or I was back to square one, a novella with a suffix to nowhere.

So there went women, several women too, back and forth or just standing under Ramsey's portrait of the 12th Earl in his scarlet jacket and kilt, fluted glasses coloured by what must have been some cheap skink the way they lipped it, all dink and fite-iron gentry-like, costume jowels flashing by the glim of twenty-four electric candles on the chandelier. It made me sick if you wanna know, like my parents at the village Conservative Wine and Cheese evening, the only council tenants, the only guests who walked because the old banger would show them up alongside Councillor

Woodyard's livery Jag. So they got my old man to sell the raffle tickets down solid Labour Barratt's Road and he ended up having to buy them all himself. Didn't even win the sixth prize dinner for two at Tang's Chinese Restaurant, or the tenth and last bottle of Sherry from the Councillor's own cellar.

These Boots binoculars missed nothing (10 × 50 with a plastic strap) exposing Millicent and Ethel from the Charity Shop. Some bric-a-brac this, Millicent. Nice Kharassan under these covers out of harm's way. Adorable Stuart chairs, Ethel – best not sit on them, had we? Well I might have got the Duke's breeks, but Millicent missed out on the Duchess's ball gown, preferring her own of black and red tricel with gold lamé clutch bag dangling off her thick quivering arm by a thin chain. They were talking with a very old woman whose grey hair sat like a whole tray of buns on her head, fat pearls like golf balls rolling on the folds of her gathered neck. This was a George Grosz/Fellini production so far, and I thought we were in *The Third Man*'s version of Cedric Lily's *Casebook*, a little adventure from Volume One entitled: *Museum Piece* or something more detonating and action sequenced like: Milky White on Ice: An on-the-Dole Mystery.

Bad jokes wouldn't help find Milky and Semolina White so I resumed my targeted surveillance and swept the powerful binoculars across each window. Bear in mind I was up a steep bank in this wood and the castle drive slopes downward so I was not in the stalls. I could see the dining table buffet, the covered carpet and the Stuart chairs arranged along the panelled walls. I could see high heels and patent leathers, keeping an eye out for Milky's Hush Puppies. At last I spotted them, Mr and Mrs White MA BA Anon., nibbling fondue and celery sticks alone in the last window, at the back of the room beside one of many doors. They look like gnomes on a wedding cake, so tiny and insignificant beneath a magnificent portrait by Lawrence of Gertrude Duchess of Northinterland with her eldest daughter Jane, later Duchess of Muir, on her knee. Jane pointed at Selina's neck. Binocular bloated, it looked off a butcher's slab or a thigh with garter, not one of those velvet chokers with velcro fix and plastic Wedgewood bust on a slender neck. Hung-pig red, her crushed-velvet dress featured puff sleeves, low neckline and slung back. If she turned round, the viewer saw her bra strap clear as a bridge across her back, hair sprayed tight as a bird's nest, pure bum's rush. Then she turned back and you'd never seen such an expression of morbid humiliation and furious pride on any face. It was so painful I could have rushed in there and suffered greater humiliation just to relieve her. Looked like social suicide when I focused on Mr Melvyn White too and irrationally my heart hardened against Selina, the way he stood like a cardboard box beside her in his grey bridegroom suit, pretending to look with expert scrutiny at an Italian frieze, ignoring Mrs S. White. No one spoke to them anyway. Done with the frieze, he examined the nearest corner of the painting. A maid took Mrs White's empty glass so Mr White quickly cleaned the edge of his with a napkin after sipping from it with a full mouth of food, looking round to confirm his anonymity. Sweeping the binoculars over the entirety of guests, I failed to identify the Lords and Ladies. It wasn't that I'd seen enough – my attitude would not have progressed if I'd stayed at my post true enough – and I know any hold I had on my surveillant language has slipped as I feel you question this voyeurism now the detective persona has worn off. Adopting it in the first place meant impunity. Motif into motive. The point of view problematized. No, the reason I abandoned my surveillance was to implement Stage Two because the way Mr and Mrs White's social life went I didn't have much time before they chucked it. Pity about the Duke, though.

Up at the Slug Sheds I stationed myself behind their back wall and waited, dripping sweat, a chest full of driven nails from the haulage up. The air was still and cold and the sound of voices would carry a mile. I even dared to roll a fag and light it, the scratch and flare like an explosion but it was worth the risk. I've read hundreds of old green Crime novels and a good smoke at vigil never seemed to jeopardize the plot. This chap Merriman in Wills Croft's *The Pit-Prop Syndicate* actually burns through several good pipeloads on a perfectly still, warm summer night in Bordeaux while sprawled under an open bedroom window of a house in which a dangerous criminal insomniac paces to and fro with a loaded gun. At one point in this vigil the dangerous criminal insomniac comes out into the perfectly still night air and passes within feet of our pipe-smoking vigilante, none the wiser.

However, I stubbed me roll-up out on the wall when I heard the
Mini chogging up the Slug Sheds hill. The driver parked with
careless, angry revving and a slam of brakes and doors, damn and
tut from Selina, not an actual word passing between them. The
bathroom light comes on. Milky stays in the kitchen with a glass
of Alka Seltzer. My binoculars reveal every bubble in the glass,
every crease on his forehead. A running bath, the small top
window opens a notch. Milky leaves the kitchen and I hear him
shouting.

'Selina! Selina, open this blessed door.'

Selina says she's having a bath, thank you very much.

'You haven't even run the cold yet,' he says, trying to sound
angry but there's no disguising the pleading in this voice. 'What
did you mean you've had enough, Selina?'

'You bloody well know what I mean.' Such contempt in her
voice too, the authentic sound of the face I'd seen through the castle
window.

For the moment the argument gets nowhere. Open the door.
No. Open this door. Why should I? and so on. So I creep up to the
window of these dangerous historians with aristocratic connections. The steam bundles out with the smell of bluebell bubble bath.
Milky belches like a schoolboy.

'Oh fer Christ's sake, Melvyn.'

'It's that damned wine.'

'No, it's not. It's the damn Alka Seltzer, you moron. I told you
not to take it before but oh no, you have to try and prove me wrong
when you know all the bloody time it gives you the wind.'

She flops into the bath with a great slap and surge through the
overflow pipe, sighing like a puncture.

'I want to know, Selina,' Milky croaks, trying to sound at the
end of his chain, 'what you meant when you said you'd had
enough. Is that clear? Do you understand me?'

'Oh, do stop rubber lipping, *please*. I'm in the bath, if you haven't
noticed.' The taps come on again.

'Selina. Selina. SELINA, TURN THAT TAP OFF.'

She doesn't answer so he beats on the door with his fists. When
she's ready the taps are turned off and she laughs. 'You creep. You
idiot.'

'Selina, you fat cow OPEN THE DOOR . . . oh God, OPEN THE DOOR QUICK. I'm going uhhhh I'm gonna-be-sick . . . '

Now comes a crump and scuffle, the kitchen door flies open as I dive head first over the wall just as Milky throws up near the clothes line pole. The bathroom window opens onto another retch.

'You filthy creep, Melvyn. Why the hell didn't you spew up in the sink? Now that idiotic Watson cat thing'll eat it up if you leave it there.'

Selina's voice is a Tannoy announcing Milky to the world. His record-breaking SSSSSSSHHHHHHHHHHH is equally megaphonic. 'Of course the cat won't eat it,' he says with several spittings.

'How do you know? You're not exactly Mr bloody Zoo-Keeper. You've never fed the frigging flea cushion properly in your life. It's a daft spastic, that cat. D'you know what I caught it licking last week? Sheep shit. Sheep shit, Melvyn! And I know for a fact you let it lick under the toilet seat . . . '

'I've just been ill for the love of Mike, Selina. Can't you show any concern? I might have food poisoning for all you know, and all you manage is some fantasy against Watson.'

'Fat chance you've got catching food poisoning eating off one of Lord Muck's silver plates.'

The bathroom window slams shut and she plops back into the bath humming. Milky tries to spit, only his sputum lengthens into a two-foot string and swings down his trousers. He scrubs his chin and trousers at the kitchen sink with the best tea towel. Outside again he tries in vain to kick some loose earth over the sick. Now he sits on the doorstep for a long time and I have to keep still, wet arsed, shins barked, mud and Watson's Sheep Supreme on my binoculars, which lay where I've chucked them in the rush. I wonder if this might have worked better as a Private Detection Agency with a novel spin-off. This way I'd stick to motif and opportunity avoiding the Faith of Language & Expression, so you'd stay client instead of reader/critic and I'd get the flat rate with expenses instead of just the dream of royalties, a humble subject of the Publishers Monarchy . . . But here's Selina out the bath at last, coming into the kitchen, Milky shouting at her, wanting to know what she meant. Tell me, tell me, he keeps saying, what you meant by *I've had enough of this.* I can't get enough of this so I poke an eye over the wall to see Selina stamp her pink fluffy slipper on the WELCOME mat as Milky paces up and down outside, his trousers in a thumb tweek.

'YOU!' she bawls at him both barrels, 'YOU! I've had enough of YOU and THIS PLACE and the friggin' CHEMISTS and your bloody MUSEUM SCHEME. Understand, thicko? I HAVE . . . HAD . . . EN . . . UFF. A gut full. Up to bloody here. Get it? Savvy? YOU! WHY OH U.'

'What do you mean? Don't be so stupid, you've only been here two weeks,' Milky says, shaking his fist rather weakly.

'Two weeks,' she says. 'It didn't take me two minutes to discover what a moron I'd married. You and your great opportunities for us both! My God, Melvyn, of all the self-deceived, lying creeps I've ever come across, you take the biscuit, you really do.'

What follows is shocking, not because you or I haven't heard wives and husbands abusing each other before. Me, it's all I've ever heard them do in a way, usually through walls at night when trying to sleep or read, but always uninvolved and unconcerned. This Milky–Semolina clash is new to me because I'm inseparably of it. Selina's every word goes through me before reaching Milky as if I'm a filter, not for detecting or removing impurities but for multiplying them. Like wild dogs at sheep I drive them harder and the depth of her betrayal is mine, her fury and disappointment too. And my ambition is to achieve her great spew of words as simply and as naturally. If a feeling doesn't settle in her stomach, up it comes, not processed into abstraction but organic and corporeal. With me it sits heavily for years causing progressive discomfort.

Selina begins her lament by mocking and gloating over her accusations. In awe, I gloat with her, my own mind for once emptied of its own thought, silenced at gunpoint or an equitable force. I can't imagine it possible to strip anyone so bare and so completely as Selina strips Milky in these few minutes. Here is someone prepared to reveal her weakness and the illusion of her husband's life in Kildaggie, to admit she is left with nothing.

Then my identity with her is confirmed. I'm amazed to learn that Selina arrived in Kildaggie about the same time as me. Milky has only been here two months. Selina stayed in Wick while Milky prepared things for her coming, setting up the Museum Scheme, finding a house, spending her money. She hadn't wanted to move from Wick. She agreed because Milky promised her an assistant curatorship. She'd been deceived. In fact, she'd deceived herself too . . .

'God, Melvyn, do you know why I finally agreed to come and live in this dump? Do you? Do you? No, you don't, do you? You think I came on your behalf, I bet. To stand proudly at your side, my boss and my superior, Mr Black and White's museum piece. Well let me tell you, big schemer, that I came because you and your great new chum and social equal Lord Donald the well-known keen historian would be running the museum together. Oh think, you said, of all the jolly tête-à-têtes we'd have wi' Lord Donald, weeting our thrapple in the gloaming ha ha ha, knocking on the castle door instead of Pete and Sue's, you said, having our scrambled egg under his Canalettos. And who knows, we might even compose a jolly monograph what!, all three of us together in the ole history boat. Jesus Christ, Melvyn! I believed you – oooohhgghh I could hit myself, I really could. I still believed you even when those diz-GUSTing overfed tarted-up vultures round the buffet table ignored us – just jealous, I thought. Wait till Lord Donald blah blah blah and this is my wife Selina, ow CHARmed I'm sure Melvyn's told me SO much about you UUUGGGHHH it's me should spew. YOU HAVEN'T EVEN GOT A JOB. There is no BLOODY MUSEUM. The Duke of bloody North Shitshire hasn't ever clapped his toffee-nosed eyes on you in his whole chauffeur-driven life. Fuck-a-duck, Melvyn, he hasn't even heard of you. Can't tell a White from cow's udder coz he's just come back from the Canaries where he's bin prancing in his jolly sun shorts since the bloody summer. Oh Mel, you despicable liar. Yes, Selina, guess what Selina, Lord Donald actually in the flesh himself said a few kind words in my ear, jolly nice chap, you'll like him, oh yes, so how shall I say? down to earth, accessible, really thinks the scheme's great. You should have seen US, US, standing there like beggars in disguise, twiddling our delightful glasses, aren't they, Selina? with these unique fluted stems when up comes Lord Jack-in-the-Box who've we got here then? Live in Kildaggie my man, or just passing through? I'm Mr Melvyn White BA MA, sir Lordship, you may recall a slight communication regarding my Museum Scheme. Bai

Jove yes, White . . . White? White? Seem to remember my secretary passing something over with that name on it, ha! Grand scheme and all that, White, but afraid it's not on, old chum. Closed the museum down, you see. Havin' all the ole stuffed fish and deer heads carted up here where as you probably know we have one jolly wonderful curator already. Local man. Old family, ha! Oh but there might occur a little temporary opening if you're interested in this sort of thing, you know, inventories and whatnot . . . And what does Sir Melvyn White reply, eh? What does he utter with his new chum and collaborator? YES, SIR. You said, yes, sir, I am quite interested actually in this sort of thing as a matter of fact.'

It sounds like Milky punching his own head and slapping himself.

'You never *listen*.' He tries to sound angry but his throat dries and he has to lower his voice to avoid coughing. 'I tried to explain. Why don't you ever listen and let me explain something? You know I wouldn't have come here if the Estates Office hadn't backed the Scheme in principle. The Director of Caithness *told* me he'd discussed it with them. HE fixed it up with Manpower Services. Not me. Listen, the Office said they'd back me when the Duke returned. They said they didn't foresee any problem. Selina? Did you hear me? Don't you ever understand anything, you stupid cow? It's not my blasted fault.'

'Christ, Melvyn, you're so thick. My *sister* told you it was dodgy, *I* told you it was dodgy. Caithness wanted you to resign so you couldn't sue them for breach of contract. Not that you'd *dare* stick up for yourself, oh no. I'm not an agitator. They made it UP, Melvyn. It's pie in the sky. I know, they said, let's tell him there's this nice wee abandoned museum in Kildaggie. Mention the Duke. Say we'll put in a word. Good as yours. Curatorship for life. Great opportunity. Ooohhh they knew their MANNNN alright. JEEE-zus. They knew him more than I did. And what else did they know relevant to our case? Hmmm? Eh? Eh? That old Lord Jet Set wasn't due in his castle for another six months. Right? By which time they'd be well shot of you. Well they've set an example we might *all* choose to follow . . . '

Horrible silence now. You'd think there'd be a puff of words floating off into the sky like smoke after an explosion. Milky's cracking his fingers. Selina's playing tiddly-winks with her nails. Now spit, spit. A windy, ineffective roar from Milky. I must see this so I shift a few feet along on the edge of the light pool and put an eye back over the wall. Milky's standing with his neck stretched forwards, spitting at Selina from a distance. Never learned to gob as a boy, Milky never. Nor'd he bulge water from his mouth or pistol it through the gap in his front teeth. So he falls short every time. Hasn't even got any spit up to shoot with so he hisses through his teeth and does an infuriated jig.

'Youuuuu STEWpid COW-OW-COWWWWWWW, SELINA. You PER-PER-PER,' dry spits in threes and more pantomime hissing. 'SHITBAG!' He works loose from his moorings and clenching fists runs forward. Selina's holding the towel round her head and I'm ready to jump over the wall and get Packham'd. She backs into the kitchen ready to slam and bolt the door. Milky stops short. 'HAH HAH. That bloody scared you, didn't it, you bloody rat-cow! Well, you can go to hell!'

'Don't concern yourself, chum, I am going. I'm leaving hell. It's all yours.' Her contempt is so huge now I feel it include me and glow and singe like a bush fire trapping us in. 'I'm going back to Wick, Melvyn. I don't care where you go. Just don't come near me, you or your bloody fantasies or Cedric-type creep friends. I hope you enjoy telling him what a shitbag I am. I'm going to pack now and I'm taking *my* car first thing in the morning. And if you've broken that dishwasher you can pay the rest off out of your own money. Oh, and you sleep on the sofa tonight. I don't want you anywhere near me. EVER!'

One doors slams. Then another. I slump exhausted against the wall, my throat aching in couvade for Selina. But it's not over. There's muffled shouting in the bedroom and Milky runs back into the garden. 'You bastard,' Selina shouts after him.

I can't see what he's doing. I wait for ten minutes till he's finished, the door slams and the house is dark. Milky's marching up the lane, torch beam smashing everywhere in a temper of light. Climbing the wall into the garden I find that Milky's emptied the entire contents of Selina's make-up bag into his pool of sick and stirred it into the most disgusting mixture.

I set off in the other direction to a sleepless night. I hear cowman

John unhitch his gate at creek of day. His dog scuddles and yatters after him.

Chapter Thirteen

Walking along the promenade I heard Milky call out behind me.
His hair was rucked along the crown from his sleepless night on
the sofa, eyes like shaving cuts. I was not pleased to see him. There
was a spot growing on his chin he didn't know about too. I mean
there comes a time when you have to tell him something.

'Having a stroll,' he said, unquestioned.

The school bell rang. Coaches revved up in the carpark.

'Nice day,' he said. 'Balmy. Can't stand the wind myself.'

I slowed the pace, leaning on the railings, waiting for the girl to
appear. Milky pretended to breathe the sea air, deep inflations
through his nose. I jumped down onto the beach to examine a shell,
burst a seaweed pod, disconnect myself from Milky, who just
wouldn't go away. At last the spaniel ran onto the beach, nose to
the sand, setting off along its regular trail. The girl kept to the path,
rounding the point towards the bench. I started after her, Milky
trailing behind and wondering at my sudden spurt. I made up his
conversation to myself, things like: 'Ants in your pants, Watson?'
And: 'I say I say, old chap, what do you use to part the waves? A
beachcomber, haha . . . '

Anyway, she'd gone by the time we got there, already striding home along by the kirk wall in a hurry. She couldn't have sat on the bench. Why? Who was she meeting? Or had she seen me coming after her? I started off along the sea path towards the castle without thinking. Milky said he'd rather cut through the woods if I didn't mind. My feeling for him wavered between sympathy and hatred. The events of last night were as visible upon me as they were on him. My lines of thought were tangled. I felt the same hopelessness about the future. The fear of failure. The knowledge that I may have gone too far. The inevitable question: where next? And why? Don't forget why. These are conventional questions I know, moral and social questions which condemn my activities in Kildaggie and force readers to assert their values over the text just in case I'm going to strangle the girl or the reviewers call me a perverted voyeur and so on. Milky surrendered himself then, only to find me unresponsive, my mind on other things.

My heart was against him so I asked how Selina was, and how the buffet at the castle had gone.

'Fine,' he said. 'You know how these things are. Nothing special. Just a lot of educated chinwag about nothing.'

We crossed the burn, over the wooden bridge. In the lips trout too quick to be described flipped rings on the surface, diving and ruddering over dark scridden. We leaned over watching them in silence, rising in our own broken reflections. Then we dragged ourselves through the dark-brown light of Kildaggie Wood as far as the obelisk.

In memory of Capt Lord Alexander Northinterland Crumwyel St Rex died 8 August 1925 of fever in East Africa after four years' service in the Great War aged 34.

I felt my life draining away with them both. I felt I'd been here before, many times; or this was the last and only time. The obelisk stood high on the edge of the wood overlooking a paddock on the links where a cob and foal grazed ten yards from the sea shore. Milky came to the fence and pointed. 'Have you seen that?'

'Seen what?'

'That . . . that mumbo jumbo thing down there.' His voice was strained.

The tide was in, running up the chucks and almost down the first line of burrows. Milky showed me the miniature henge of clinkers gathered from the shore, some split recently. They were in the grass near the bench, some two feet high and weighing a hundred-weight.

'Don't you think it strange?' Milky asked.

'It wasn't there yesterday,' I conceded.

'There, I knew it. Cantrip. There's glamourie in these parts still. Mean, superstitious people.'

'Doesn't have to be malicious,' I said, thinking of the girl. I knew she'd done it, her and an accomplice. It's why she'd hurried off just then. She must have planned it on her walks, sitting on the bench till I disturbed her.

'Calm down,' I said. 'Let's see how they like this,' he said, kicking one of the standing stones over with the heel of his wellington.

'That'll teach the bastards,' I said.

Through the swing gate I cut across the paddock, shoes chaffing on the yellowing grass. Milky stuck to the thin worn path till once again we stood in the dark brown light of the wood, beside the memorial to Viscountess Clarran.

'Excuse me,' Milky said. 'Call of nature, old man, ha,' then beating his way in the undergrowth he took a slash with his back to me. I remembered another grave then like a flash of past dream. I'd just left school, one of my long walks with a book out towards the next village on the Old Rye Road. I knew she'd not been buried in our village so as I'd passed the tiny churchyard at Silverden Cross I decided to begin my search for her grave. I walked to all the churchyards and cemeteries within a five-mile radius. She was at Hurst Green, St Kit's Parish Church. A stream ran through the churchyard. Trees had uprooted graves and toppled several crosses. The newer graves were to one side on a sort of bungalow lawn, but hers was in the shade the other side of the stream, a tended space among the brambles and yarrow. SACRED TO THE MEMORY OF YVONNE SHARPE. I felt sick at the sight of it and the living/dead presence of the fresh flowers and this awful little photograph cut out with nail scissors into the shape of a gravestone. A girl sitting on her bed, feet dangling above the floor, hair turned under her chin on one side, turned out the other. A smile hardly alive enough to show. The bed was like a hospital bed too and Yvonne was sitting on her hands. Beside the photograph hung a chain and plastic tag. CINDY DOLL.

> AN ANGEL TOOK MY FLOWER AWAY
> YET I WILL NOT REPINE
> FOR JESUS IN HIS BOSOM WEARS
> THE FLOWER THAT ONCE WAS MINE

I waited in the churchyard all day the following Sunday but her parents didn't visit. I tried again on Wednesday afternoon then gave up.

The sixth anniversary of her death was a bitterly cold November day, the first heavy ground frost of the year, puddles frozen solid, ice like big toe nails. I arrived there midday. Her grave had wintered over. The photograph was of a dead girl, a blank shape. Her parents came about the time Yvonne was strangled. Mrs Sharpe in a heavy grey overcoat, Mr Sharpe in an anorak and a yellow rollneck sweater, his face red, a fag in his mouth. They saw me but took no notice as I poked about round the back of the church pretending to take photographs of gargoyles. The skin on Mrs Sharpe's face looked so flakey and loose it seemed to catch on overhanging branches. She chipped the rind off the plastic tag, its inscription like a fossilized worm. She cleared blackened leaves away by hand. I took two photographs but didn't develop the film. It's still down Barratt's Road in a drawer. As Mrs Sharpe placed fresh flowers on the grave, her husband rubbed his hairy knuckles and went into the bare bushes for a piss.

Milky was impatient. I suspect he'd pissed down his leg because he was holding out his hand and looking at the sky over the sea.

'I'm sure I felt a drop.' Of course he was right. The wind was picking up and a dark sky over the Dornoch Firth was moving our way. I said he must have spat on himself.

'I hadn't spoken, had I? Of course it's rain. Anyway, this wood's too gloomy to be loitering about in.'

We followed a wider track with a flint verge, winding through the spruce, metal arrows at each junction.

'There's a broch up there,' I said.

'I know *that*' he said.

'Can you tell it's a Wednesday?'

'It's not Wednesday,' Milky said.

'It's a Wednesday wind,' I said.

'It's always windy up here. Listen, I know people who have left Scotland for good because they can't stand the wind.'

I invited him to Middle Cottage for tea. He sat on the edge of the chair and more or less refused to talk, looking into his tea or onto the floor, showing no curiosity over my way of life. When he went to the toilet he put his wellingtons back on discreetly so he wouldn't get fluff on his socks. He'd taken them off automatically because I didn't ask him. Outside, the wind slashed through trees and crushed the grass, leaves and rose petals whipping by, driving the Rayburn dial to moderate already. The kitchen smelled of coal and Milky grunted about pulling the blankets down off the windows and letting in more air. Bad for the lungs, he said, coal smoke. I banged his empty cup down on the table and poured him another, my fascination for him equal to my hatred and dependence on him. Then he took a final slurp on his tea and stood up. This time he'd kept his wellingtons on.

'Early night,' he said. 'Have to go to Wick on business for two days.'

Then the postman came up the path and the letterbox clapped. It sounded so desolate, the echo of wasted time and hollow afternoons in unfriendly places I never wanted to be in again.

I saw Milky to the door and picked up the letter, ripping it open and waving it in his face with visible relief. A cheque from Social Security for twice the coach fare to London. You should have seen his face, too. He guessed I was leaving. In turn it dawned on me why he was going to Wick, apart from to plead with Selina. He was going to the Benefit Office.

I followed him down the garden path shutting the gate behind me and saying I'd walk some of the way with him. Half way up the slither the wind barged down in our faces and we turned our backs simultaneously. A sweep's brush cocked from Cowman

John's chimney top. As we entered the forest Milky was ahead of me. I shouted after him. ' 'Ere, did ol' China ever sweep your chimney?' The wind swiped from all sides bowling us four ways. My shout was like a gum bubble flatting back into my own face. China Thomas was the last chimney sweep in the village and lived down Barratt's Road. I couldn't hear what Milky shouted back, neither could I keep up with him the way he kept skipping ahead and jumping from side to side to avoid the grummel and ruts, even in his wellingtons.

'I SAID, DID CHINA THOMAS EVER SWEEP YOUR CHIMNEY?'

'Of course he didn't,' Milky shouted back. 'We always had electricity.'

The tree tops whipped and spun. The sound of antlers clashing and our voices wadded down our throats. Milky's macintosh had flattened against his chest and I bent forward to keep my jacket being ripped off my shoulders. I wished the wind would hurl me against him like paper on a fence so I could stick there and force a confession or smash his head against the ground and give him some facts: like NO MUSEUM or NO WIFE and NO CAR, so stop pretending and FACE ME. But how could I? You always need that last push, that last shred of feeling peeled away before you can hurt someone else, especially when they're hatched from the same social egg. Let's face it now: we're just two working-class plonkers, me and Milky, out of our depth and drowning in a bottomless inferiority complex.

'Crikey,' he shouted, 'look at the sea.'

I stood beside him and made a peak with my hand to keep the dust from my eyes. Far below, through the trees, I saw the white topped sea beaten to a froth across the whole Dornoch Firth like a stampede of horses. Milky's unimaginative remark came next.

'Hmm, like rice pudding, Watson, eh?'

I said no way did it resemble rice pudding. In fact, I said, I hated rice pudding so this influenced my comparison.

'We never had rice pudding,' he said.

'You liar,' I said, at first quite lightly, but in case the wind blocked his ears I said it again like a hammer brought down on a mis-hit nail.

'Who are you calling a liar?' he said. One problem I have with people is my intolerance of any lack of actual talent in people who write. With Milky I felt I didn't need to read anything he'd written. Standing there watching the sea at the most painful period in his life, all he could imagine was that the sea looked like rice pudding. I was calling him a liar because he'd told me, Daz and Skinny that Saturday afternoon we went down Little Nineveh that he'd had rice pudding for dinner. This is something I can't verify. Something I might have convinced myself was true just to call him a liar when I needed to.

He half faced me, like I was the wind and might blow his eyes inside out.

'I knew you were going to bring this up.' He strode into the wind like a kite which stubbed the ground and wouldn't lift, arms stiff ape length from anger. I chased after him, shouting with no sense of logic, throwing out sentences like I was trying to hit him with one.

And what had driven us both here too? I asked. Hadn't he thought of that yet? What the hell did he think I was writing about? Why did he think that I, Swattenden and Barratt's Road, how come I was writing a novel in the first place? When I stopped running so did he, shouting back and taking a little false charge at me like he had at Selina.

'You jolly well better leave me out of it. I don't want you writing about me, you sod.'

He stumbled through some mud like a spooked cow. Then this pine cone fell from a tree and bounced off his hunched back making him spin round because he thought I chucked it at him. I couldn't exactly hear what he said but it was probably 'RIGHT!' He couldn't find the culprit cone so he scavenged for a clean one but finally had to pick one with a pliers hand from the mud. Like a cheat at cricket or darts he edged forward to get nearer the target, but I backed away. Old blunderbuss shot it hard as a rocket but it missed by a mile and whizzed off into the bracken. When he saw I didn't intend chucking one back at him he stomped off home.

On the kitchen floor I began half-heartedly packing my books and doing the washing up but there seemed no point doing it now as it could be done with more enthusiasm at the last minute, so I walked down the phone box by the Post Office and rang the coach station at Inverness.

I woke late, the light pulling at my eyes like unsteady hands on the shutters, grey, gloom-blue light, the sky a mortician's cold shave. Winter had begun that night. Petal-torn rosehips flapped at the window like stranded fish. Trees turned porous in one night, the track drenched in twigs and, but for a technicality, last year's leaves. I sat in the window drinking tea, glancing out at this inswept and stunted place while I wrote Milky a stunted letter telling him I'd be leaving Kildaggie on Saturday for good and would not be troubling him again. Good luck with the woodwork, I ended, but crossed out woodwork and put writing. I addressed it to his bungalow.

I kicked my way along the beach. Broken sky, sea like a moss pot, gulls riding in like ducks. Perforated clouds. Pale, quiverstill shoreline. For God's sake, I said, but waited another half hour, rose, then sat down again. Miles out to sea gulls flashed like white and yellow butterflies. The low tide sobbed and dragged over slick sand, a faint song on the far-off rocks, swilling like a slow dream. Two jet fighters honed to a point along the horizon half a mile apart before twisting high into the cloud BOOM . . . boom, breaking the sound barrier. Over in Ross and Cromarty plumes of smoke from burning stubble as the day drew in.

Chapter Fourteen

The fuckin spaniel won't stop yapping and tries to bite me when I clamp my hand over its mouth. Voice from the kitchen – Raif's voice too, that Oxonian from the Estates Office (so *she is* his daughter then) says, Archie, do shuttup, there's a good chap.

A strip of blue, nylon, splintered rope from a washed-up lobster-pot stinks of salt, shedding sand grit which clogs everywhere. Noose Archie's neck and bundle him under my arm slapping me leg like a cowboy horse.

LEZ GO ARCHIE LEZ GO LEZGO LEZGO

High in the wood an obelisk on the drop's edge over the paddock. Tie Archie to the obelisk then run along the beach to her bench. She's crying and trailing an empty lead along the path. Feeble ARCHIEs Archies Archies in her voice.

Have you lost your dog? Yes.

She won't look up. The moon catches her parting, a white line.

I'll help you find him. Wait there, they sometimes like to cock their legs round the obelisk Milky's standing at the obelisk marble like the obelisk white faced moon peel on his skin nothing more horrible than the way he screams silently.

Thursday afternoon I was walking across the farmyard when Marine Cormorant walked out of the milking shed with a man I'd never seen hanging back behind her, taking his tobacco tin from an overall pocket and choosing a stub in the doorway. She carried an empty blue bucket in her right hand and shook the bucket at me in lieu of her fist. Marine Cormorant looked ridiculous, tottering on the stones, black cords ironed the wrong way and sticking out sideways like cowboy chaps. Cigarette in her fingers, rally jacket zipped to the neck, brow lowered over bleedy slash eyes.

'A wurrd wi'ye, Cairdric,' she said without breathing in or out.

I frowned back, hands in pockets.

'Aye, thez noo greeter wrrath th'n thart of a wumm'n scoorned,' she said from several yards off. 'Cairdric,' she began a second advance, 'when ah walk past ma hoos a wee while agoo, what do ah see noo when looking up inta yewer bairdr'm wonder?'

She didn't want an answer so I watched the light catch the fluff on her chun, the brooken vassels in her chicks, the bloatches under her lugs. 'Ah'll tell ye what ah saw . . . Bairdcovers. Aye. Ma bairdcovers.' Her companion had edged his way back into the cowshed to light his tabbie.

'An what d'ye think ah say t'maself? Marine, ah say, a'three o'clock in the noon thez ma bairdcovers across the wonders like some tramp w' kippin' in ma hoos. Noo tull me this, Cairdric. Is it reet or noo?'

'Is what reet or noo?' I said.

'Why, mun, the way yewer luvin', Cairdric. Turning ma hoos inta' squatt. Aye, the bairdr'ms like a squatt.'

'How do you know? Have you been in there?'

'Ah c'n guess, mun.'

'You have been in there. It was you pinched my money and left the bathroom door open once and shuffled the papers on the table. Well? What did you read about yourself?'

She tried to summon the man from the shed but he wouldn't budge. She said she wasna having this from a keeker like me.

'Get oot o'ma hoos, mun! Ah doan wantyin ma hoos, you wi'yurr scodger's creep . . .' Least that's what it sounded like. I told her I was leaving anyway so she couldn't flatter herself over my eviction.

'What did ah tell ye? Yewen yurr bl'dy stewpitt ideas. Ah seed y'd nairver luss th'wunter oot, an' yurr canna iven luss the bl'dy month. Ach, goot riddance t'ye . . . '

On the bench I watched the sea. Thin yellow sky, a bank of cloud greying the corners and coming down off the hills, bringing rain once more over the runt houses of Kildaggie. I sat on until the daggy soaked my back, the grass began to lift and bow and darkness fell. That night I dragged the furniture from one room to another until the cottage was exactly as I'd found it, my belongings piled in the middle of the cold kitchen floor.

Chapter Fifteen

Friday evening, killing time while autumn killed its insects, sitting in the window drinking tea and smoking tobacco when Milky appears at the garden gate, shining his torch beam up the path even though it's dusk enough to see. I was thinking of these African flies which used to hatch on my verandah at Mbugazali. White-winged, they rose fully hatched for a maiden flight from the ground to the porchlight (if Grimble let the school use his generator) or the flame of my paraffin lamp, a lifespan of nine seconds. Some didn't even reach the light. For a whole month during the rains they hatched every night. In the mornings a boy came and swept them up for five shillings a week, the price of a box of matches. These flies were so numerous they blew into white snowdrifts along the walls. When I put one under a magnifying glass I saw two beautiful white wings like micro-stained glass windows.

I went to the door and stepped into the beam of his torch. He snapped it dark and tried to smile as I nodded. He smelled of insect repellent and must have walked down through the forest where the midges are thick as hedgerows.

'I, uhm, received your communication . . . ' he said, standing in the middle of the path and looking up at the sky.

'I didn't chuck that pine cone at you,' I said. 'It fell out the tree.'

'Ah,' he said. 'Heaven sent, eh? Ha. Well, everything comes out of the blue nowadays, man.'

He followed me in and sat on one of those hideous chrome chairs I'd re-introduced, warming his hands on a mug of tea. Very politely, I offered him toast. He looked famished, so I cooked up what food I had while he sat and flicked through a tourist booklet which went with the cottage. I told him of my relations with Marine Cormorant and he said the Scots were a funny lot. He'd seen her name in Wick on the sides of fish lorries. Our meal was as frugal as the conversation. Milky didn't allude to my departure or himself. He was like a stray animal creeping towards the fire to warm itself, hoping it wouldn't be spotted and turned out. I made coffee. He wiped his mouth with a handkerchief. He'd come to give himself up. I fumbled a cigarette into the proper shape and burnt my nose lighting it. Then I told him I came to Kildaggie knowing he was there. *'Because* you were here,' I said to avoid ambiguity. He clutched his mug and watched the floor, his lips working in and out in a world of their own. I stared back out the window trying to find the sea but Milky's reflection stood in the way. He moved his chair nearer the Rayburn and tucked his shirt in properly, sitting down again with his mug.

'Why?' he said at last. 'Why?'

For a few seconds his eyes fixed themselves on my face but as I didn't reply he lowered them again, leaning forward, legs apart, elbows on his thighs, sipping at his tea quickly as if he'd just remembered it.

'Why?' I repeated, asking myself. Not a single word came into my head. I really couldn't tell him why because this novel had grown around the question long since. What had happened in Kildaggie was as much part of things as Little Nineveh. Truth didn't interest me anymore. It interests me even less now and I'd have to re-read this re-writing to formulate the question which might once have applied itself to the truth demanded of an answer. I was also trying to interpret my feelings towards him. The humming in my ears and the sticking of my eyelids each time I blinked might have been boredom. Milky didn't puzzle me anymore or worry me. He was an element of fiction, an umbilical link, a character in a novel which had taken over from him. He waited for me to breathe life into him once more. His biographer.

'Research,' I said.

'Are you really writing about . . . all that?' he asked.

I told him I was on Chapter Fifteen and what that's about is up to you. 'We're both in it up to our necks so far.'

'We,' he said, sitting up and looking at the manuscript on the floor, wiping a tea drop off his trousers. 'Doing what?'

'Don't you ever write about yourself, for God's sake?' I asked, but he gave me what other novelists might call a queer look so I picked up the manuscript and dumped it on the table and extracted Chapter One.

'What's that?' he asked, but not so stupidly as you think. More like he might ask of a surgeon who'd just removed something from his guts.

'I'll read it to you,' I said. 'It's about our adventure down Little Nineveh. . . .' waiting till he motioned me to begin because it was important I had his full consent, straightening the pages, parting the air between us. A sense of power, real and independent; a love for what I'd done and written, of hate, confession, self-destruction; and more than anything of irredeemable isolation, because I'd never written to anyone before. Old feelings rising in new places. There was no way to get at them and cut them back. They entwined themselves about me until I felt at Milky White's mercy too. My desire to read to him was so great that I felt ignorant, so dependent upon impressing him. How little I knew of him after all unless I was behind his actions or conversation . . . So before I'd even opened my mouth he'd reduced this into the shame of an insignificant gift.

'Well, go on then,' he said, 'if you're going to.' Grudging, superior, as if he thought he was doing me a favour. The critic. So when I began it was in a voice of accusation. I'd made annotations on the manuscript which overflowed onto slips of paper, stepping stones through Chapter One, points of law, interrogations in the second person. The first appeared on Page 2:

'Each Saturday morning about this time, *you* received five shillings pocket money from your father. *We* got two bob from our dads. You didn't rush like us down to Pullins for a pike float or up Baldocks for bubblegum cards. No, you put yours in the Post Office Savings week after week. In fact, you would have been on your way back from the Post Office when I caught my first glimpse of you that Saturday morning. Then what did you do? Where did you go? Because I saw you walking down the pavement on Cranbrook Road, approaching Sandrock Villas too, a peculiar way for you to be going . . . '

He looked like I'd slapped his face, but fascinated, amazed, I don't know. I've seen that look on children when you've done something ordinary and pretended it's a trick, a worrying trick. I saw it once on a vervet monkey in Africa after it had stolen my pen from the window ledge and I climbed up a tree after it. Still, I had Milky's complete attention.

'Are you asking me?' he said. I didn't move or speak. 'Well, if you must know I was on my way to see Wormhole.'

We both knew very well that Wormhole lived in Chapel Road and the quickest route was down Windmill Lane from the Bandbox. Come on, I told him, he'd passed Windmill Lane and was in fact at the bottom of the hill two hundred yards off course. The only person he knew down Sandrock Villas was Red Lantern (Bernard Burns), a boy in his class and a mutual enemy. So why was he down Sandrock Villas?

'Alright, you obviously *must* know. I was . . . I went to see Avril Kent.'

It was my turn to be amazed. 'Avril Kent?'

'Well, what's wrong with that?' He sounded hurt.

I'd never given this aspect of Milky a second thought, always assuming he'd had nothing to do with girls because none of us had, or not so directly as to establish visiting rights.

'Now we know yer,' I gloated, increasing my ignorance.

'Oh don't be so ridiculous,' he said. He'd kept *that* a secret, I said, but he reckoned there was nothing to be kept a secret.

'She'd gone shopping to Hastings in any case. I never went round there again I can tell you. I never went out with her either.'

It still hurt him, this. I could just see him lowering a keepsake from Avril Kent down the drain on a piece of string. Stamping his wife's vanity pouch into his own puke is a later development of some earlier notion of unsullying yourself from a woman.

'So after that I suppose you called on Wormhole.'

'More or less.'

'What's that mean? You didn't?'

'Well, I did bump into Red Lantern, ha! Red Lantern! He wore that fawn dufflecoat with the arm hanging off. Did he ever come round your door with his old woman? He used to come round ours but never said anything. I don't think he really knew what a Jehovah's Witness was.'

It's a fact worth stating that so many boys in Milky's year were of different faiths. In theory and practice Swattenden was C. of E. Red Lantern was the only Jehovah's Witness in the whole school. His brother Leonard went to the Tech. Bernie Burns was known as Red Lantern because his face glowed red at the slightest provocation, apart from the convenient pun. Milky had fallen out with him during hockey practice. Milky whacked him on the knee so hard he couldn't walk on it for a week. He accused Milky of doing it on purpose. Milky said if Jehovah's Witnesses weren't so stupid and went to doctors like everybody else he could have got medicine for the swelling and might have limped for a day or two at the most. Red Lantern wasn't even allowed a bandage on it.

'So what happened when you bumped into him then?'

'Oh nothing. Him and his brother were washing the car and one of them said: "Ugh, there goes ol' White." '

'What did you say back?' I guessed he must have said something witty because he wouldn't bring anything up unless he'd been victorious in his own eyes.

'I called him Beetroot Face. Hah! His stupid brother started coming at me with the shammy leather. Couldn't run for toffee, the prat. I just legged it up to Wormhole's.'

'Ah yes,' I said slowly. 'Wormhole.'

Into a chink of silence then, came a moment like a flash of memory before it should have existed, if it had existed at all. I think it must have crossed Milky's path too, but only as a draught under the door. So supposing we were back in that morning, the memory goes something like: Yvonne Sharpe's gonna be strangled a few hours later this afternoon . . .

I read on. The next annotation concerned Wormhole: 'It's strange how all your friends were from different religious sects. Before the hockey incident you'd been good friends with Red Lantern. You were Church of England and even came to Sunday School with me, Daz and Skinny once or twice. Martin Mumps was one of your early school cronies and he was a Catholic. Baker was Methodist. Jewdrop, who you played school chess with, was something weird – 'e weren' a Jew of course – like United Reform. And then there was Wormhole the Baptist. This isolated you, your religious conventionality, because all five of your companions were exempt or banned from assembly because of the prayers and hymns. They lined up outside the hall until the headmaster waved them in for the notices at the end. Till then you stood alone in the gap which was always left for them either side of you. I used to see you by my snide sidelong glances behind and slightly to the left, saying the Lord's Prayer with real prayer book hands as if you meant it, your excommunicates stamping up and down in the cold and finding your devotion amusing.'

I didn't know any of the others, but I once went round Wormhole's myself to visit his younger brother Graham. Their tiny house was the sort they used to put on lids of Betabrix sets – green pebbledash, a front garden three strides deep behind a fancy, knee-high wall; crazypaving pink and white, a bay window big enough for two faces and a dog. I don't remember the exact details of how my visit was commissioned, but I think it was one of those things mothers arrange when they meet up the shops and waste a whole Saturday morning of their sons' time as a consequence.

Mrs Wormley opened the door. Two broken front teeth made her voice phut words, her tongue landing in the wrong place. 'Hello, Thedric. Here'th Thedric, Grah'm.'

Bo-Peep Cottage. There was even a fish tank like a jamjar with minnows and a three-foot-high grandfather clock. I was nearly as tall as Mrs Wormley even then. Full-size Graham, Worm'ole Sub-stitute, was at the kitchen table with his model galleon kit in pools of glue all stuck to the newspaper, which followed him round the house because Mrs Wormley insisted he took my shoes out the back and fetched some felt slippers for me to wear. She'd cut them in one piece from underlay and sewed them with waxed string. Graham was in a daze.

'Well thun?' his mother said. 'Lookooth come t'thee you. Thedric's come to giff you a hand with your thip.'

I was given a glass of Lemon Barley Squash and a digestive biscuit, unstuck part 7 from part 49 and stuck it to part 6. This was all I could manage against Graham's adenoidal uncorking sulks. 'Let me do it! Marm, why carn I do it meself? It's not fair . . . ' I never went back there again. If Worm'ole Substitute saw me at school or the bus stop he'd gloat a wistful 'Watcha', which died on his face if Daz was about. 'You watchyer self, Worm Face,' he'd say.

The thing is I wondered what you did round Bo-Peep Cottage with Wormhole. Play snap upstairs with those two-inch-long cards you got from Pullins, or miniature travel draughts . . . '

Milky interrupted: 'No we didn't! Wormhole had a full-size Scalectrix set. We made tunnels out of shoeboxes and Bibles.'

'That morning?' I asked, 'After you saw Red Lantern?'

My question silenced him again. Perhaps he sensed where it was leading. There was an old smell in the air. A cupboard that hadn't been opened in years.

'You must have done something,' I persisted.

'No,' he said.

'Why not?'

'I didn't even see him, did I? I knocked on his door but Mrs Wormley said he had one of his stomach aches and they were waiting for the doctor.'

So was this it after all? He'd come with us in the afternoon because there was no one else to play with? His own company must have galled him that day. He was an experienced loner. And by then he knew what we thought of him so the effort must have cost him dear.

'Is that why you came with us then? No one to play with? Nowhere else to go? Nothing to play with? Nothing to do? You, sick of your own company?'

He nodded slowly, his head like a rocking-chair someone had left several moments before, coming gently, slowly to a stop.

'How can I believe you?' I asked. 'Why do you remember it so well? I mean . . . we've both lied to each other many times over the past weeks.'

Anger wasn't the word. It was like the rocking-chair had been pulled away from under him. 'What do you mean? Christ! Christ! I'll have you know I was brought up by a man who . . . who . . . '

'Yeah,' I said, 'a man who told jokes and slashed other people's tyres.' I was sick of his decent upbringing. Arms stiff and fisted, he was off his chair like a fireman. 'HOW DARE YOU!'

His tea drenched the floor and he didn't know which way to go as the stream made its way towards my rucksack. He'd been coming at me. 'I COULD HIT YOU!' he shouted, but his upbringing got the better of him and he swiped the wet cloth from the draining board and threw it on the spillage. I took over and dammed the stream. Milky tried to apologize. 'You shouldn't have said that,' he added washing his hands and smelling them.

'I know, I know,' I said. His face expressed utter bewilderment, a hurt, angry child I'd seen twenty years ago. Milky had joined in this football match up the field, Barratt's Road against Pigs Passage. There were hundreds of us all swarming after the ball. We won 26–12 mainly because me and Nige Monk took their fifteen nippers defence apart and smashed a dozen goals each past many hopeless and reluctant goalies. Milky ball-hogged and kept losing it but finally scored his one goal, a clumsy mis-hit fluke. 'Huh,' he said afterwards, '*we* showed 'em.'

'*You* didn't, White,' Nige Monk said, turning his back on him. I actually felt sorry for Milky at the time, seeing the look on his face. That night in my kitchen he could have stomped back to his bungalow there and then if he'd wanted to, the way he stomped home after the football match or in the forest a few days ago. His own company must have galled him more than ever. He asked for another cup of tea. I knew I could read him anything, ask him anything. He was as vain as the rest of us and he'd never had so much attention. He could see how long I'd been writing about him and thinking about him, at a time when most people appeared to have ignored him. Neither could he go without finding out what I'd said of him, what was on the next page and the next. And when the book had finished, what was still in the author's mind about him and perhaps hadn't been used?

He might ask: will he want me again? Perhaps he guessed that when you finish with a character, it's dead, at least for the moment. There may be some slight resonance from the past, but in life terms the moment is worthless. I read on at Milky's prompt.

'I next saw you at half past one, pumping up the tyres of your bicycle while your brother rubbed the dubbin on his football boots. Me, Daz and Skinny pissed about with a tennis ball in the road below the wall. The Hawks fixture against Ninfield was cancelled, but we could have gone up Church Hill for a kickabout on the empty pitch. 'Barny'll be there,' I said. 'We c'n always git s'me ovvers an' 'ave two soides.'

'Barny ain no good,' Daz said. ' 'E always plays in wellin'tons.'

'I know you lot,' Skinny said. 'Lez boike t'Bodiam.'

You heard this and came down the path. 'I'll come if you're going to Bodiam,' you said, wheeling your bike like a race horse, propping open the gate so it didn't swing into its flank, settling it on its stand and leaning yourself on the blue railings which ran along the top of the wall, looking down upon us like you might spit if we denied you the captaincy of this bike ride. From your vantage point you couldn't really see the faces we made between ourselves. You might have noticed the bobble on Daz's woollen hat shaking, but his screwed-up nose and goofed mouth were visible to us and meant: we don't want 'im wiv us, do we?

'Lez goo darn the lanes,' I said, not meaning it, just to divert the bike ride. You see I won't accept sole responsibility for us going. I wanted to throw you off and the others agreed. You frowned, suspecting a trick. You go in, Daz and Skinny bike to Bodiam, I play football with Barney.

'What about the bikes?' you said, knowing I'd be excluded if you went even down the lanes on bikes.

'Nah,' Daz said. 'Sedge ain' got one, 'as 'e?'

'So what?' you said, 'He can catch us up.'

We didn't bother with an answer. Making a remark like that proved you were beneath us.

'Less get our catties,' Daz said and we prepared to run. We could have got away too because you stabled your bike up the garden shed and you never left it without locking it away. By the time we'd fetched our catapults we might have lost you, but you anticipated us and called your brother down, telling him to put your bike away for you, jumping down beside us with your wellingtons already on. You didn't turn their tops down like we did to make smugglers' or seafarers' boots because you said that little slits appeared in the fold so water leaked in. I don't see why that worried you because you never waded streams in any case and you kept your wellies so spotless they shone with little windows of light like a wellington house.

Until the Tudor Arms nothing significant occurs. We just slosh along the pavement kidding at the loose grit and conker husks, putting up with you haunting our gloom. Then at the Tudor, where the lanes begin, you take on a life of your own, Captaincy, walking ahead and doing American voices, slashing at the grass verge with a stick, poking bullocks on the nose through the fence. Daz suggests we ought to try and lose you but you seem to hear him and stick to us on the alert.

' 'E finks 'e's so funny,' I remember saying.

'Cor, oi smell chips,' Skinny says as we pass the hotel kitchen.

You say you've been to a hotel like this outside Tunbridge Wells where you ate chicken and chips in a basket. 'You don't eat off plates in posh places.'

'Bollocks, Whoite. 'Ow c'n yeat chips out baskits?'

'Huh, you couldn't, Skinny,' you say. 'They wouldn't let you and your ole man *in* a hotel restaurant, not unless you went there to sweep the chimney and your ole man did the drains.'

Skinny looks about to cry or chuck a brick at you but one moment passes into another with the unmistakeable phut and strish of an airgun pellet ripping its way across the face of trees.

'They're down there,' Daz says.

The lane forks here. Stream Lane to the left, Nineveh Lane to the right. I don't want to go down Nineveh Lane of course . . . '.

Milky interrupted me, Sherlock Holmes at last: 'Why not?' His voice is sharp. He'd made an important point in that I hadn't considered him when writing the sentence. I didn't want to tell him about Bluebird anyway until I had to. No faith in his temporary submission. Still clinging to the author's secrets and intentions. The problem of wishing to remain a private being contradicting the desire for a reader – both leading in my case to accusations of, well

. . . accusations. So I told him I just didn't want to go down there, cutting off his chance to answer back.

'Stream Lane is high-banked, dark under the trees. Another shot, just round the bend, the brack of a pellet aimed through the hedgerow. You hang back . . . '

'I did *not*'.

'Oh shuddup, will yer! You hung back, scared all over your face. It is unforgivable . . . '

'What are you talking about, man?'

'Just let me read it and you'll find out for Christ's sake . . . It is unforgivable the way you push Skinny forward, saying they'll be more scared if they see his face than yours. Skinny says that if you go they'll shoot you in the pants because they'll mistake your arse for your face. I'm wondering who it is with the airgun and Daz reckons it might be Cackitt who lives down here on the farm. Then we hear their foreign jabber, another shot, rooks caw, starlings scatter. We dare ourselves forward and peer round the bend, the adventure of curiosity. But without you. Your lack of curiosity, to put it simply, roots you to the tail end. We see the three Italian waiters from the hotel, shooting sparrows. 'Ugh, they eat'em,' Daz says. Another shot. This time a pellet thicks into the bank nearby.

'Cor, oi'm geddin' oud ov'ere,' Skinny says, legging it back up the lane. You're streaks ahead in a futter of hope-me-dad-don't-find-out wellingtons. Either this or you're rushing home to tell him more like. Then you turn down Nineveh Lane instead of back to the road. Oh yes, you lead us, Captain Milky, into Nineveh Lane . . . '

'I didn't *lead* you anywhere.'

'Why d'you go that way then?'

'That's the way we were going, wasn't it? I don't see that it matters who went down there first. *You* suggested we went "down the lanes".'

'Oh, yeah? You didn't stop to ask us, did you? My inclination would have been to carry on along the road and go down Foxhole Lane. I didn't think we'd decided, any road.'

'Well I don't remember you objecting. In fact, yes, if I remember correctly, I wasn't even past the signpost to Nineveh Lane when you shot past me going like the clappers.'

'Yeah, only because Daz was aiming at my arse with his catapult.'

'Well then, you led us there as much as I did. How do you know
I might not have stopped and gone back to the road? I only ran off
because Skinny pooped his pants. And you only ran off because of
Daz. It seems tò me, *Watson*, that we all ran down there because of
each other. You're just trying to blame me.'

As far his explanation goes I know he's right. You can't avoid
the self-created pains; such failures taint the whole moment.

'Alright,' I told him, 'have it your way. But it doesn't alter much.
You were the catalyst that afternoon. Our thoughts never met at
any point. Your psyche wouldn't link with ours, would it? I'm not
reading this. It's become a passage I recite from memory. Think it
or write it, it's the same: you even divided *us*. We thought the same
about your presence, but it separated us into worlds of our own.
Even our resentments towards you were individual. By the time
we'd reached Little Nineveh you'd so disrupted us that for the first
time in our lives we doubted what we saw and felt, doubted who
our friends were and began to wonder why things happened. We
were vulnerable, thanks to you. There was no comfort to be had in
each other's presence. Don't you remember? Couldn't you feel it?
Didn't it bother you?' This time *I* could have hit *him*. The way he
just stared at the window in silence, then at the floor, his open
mouth shutting slowly upon itself like a fish on hunger strike; a
sigh during unction, a minute shaking of the head. He didn't even
try and fool me into thinking he hadn't understood what I meant.
Sheer helplessness made him say: 'You make it sound like a novel.
Well it wasn't. You can't really believe what you've made up. You
can't know what went through our minds. You've made it up. You
put it there. Haven't you ever thought of that?'

Sheer helplessness against him made me reply: 'Of course it's a
novel. Of course I've thought of that.'

Fascination easily turns to boredom; self-obsession to self-
disgust. The spirit of enquiry can evaporate anytime. Post-modernists
have constructed us this option.

'The St Dunstan's School Lodge has a wooden spike Daz wants
to try quoits at one day. DRIVE SLOWLY. PRIVATE GROUNDS. Both
Lodge and grounds look deserted. On the verge beside us is an old

brick pillar with a postbox set into it. Skinny wonders if there's a letter in it. I tell him to put his hand in and find out. 'Nah,' he says. 'There moight be summin in there.' I suppose he meant spiders, but Daz says, ' 'Course there is, Postal Orders prob'ly.' Skinny rolls his sleeves up to the elbow but you're here to keep the Law. 'Don't. Someone might look out the window and call the police.'

Above the long hedge we can see a tiny, leaded window. A spinney runs the length of the school drive. ' 'Course they won't scarecat,' Daz says to you, but our heart isn't in it now. Yours is the one odd beat. 'This is boring,' you declare.'

'Oh get on with it for God's sake,' Milky (and the only word I can think of is blurted). 'You're not a very good novelist, are you? You keep diverting up this path and down that lane. You're worse than that Conrad, all this, this significance like a huge . . . I don't know, dumpling on the side of the plate. Why can't you just say it was three o'clock and we just pushed on up the footpath and I don't know what! . . . '

I said I bloody well had written it was three o'clock, but hadn't it ever struck him that it might have been quarter to four?

'So what?' he'd said.

'Because the clock struck quarters.'

'So what?' he repeated. Only, I told him, that it meant a lot to our parents at the time. They'd gained comfort from thinking there'd been no possibility of us being murdered, or being any-where near the murder. At three o'clock Yvonne Sharpe was still at home. Quarter to four was a different matter. She might have been there by then. Partridge certainly was. We'd seen his bike, hadn't we? Leaning against the fence, wasn't it?

So Milky was right. I'm not a novelist. I came in my trousers just now, ex-text at that. No sense of duty, crescendo, plot. The kind of writing Milky demanded was ex cathedra. I'd only provoked his sullen anger once more, without revelation or consciousness-piercing. Worse, I'd showed no faith in the work and the scene went flat. Like poisoning someone's drink and giving yourself away because you think it's not working. They call the police and you're caught.

One of my talents is relevant. I can see a thing through and won't abandon it. This way I found I could route march in the

African heat by looking forward to that drink at the very end rather than surviving on refreshment along the way; for the traveller, once supped, never feels like leaving those tin huts selling juice. So, as I'd come at last to the bike, the lie at the heart of them all, I must have imagined it appropriate to use my own voice and shed the text. In that sense I'm not a novelist. Let me go back to being me after all.

When I see the bike I say: ' 'S Partridge's.' It's you (I recall this very clearly now) who says it isn't. This can only mean one thing and is contrary to all you claimed afterwards. You give yourself away a second time now. Daz says: 'Bet 'e's watchin' us.'

'Who?' you ask.

'Partridge,' Daz says.

'Who's Partridge?' you ask. I'm not suggesting you knew Partridge by name *because* you denied that it was his bike. I'm certain you knew whose bike it was. You just didn't know his name. At the time I don't pick up on any of this. When you ask: 'Who's Partridge?' I feel it's a natural question. Of course you haven't met him. You were never with us up Church Hill when he was. Several times, in fact, we all assumed you'd not met him. You tell the police you've never even seen him before. They show you this photograph. 'No, I do not recognize this man.'

So: 'Who's Partridge?' you ask Daz.

Daz says: 'That bloke what use'ter 'ang about wiv Gibbs 'n them.' No, you still don't know who we mean. Then Daz points at the bike.

'The one what rode this racin' bike.'

'Oh,' you say, 'that twit,' but not in the manner which means you've placed the *man*. No, you already know him; didn't you? You'd recognized the bike, hadn't you? What you mean is: Oh, so *that's* his name. You see how deep this goes? How much more you denied than the mere existence of a racing bike?'

To my surprise Milky nodded. He did see. Standing up and stretching, he came over to the window and tried to peer out but the table blocked his way. He couldn't get his eyes near enough, so all he saw was himself. At the table he drummed his fingers on the glass top. I think he was looking at me. My own face was somewhere reflected in the table top so I pulled my manuscript in closer and stared at it. I was reminded of this old Scottish proverb I'd seen on a tartan postcard at the newsagent's: A friend's eye is a good looking-glass. I went and leaned against the hot rail on the Rayburn. Distance settled us once more. Yes, Milky confessed, his flat voice without the relief of unburdening, he did see the bike. He did recognize it. And yes, he had known who Partridge was, though not by name until the moment Daz had mentioned it.

He'd only seen Partridge twice. Once the day they came back from holiday in August and Milky was sent out for fish and chips. Partridge and Basil Latter were lolling about the railings outside the chip shop. Milky didn't like the look of Partridge. Said he'd crossed the road and walked down past the Smugglers Den then recrossed and come back up to the chip shop below them. Partridge had still said something disgusting to him. Took a lot of coaxing till Milky told me. Apparently, Partridge had shouted through the chip-shop doorway as Milky was about to order: 'Six penn'orth of 'is mother's cod!' I wondered if Partridge had the bike with him. Milky hesitated and tried to laugh it off, twitching eyes, licked lips and bloodless skin.

'I saw it next time, hah. I'll never forget it because he ran me over with it.'

My laughing put paid to Milky's sense of humour. I suppose if I'd ridden Bluebird myself I'd have enjoyed running Melvyn White over. As it was I'd made this possible by stealing Bluebird in the first place. There was still no point telling him about it. He'd have blamed me and told me nothing.

'It's not bloody funny,' he said. 'That nutcase ran me over deliberately. The bastard. Going full pelt.'

He was impatient to tell me about being run over deliberately, like a xenophobic who's been overcharged on his fags in an Asian shop.

'Yes. Deliberately. Up by the Two Trees.'

Now this really interested me, and Milky acted like he'd pulled off a trick. Well, I hadn't known or even thought it possible that Partridge came down Barratt's Road. I asked Milky why he hadn't told anyone but the question irritated him. He picked at a stain on the glass table, left it a moment, picked at it for the last time then cleaned under his fingernail with a handkerchief. 'I couldn't tell anyone,' he said, falling into silence like it was a hole he'd dug for himself. I sat drumming fingers on the chrome chair leg. It had got too hot over by the Rayburn and I needed to prove I could walk over and sit with Milky at the table. I must have sounded insensitive when I asked why on earth he couldn't tell anyone. He flew at me. 'I was embarrassed if you must know!'

'I'd have been furious,' I said.

'I was bloody furious,' he shouted.

'So why didn't you tell anyone?'

'Because I wet myself, that's why, for Christ's sake!'

Another problem I pose other people is my failure to react to their emotions with more sympathy than fascination. Either I probe for details, or laugh, concentrate intensely, or weep with boredom. Before I meet them I've usually drafted the scene out and spend the encounter guiding it by paragraph towards some point of interest. I know my own dialogue by heart and offer few genuine reactions; I'm mostly governed by a burning and uncontrollable desire to get away at the earliest time I decently can to write the whole thing down exactly as it has taken place. I must have communicated something of this attitude to Milky because my probing him led to a request for a cup of tea and more fuel in the Rayburn so he could warm what he called his 'nub end'. He was digging in and I felt uncomfortable but complied with his request.

'Well?' I said. 'Come on, didn't anyone else see what happened? Who was you with?'

Only Wormhole, or so he said. Milky was in goal between the two drains. Wormhole was taking penalties, God knows how. Mrs Wormhole made them wear plastic sandals in the summer and Wormhole was a toe-puncher. If a car turned in at the top of the road Wormhole shouted 'Car!' We all did it that way, standing aside to let it pass. But instead of shouting 'Bike!' Wormhole simply stood there, the ball placed on the spot with a stone to stop it rolling. Naturally enough he expected the rider to avoid Milky, who thought Wormhole was just taking his time because he could be gormless without warning. Milky had no reason to look behind until Wormhole shouted: 'Look out, Mel!' And there was Partridge putting on a spurt the last few yards and coming straight at him. Milky was flattened under the front wheel, hands grazed, seat torn, winded. I pressed him to recall the exact moment he wet himself. The moment before impact, he said. The second he actually caught sight of Partridge.

'He came off too and hurt his foot. Then he just picked himself and that bike up and rode back the way he came.'

'Didn't he say anything?'

'He called me an effing little twerp. I told Wormhole to keep quiet because I had to run home and change my pants. I was shaking like a leaf too. Told my mum I'd fallen out of the conker tree.'

He looked at his watch, said it was late but it didn't matter. I said that Partridge was certainly a nut and they'd never let him out. He'd probably hanged himself in his cell. Milky hadn't thought of Partridge being alive and paroled. He excused himself, locking the toilet door behind him. Do people really think you're going to join them in the toilet? He came back smelling of soap and sniffing hard. 'Cold night, Watson old man,' he said, bravely (I think he would appreciate me adding). I agreed. It was a cold night. I looked out of the window and the sky was clear. Owls screeched over the biggins. Painful tiredness. In twelve hours I'd be on my way to London. After that I didn't know where.

'So, you recognized the bike as the one which ran you over?'

'Yes,' he said. 'Don't you see now? Can't you understand why I lied about it? I was really scared. I thought you lot were just pretending because you knew I was scared. You couldn't trust Wormhole. I thought he must have told someone and you'd found out. I was never accepted, was I? I thought Partridge only hated me, didn't I? Stands to reason, doesn't it? Anyway . . . I just wanted to go home when I saw his bike.'

So, did I understand? I said I supposed I did and that it probably didn't matter now. I said I would've let a murderer go rather than have people find out I'd wet myself, aged twelve. Yes, I said, I honestly understood that. But no one let Partridge go, Milky reminded me. They'd already got him.

'*You* made sure of that, Cedric. So what was the point of *me* saying anything, eh? It wouldn't have made any difference.'

'It would to me,' I told him. 'Oh yes. It would've made all the difference to me. I wouldn't have felt betrayed. I'd have led a normal life too. Wouldn't be here for a start.'

I was only saying this, without feeling or meaning it, regardless of its potential as fact. The thing was, something far more interesting had occurred to me just then. Supposing Partridge had run Milky over by mistake? He could easily have mistaken Milky for me. Up the crossroads that time he'd shouted at me: 'Lillywhite,' he'd called me. 'Lillywhite-'ad-a-fright? Wet yerself agen? Fallen off yer bike? Gone over yer 'andlebars?' Whatever he said it applied to us both. Cedric Lily. Melvyn White. And who did Partridge think the other was? Perhaps he even thought Milky had pinched Bluebird. Better for us both if Partridge had hanged himself. Then I began humming 'Green Grow the Rushes-Ho' until I remembered the words and made them just audible:

> 'Two, two, the Lillywhite boys,
> Clothed all in green ho-ho.
> One is one and
> All alone
> and
> Evermore shall be so . . . '

'Oh ha, yes,' Milky said, 'that's clever.' I wasn't sure how he'd taken it so I looked over the rest of the manuscript. Only one page left I wanted to read him, the best bit too where we all come to the hedge and . . .

'I don't want to hear anymore,' he said.

Why hadn't my writing impressed him? I'd wanted his praise and the endowment of official biographership . . . His face was a blank skin. Partridge was a dead man, Bluebird a name gone cold. I'd come close. Narrating without a licence.

'I'll walk you to the gate,' I said. He put his coat on. We walked down the short path taking deep, relieving breaths. We might have just left the theatre. He stood at the gate, rolling on the balls of his feet, hands behind his back, staring up into the sky. Then he changed his pose as if something was bothering him about the play he'd just seen. He scuffed the ground, his hands back in his pockets. I felt as if I'd just woken up and found myself standing there with a stranger, moon on his face, his hard shadow cut like rock on the track.

'Well,' he said in a voice neither coming nor going, 'don't you want to know what I saw through the hedge on your last page?'

He surprised me. What I really wanted to know was why he thought I'd written it, but the desire rose and fell. A pact in which you do not voice your perplexity or doubt over the unanswered question at the end of the text. A self-deceptive strategy . . .

'No. After all, can it really mean anything?'

He agreed: 'Not to you it won't.'

Then I tried recalling the scene thinking it might help disarm this weapon I'd built. But it was like an idea I'd once grown out of. Like traces in your old bedroom, some of which your father has removed by painting over. Others which your mother wraps in tissue paper and puts in a drawer. You sleep in that room on visits you detest. They say you get over this imaging the umbilical link in the first novel. There's a kind of seed novel which enters you long before this. It can be any age. In boys it's usually when they're about eleven or twelve. It grows slowly till it splits and leaves the body, entering the mind in crisis, through dreams and daytime images, turning memory into imagination. What it produces dies off eventually – in seedy poems or unwatered novels. Some die off at front gates as the cold creeps in from the sea and the moon's like a lamp in the mist. Didn't you feel it too? But it's strange what you saw nonetheless. You had to tell me. It wasn't what you saw exactly, you said, because you saw nothing. Absolutely nothing at all. You didn't know why but something made you pretend to see something. In fact you'd pretended to have seen it all those years, right up until you stood at my garden gate. You even wrote a story about it and thought of showing it to me but changed your mind after hearing me read mine. You'd pretended to see a dog on a length of rope tied to a stake which had been knocked into the ground. You were already frightened. What terrified you was the idea that you could pretend such a thing at that very moment. It didn't seem natural. It terrified you for years after.

Then you told me what you really thought, that you believed in evil because there'd been evil down Little Nineveh that day. The dog? Oh, you said, the dog was alive. A little black spaniel with a tartan bow tie, jumping up and down on its hind legs. You lot couldn't hear it barking because its mouth was gagged, you know, like it had toothache, a handkerchief wound round its jaw. This was all really, except that one of the reasons why you gagged yourself about the bike and all that was because you'd so convinced yourself that you'd seen this dog. Yvonne's dog. The police would think me mad. You'd even worked out a decoy theory. Partridge had used the dog to lure Yvonne down there. He stole her dog and she went with him because he said he'd found it or he'd help her look. You even gave it a name. Angus.

You saw the look on my face. You couldn't resist saying you only wrote the story after I'd come to Kildaggie because I reminded you of it, that day I first looked through your kitchen window and the old Little Nineveh shudder went through you. Just proves how ambiguous imagination is, you said. On your way up the moonlit track you seemed to rise above me, transfigured. You bade me a simple goodnight, and said you wouldn't see me again.

Chapter Sixteen

Where to emerge from behind this Trojan Horse, this camouflage? This isn't another chapter. The reading is over and this is me, alone.

Until now events have superseded any postscript. Let me explain. Demerara is a border town in the desert scrub of north-east Africa where the rainfall is five years late. When the waterholes began to dry up, nomads slaughtered their cattle and took to smuggling. Some armed themselves with rifles and took to banditry. The NE Province became dangerous: tribes raided across borders; pitched battles broke out between smugglers and police and eventually between the tribes themselves. In exasperation the government began a disarming campaign which failed, so they built a new airstrip at Demerara, expanded the barracks, and let the army loose. Villages were bombed out and waterholes poisoned to force nomads into towns, where they were denounced by informers and rounded up. Helicopter gunships dropped napalm on the few remaining cattle herds. Parents abandoned their children. Two thousand families fled from the desert into Demerara. I arrived here in the midst of this, a year ago, when the Children's Town took in its first two hundred orphans of the war.

Today, even the recent past feels remote. It's the beginning of the Haj and the fighting has stopped. It has cost the government too much money. Half a battalion remains in permanent garrison, confined to barracks or routine border patrols. The Brigade has gone south, leaving the desert for those human hyenas desperate enough to remain. We've been sitting in the courtyard speculating about 'the ghosts'. According to soldiers on patrol, these ghosts come in as near as the cattle market and try to drive the camels out into the desert. This past week, when taking our tea in the last heat of the afternoon, the subjects of our conversation ranged over ghosts and smugglers, the slow progress of our plot to recover some of the diesel fuel for the mission's Bedford commandeered by the army; or the state of Ibrahim's leg or the continuing mystery of the missing blankets. I keep meaning to ask Father Giuseppe why there's a typewriter ribbon draped and tangled in the branches of this Chinese rose tree beside us, but it becomes of less importance as the days pass. It was there when I arrived, so I've had about three hundred and sixty days to ask who put it there.

Today is Father Giuseppe's turn to eat supper with the sisters over at the TB mission. After tea he changed and showered in his room leaving me in the yard with nothing to do. Ring doves flirted in the pink blossom and tonic-green swallows dipped in the bird bath. Mamoud came in wearing his little yellow sash to ask if I needed more tea. I said I didn't know what I needed, I only wished those books would arrive. There's been nothing new to read for months and all our parcels have been held over, two thousand miles south. This war has disrupted the mail. Only military or emergency supplies have been allowed through. There's a Greek pilot who flies a sporadic charter, but for contraband, the black market; like sacks full of *mirrah*, these green shoots the men chew all day and which the army smuggles over the border, where it's banned as an illegal drug. In Demerara the women work while the men sit on the edge of bedsteads in places like the New Friends Hotel and a hundred other mud-walled dives, wrapped in table cloth *kikois* from China, chewing from dawn till dusk, eyes glazed, minds emptied, a heap of stems, Pepsi bottle tops and dog-ends on the floor. If we raise fuel for the lorry, we'll go down-country ourselves. We've run out of just about everything we need . . .

but I've strayed, without point, rusty victim of the uncompleted.

Father Giuseppe has done his rounds in a clean shirt and is about to trudge on foot the mile or so over scrub and through the town to the north side where the sisters live.

I keep looking out across the scrub in case he's forgotten something, or in case the plane comes and I have to run up to the airstrip. There might always be something on it for us. It was due this morning but it won't come now. The Greek hates flying back in the dark and refuses to spend the night in Demerara guarding his plane from soldiers who are there to protect him. But a great crowd still waits and an army Land Rover comes and goes with its impatient government official who was due to fly back today. Everyone is restless and impatient by now. The police are there with clubs and batons. When planes arrive they have to beat the crowds back and the fence always caves in. There'd be a riot if old Kostus flew in now. They're all smugglers and the bribing lasts all day. One man bribes another into promising to bribe the Captain to fetch or carry his contraband. I can even see two sisters from the Irish mission standing under the acacia in their safari habits, whispering to each other. Out front in Children's Town, some of the boys are playing football, barefoot in the filthy sand with a ball made from hundreds of strips of rag and polythene and string lumped together into an egg-shaped globe. They wear only a pair of shorts themselves, the same ragged strips like the rag you keep in the boot for wiping the dipstick on. Ibrahim is here, his leg now thick as a barrel, holding it like a cricket bat every time he wants a swipe at the ball. We've told him that when the doctor comes he'll amputate it. The others say they'll have a decent goalpost when he does. The sun begins to set now. The sky turns yellow and green. Our ten-ton ex army Bedford is parked like a rock beside the glade of frangipanes. One of the girls sweeps the path with a brushwood broom. All our paths are lined with painted stones and the driveway with whitewashed rocks. Our long, low buildings are also white, with green tin roofs. On our flagpole the Children's Town flag is limp this evening. Beneath it, arranged tiny white stones set in double rows into the sand, the words: DEMERARA CHILDREN'S TOWN.

The shops will soon open for the evening. The men are drinking tea and boys wheel their plastic water barrels from one Hoteli to another. A convoy of them marches to and from the river a mile away. Paraffin lamps are cleaned, trimmed and filled. Some already hang in doorways. These lamps are the only things people here bother to keep clean; Demerara is a town where the cockroaches are big as matchboxes and the streets are caked in shit.

I have a tiny room, walls painted a cold green, two framed photographs of the Italian Alps, and a crucifix, details of a former occupancy. My window has a shutter, wire mesh and an iron grill. I sleep on an iron bedstead, have my table by the window and a hook above me for the paraffin lamp, which is cleaned, filled and ready to light. The manuscript is beside me, yellowed and covered in a film of sand and dead insects. My throat is dry and my hands begin to tremble. At this time of day I usually tell the children stories about England, which brings me finally and inexorably to Milky White.

When I arrived back in London from Kildaggie at six thirty Sunday morning, I had enough money for three days in a Holloway Road bed and breakfast. What happened next was unimportant – I mean I refused to shed blood about my future. I needed a day's sleep, then spent the next forty-eight hours writing Chapter Sixteen certain that when I reached our parting at the gate I'd understand the nature of my failure and know what to do with the rest of my life. In fact I assumed I'd consider suicide and add a Holloway Road envoi before submitting to a London publisher. Milky seemed so convinced I was evil that its enormity as a perception I could trust seemed a splendid place to end a novel. Transformed by his own revelation, Milky might appear my ambiguous comforter, my moral editor and linguistic pissing-post. Who knows, my confession might be read as transformation too – only I had nothing to confess. The state of permanent incompletion. This was a true source of despair; that literature fails you because writing is psychic haemophilia, one cut and the language you were born with floods away. Transfusion after transfusion until your whole language and life's blood of fiction is corrupted by a hundred donors. Not a drop original. An elaborate deception is being played on you. It makes you capable of believing anything to survive. In Holloway Road I soon found myself reading through my manuscript convinced I carried the sins of the world through my language. By fighting one thing to the exclusion of everything you allow that one thing to emerge. Milky had witnessed life turn into literature like a miracle in the desert. It had made me too vulnerable and his own failure had been a destructive influence upon my novel. Ah, that was it: THE ANALYSIS. I identify with Milky and at this point he twists the table on me and . . . Little Nineveh is my creation. I am cause and effect.

In this state of mind I discovered his letter shoved to the bottom of my rucksack, well-concealed but done with foresight, presumably when I was in the toilet that last night in Kildaggie. In any event, he'd arrived at Middle Cottage with the thing already written. I have it beside me now. Written on several sheets of cheap blue writing paper in a perfectly clear, steady hand, though the imprint of his biro has indented the paper to such an extent that it has almost changed the shape.

Dear Cedric,
By the time you read this I shall be dead, I hope. I wish I could describe to you of all people how it feels to write words like this and really mean them because you would probably appreciate that feeling and even be envious of it. I have sat for a long time hesitating over writing this letter at all, trying to disassociate what I would feel if you read one of my stories from what you will think of the way I write, technically, as indicated in this letter. But the enormous strength I've gained from the first line has encouraged me to continue and risk your criticism, which I am sure is natural to you and, after all, can make no difference. It is just a shame that for the first real moment of my life I don't have the skill to render these thoughts with the perfect clarity I think they deserve. Therefore, to enhance artificially what clarity there is, so to speak, I shall hereafter refer to myself in the past, as a dead man.

Would you like to know why I killed myself? Or do you know already? It seemed to me you considered everything as obvious. Well, apart from the obvious fact that I had nothing left to live for. You were the one who showed me just how little I had whatever your intentions in coming to Kildaggie. I admit I never loved Selina, but I'd never considered hating her until you arrived, in the same way that she hadn't considered hating me. I didn't blame you for any of this. I merely draw your attention to it so that I keep the idea in my own mind that I have your full attention. This will help me explain this question of hate.

Hate was the first important aspect of your influence upon me. It came like a smell from your soul and was sometimes so disguised that even at its worst it passed for a violent reaction against what you considered, after experience and analysis, of course, was bad. Ordinarily I might have withstood you and concluded that life was too strong for you and in failing to conquer it you'd become bitter and isolated, turning to compensations like authorship and parasitical intercourse. But it was too late. You'd made me hate myself and loathe my own failures, feelings so new to me that almost from the first day of your arrival my only means of regeneration was to curse life and Selina and everything. These feelings for Selina made sense at last; and my hatred of you was pure joy after all the miserable years I'd spent in Scotland, pandering and being used, ending up as an outcast in Kildaggie with absolutely nothing to expect. Until you came I didn't see it that way. But don't get me wrong. I might have been able to live with that. It might have given me the spunk I needed to leave Selina and move south. Then she left me and I felt humiliated instead of relieved. I saw myself ending up like you, a vagabond nobody likes. Even so, I might have lived with that too. I've made few friends along the way in any case. *What I couldn't live with, the thing which finally made me so afraid to live, was the discovery that you were writing about me.* I became obsessed with imagining the kind of things you'd write, the ridicule and lies and contempt for my own ambitions to write. Being the subject of your pretentious questions about the past disgusted me. I began to see things as an author too, manipulating events and substituting this other hero for myself, thinking in different pronouns, encountering boundaries and spaces I'd never thought existed. I became jealous of myself and envious of your written creation of me. I wanted to steal myself back. I did not want a biographer or a ghost writer. I *knew* the words.

That day I threw the pine cone at you in the forest I thought of killing you, but realized it was a fictional event. So I walked home like in a narration, pretending it was the opening of Chapter One, pretending I was going home to fetch a gun. I sat in the kitchen and realized you were already at home writing it up yourself and that you'd probably imagined exactly what I'd just done. I might have killed myself then. Or the next morning, or in a minute's time. There is no escape from such ordination. Can you understand that? From then on I was at the point of death every moment. Life was precious and each thought an insight. It is one of these insights I wish to pass on to you now before leaving you the responsibility of informing the authorities or not, the choice is yours, that I am somewhere hanging from a tree in the middle of the forest above Home Farm, my coat neatly folded nearby.

At the point of death I was able to pity you because I was faced with hatred of you/me. In Christian eschatology there are two things to consider from the point of death. My human soul, having been converted to light and love, reached out to the spirit of hate and falsehood in friendship. This was ultimate humanity. By realizing itself totally defeated, with no human body left to possess and everything immune to its power, the hatred broke down and out of utter loneliness accepted the offer of friendship and was converted to love.

On the point of your death, your soul will refuse to lose. You will find friendship humiliating and reject it and you will suffer in solitude until the end of time.

M. White.

I must admit, my first thought was the simplest. Milky White was mad. That transformed look on his face when he'd told me about Yvonne's dog . . . His precious moment at the point of death. Oh, I didn't doubt for one moment that he was still hanging neatly from a tree like a ready-made suit at John Collier's. But what could I do about it? I didn't possess enough money for another night at the bed and breakfast so I had to leave and spent the afternoon in a café. I tried understanding his insight and behaviour. Why hadn't he realized what a perfect ending he'd supplied for my novel? What should have excited me puzzled me. His suicide was such an indifferent act of frustration. Once again he appeared in possession of knowledge which eluded me. I couldn't concentrate in that café. I felt angry that he should think I'd feel envious of his privileged authorship. The stench of cigarette butts and frying fat made me feel sick. My head ached. Huge boredom because I'd been there before. With Milky dead it was like an Arts grant had dried up or you'd forgotten the combination on the lock. No reader, no human signifier. I was a bigger fool for even trying to disguise his name in parts of the manuscript. At one point I'd called him Victor Wickstead and made him a librarian at Golspie.

At five o'clock a gang of muddy Irishmen came in for their tea. I surrendered my table and shoved off. Desmond answered the phone after fifteen minutes' ringing. I asked to sleep on his floor a couple of nights but he said 'Fuck off, chav, me girlfriend's 'ere.' What about my old room? 'There's some black bastard in it,' he said. 'Shall I get him for you, mate?' The money ran out.

I took a bus to Charing Cross and dodged the fare, caught a train to Orpington without such luck. That was the end of my money so I hitched down the dual carriageway, standing for hours, cursing hundreds of passing cars until a lorry took me all the way to Flimwell crossroads, flattening dozens of rabbits down the A21. Walking the last few miles I reached the village at half past ten. My parents were taking first sips on their bedtime cocoa and the dog was up the back garden 'working out the day's takings,' as my father would say. Could I have a bath? No, they said, it was too late for a bath. And what did I mean by turning up like this, scaring the living daylights out of my mother? My father wound the mantle clock and my mother put clean nylon sheets on my old bed. I sat up half the night writing to Father Giuseppe. I said I'd like to go out and work for him. No wages, just room and board and pocket money. I'd earn the fare out. He'd just need to arrange my work permit. Life in England, I said, had become a problem. I needed a lift.

I was woken by the Radio 4 news blaring through the floor, my father frying his egg like a workman putting up a tin roof. My mother unslid the four bolts on the back door to let the dog up the garden for its 'early shift'. It was impossible that after everything which had passed I was here again. Life was retching on its own bile. Downstairs, I plucked the *Daily Express* from the letterbox and entered the kitchen like an eclipse of the sun. My father said: 'You can put that paper down and boil a kettle. Give yerself a shave.' My mother said: 'Mornin' boy. Bedder do as yer father says.' By the time I'd shaved and made myself a cup of tea, he was up the garden shed tinkering with his models before going to work. My mother was washing the kitchen and kept saying: 'Mind where yer put yer feet, boy.'

I sipped tea in the front room watching the mantle clock advance ten minutes, trying to catch the hand actually moving, counting three hundred strokes of the pendulum before snapping out of it. In one jacket pocket I shoved Milky's letter. In the other Father Giuseppe's. 'You 'aven't washed, boy!' my mother shouted after me.

Barratt's Road. You'd think it had been evacuated. It was greener than I remembered, now that saplings had become trees and hedges had plumped out. Only the emptiness was stifling. No children playing. No mothers in the kitchen windows. All the cars driven to work. No delivery vans or council workmen. I felt like a giant on the tiny pavement. As kids, it had taken us three whole leaps to cross the road. Now it was so narrow I got most of the way across in one. And the drains we'd used as goal-posts weren't even opposite each other. The marbles hole had disappeared under a new coat of tar, but the wall seemed the same size as it had always been, its railings still blue and chipped, the concrete slope to Number thirty-nine perhaps a little steeper under the circumstances. Milky's dad had put up a new gate. Borders were freshly turned. When I reached the front door my hand refused to knock. What eyes there were must be upon me and my own joined them, watching a hand snaking on its thin wrist from a cuff, a long boney white hand I couldn't place, three knocks which announce the death of Melvyn White. This was sentimentality. Best to feel nothing first, so I took the last page of Milky's letter and prepared to show it to the recipient of my visit. Just that passage about my responsibility to inform the authorities about his hanging body.

The longer I stood there the more I thought about the letter, how well written it was, how progressive his attempt to subvert my own writing actually was, how in a sense it illustrated my own ideas. I felt gratified by this, knowing that Milky had probably realized this himself. For once he was the centre of his own work, owing nothing to Dickens. Sweeping, instead, across post-war European trends, his writing may have even induced his suicide: you can be so appalled at what you didn't know was there. And once that voice is born you have to nurture it and comfort its screaming and protect it. He wouldn't have known. Self-consciousness and sleepless nights were new to him. Symbolic language or artificial text – what awful conflict. Poor Milky's first mental illness. Christ, he'd only written one suicide note. I've been writing mine for, well, you know how long and it's still unfinished. Thought I'd forgotten you? I had. Remember, I'm not entertaining you anymore. I'm not challenging or questioning form. That came to nothing because you and the author as blood/text relatives can't marry. The incest produces spores of degeneration; or signed copies. I'm not a family man, neither do I crave for institution. Old Mallachie got one thing right though. About my soul refusing to lose on the point of death. Stop writing and die? Was I about to close the case?

I don't know exactly how long I waited at Milky's front door before I decided nobody was home. Mrs White was probably at work up the butcher's. Mr White's Driving School was on the road. I didn't expect brother and sister White, in their twenties by then, so I put my hand away with the letter and took my first step back down the garden path. A soft step behind the door. The click of a well-oiled latch as the door opened. I took a deep breath and faced it, recovering the letter and holding it like Psychopompus with a telegram. Regret to inform you. Son killed in action. Only the dead son appeared himself, through a gap in the door big enough to shove his face through, like a man easing open his own coffin lid wearing suedette life-like cardigan and grey-trousered shroud. My solemn hand with its letter shook under his nose like the police had planted it on me. His white, unmarked, unhung neck and flat smile resigned to life. Whatever I said was foolish. Something about return to sender. You could see he felt he owed himself the satisfaction it gave him.

'No need,' he said. 'I made a photocopy.'

'Didn't you mean any of this? Didn't fall out your pocket, did it?'

'No,' he said. 'I simply wished to return your confidences. It's an extract from my novel. Now, if you don't mind, I'd like to get on with it.' The door closed.

I looked through the front room window. What I expected to see only counted if Milky were alive in the ordinary sense, without super-resurrection and literary apocalypse. So there weren't a cold mug of tea and a saucer of ginger biscuits on the low table, or the *Radio Times* dishevelled from boredom. Instead I heard the cackling of Milky's typewriter from upstairs, the typewriter his dad gave him as a graduation present. I made note of the tropical fish tank in the corner and a framed photograph of Melvyn White BA in graduation gown propped solemnly on top of the TV.

Up the village I posted my letter to Father Giuseppe and read the cards in the newsagent's window. A warehouse out Staplehurst way wanted packers. I started work Monday morning. The months that followed are best forgotten. Dumb toil ramming cardboard boxes full of Christmas rubbish into bigger cardboard boxes while enduring non-stop Radio 1 through loudspeakers. Even the toilet was wired in. Still, by the time Christmas passed I'd saved the fare to Africa but hadn't heard from Father Giuseppe. Worse was having to work alongside ex-Swattenden boys who remembered me. It was only a matter of time before one of them pulled up a crate to eat his sandwiches with me at dinnertime. ' 'Ere Sedge, wa'n't there some murder you was in?' So I went over it all again. Out came the manuscript. The author at home. Did I have to make such a din with that typewriter? my father said each time he came upstairs for a piss. Our only point of contact.

Of Milky there was hardly a sign. I thought he'd probably gone but then I saw him one Saturday, sneaking up the back path like he had as a grammar boy. Weekends were my only chance to see him. During the week I set off for work in the dark and came home in the dark. My parents and I ignored each other. They got their keep but I never joined them in the front room, neither could I bear taking meals with them. After work I ate in a cafe. I took my washing to the village laundrette. In the spring I drew the line and moved out, taking a room in the village and writing a second letter to Father Giuseppe. I switched to part-time at the warehouse and began to take long walks again, catching sight of Milky quite often now. In fact, he seemed to take as many walks as me. Down Foxhole Lane one afternoon he appeared two hundred yards behind me and followed me for several miles. By June he appeared to follow me everywhere I went. One evening, I looked up from my table to see him peering at me through the window.

The day I decided to have him follow me down Little Nineveh I went into the Hardware Stores where his mother worked. She'd left the butcher's under a cloud, apparently. She served me at the counter where I paid a fiver for a garden spade. There was nobody else in the shop, so from embarrassment and my undetected prompting she started chatting to me. I couldn't see if Milky was observing this or not. Doin' the gard'nin' then, was I? How she wished Melvyn might show more interest in life and *doin'* things too. Not like him. Course it can't be easy being . . . you know. No reason to forsake the chores and duties of a son, mind. Did I ever see him? She was sounding like Wormhole's mother. Maternal anxieties ready to grasp any straw. She worked in a green housecoat and pink rubber gloves, which squarked and stretched in hideous distortion as she wrung her hands. Perhaps I might like to pop round one day and have a nice chat with Melvyn? Might perk him up a bit. Weren't we good friends once, at school like? No, I said, we weren't ever friends. Oh well, she said, it was wrong for a grown man of his capabilities to stick in his room all day doing God knows what, hardly opening his mouth from one day to the next, disappearing at all hours without a word. She couldn't imagine where he went or what he did. Can't be courting, not with a face as long as a poker. I suggested that he might not want to see me. Still, I'd think about it. No need to wrap the spade.

On June the sixteenth at two in the afternoon I set off for Little Nineveh. It was twenty-two years to the day that I'd stolen Bluebird. I was confident Milky had spent a sleepless night after arguing with his mother about meeting me and puzzling over the spade. His intelligence as a spy/detective-born-again-author was not in question, so sure enough, as I paused at the Tudor Arms to glance over my shoulder, there he was just visible two hundred yards behind, clinging to the cover of the bend. When he saw I expected him, as he must have deduced, he walked out into the open. I was in no hurry, needing to take in the scene after so long. Here was the pond I'd once forsaken for Bluebird, a water vole scuttering along the network of oak roots beside water now completely choked in crowfoot and pondweed. The ditch where I'd found Bluebird was also changed. Someone had dumped cinders, shards and broken fire bricks into it. The Nineveh Lane signpost was a new reflective type. The old one lay thrown into the hedgerow after a car must have smashed it. These few details were the only real changes, if you discount hedgerows and trees, some grown, others butchered. These are incomparable changes too. The past felt more than dead and impervious, though the sky was grey like any November sky in June; and here was Milky White, of course, coming along as he had once before.

In fact the weather was warm and close. Rustling leaves sounding like scratching dogs, the air felt all breathed up, like sucking it from the dustbag of a vacuum cleaner. Revulsion for the past, I turned down Nineveh Lane as Milky caught up with the pond. Momentary doubts, but Milky forced the pace. It was too late to be frightened.

The sunken garden said everything. As when I first discovered it, I had to smash my way in. All that re-imagined exotica of childhood was in fact the bindweed and parasitical growth of my grown-up eye. Sycamore saplings clogged the light, greedy big-handed leaves. There was a hiss in the air or my ears. Botanical bloodsuckers trodden in. Sickly toothwort clung by suckers to the hazels, bracts and scales like tapeworm. Stinkhorns black with flies after carrion. Knotted figwort gagged what air remained uncontaminated. Forgetting about Milky, I sliced through the undergrowth and turned up the first spadeful of blackened soil. It wasn't long before I unearthed the first detritus of childhood. Either I remembered exactly where I'd buried things, or my reasoning hadn't altered. In terms of concealment I'd been advanced before my time. So the Missionary Box from the chip shop was easily uprooted. Old blood-coloured plastic with a slit on top and detachable bottom. Its paper wrapper with the writing and photograph of a starving heathen had rotted away. Tipping out the blackened water, three old pennies clunked. What had I planned to spend these on? I fingered them out. Freshly drowned white baby worms stuck to George VI's head.

I had to hack my way through to the pond, now a coat of scum and silt, a sink-sized pool of black water at its heart. Here was where I'd first hidden Bluebird. The murderer had put it back. With more than insight, I began to dig. My second incision with the spade hit something partly solid. Rotten, rusted metal on the tip of the blade. Here the ground was thick with deadly nightshade. Bluebird was mostly submerged beneath the thick of it, entwined by fleshy roots. The worts I had to look up in the *Observer Book of British Worts* but the deadly nightshade I knew about. Throwing off my jacket I began to smash the roots with the spade, tugging at spokes which snapped like dead twigs. The saddle crumbled in my hands and the rotting shreds of tyres sprinkled like seeds. Except in fragments, Bluebird would not be exhumed. It was bound and rooted to its shallow grave. So I sat and wiped the sweat away, waiting for Milky to emerge from his hide. Are you thinking that Partridge gave it back to me by choosing my own spot? Or had he buried it in a hurry after the murder, hoping to save himself, knowing I'd seen it, relying on my own guilt not to give him away too?

I wished I hadn't cared and that the past could blow itself to dust. Here is an English disease and makes writing impossible. My disgust with memory, the way it intervenes like a rule of grammar on the language, is also a rejection of tradition. Hence my loathing for the English novel. The fact is that a rural English working-class self-educated non-graduate like me is not eligible to write an English novel because I owe nobody anything. Get there on your own and you'll find you don't belong. No institution is proud of you. No one will honour you. No one will publish you because you don't know anyone you can ask to 'have a look at something I've written' after a chat about old times when 'up'. I wish to obliterate, empty, reject. Let me do to the English novel what I did for Partridge. Let's put tradition to sleep.

So I chucked a few spokes into the silt and didn't like the rapidity with which they sink. In fact they sucked under. I'm bloody furious with the bike for not giving itself up too, so I fling the spade into the middle of the silt and it goes down like a ship's mast. And fuck Milky too because he still hadn't showed. The mud must have put him off or he'd lost his way or searched too long for somewhere private to have a slash. I grab my jacket to go and look for him but there he is, ten yards off, blocking the path I'd hacked in the undergrowth.

'So it *was* you got rid of the bike,' he says. 'I read you like a book, Cedric. June the sixteenth and all.' He comes forward too, picking up the Missionary Box.

I shrug. 'Welcome,' I say, 'to the Little Nineveh Museum of Childhood. I'm the Curator. The exhibit in your hand, a personal bequest, was nicked from the chip shop in 1966.'

He peers down at Bluebird. I continue the guide book. 'Yes, the very bicycle as deduced, which the murderer used to convey himself from one part of the village to another, still in the actual grave where it was concealed, perhaps only minutes after we as young lads saw it ourselves. A fascinating subject for enquiry, don't you agree?'

'When did you do it?' he enquired. Here was a skilled investigator.

The police told me even then, when discussing the bike at the inquest, to be careful what I said. You can leave things out, accidentally or deliberately they said, and alter your whole meaning. Decide, they said, if you want us to get Partridge for the murder of your friend Yvonne or not.

'You used to make me sick,' I tell Milky, 'riding your own bloody bike about like Little Lord Fauntleroy.'

'Why did you do it?' he persists. 'What good was Bluebird to you? You weren't meant to have a bike!'

'How do you know it's called Bluebird?' I ask, but there is only one way. He confirms it.

'I was spying on you for weeks, you idiot. I knew you'd arrived in Kildaggie within twenty-four hours. You left your door unlocked, remember? You even thought Marine Cormorant had stolen your money. I read about it, didn't I?'

'Liar!'

'Prove I'm lying. And while you're at your deductions, answer another interesting question. Who did Bluebird belong to and why didn't they report it missing?'

'That's easy,' I say. 'One of them Italian waiters, of course. The ones who shot at sparrows and scared you shitless. They didn't have work permits so they'd hardly go to the Police Station for justice.'

'Speaking of which,' he says, pulling at Bluebird's firmly embedded frame, grabbing tendrils and undoing them systematically like they're knitting errors. 'Evidence, Watson. By jingo, enough to hang a man!'

'Very amusing,' I say, 'but go careful with that stuff.'

He's ripping what he can't undo from the soil, yanking on the deadly nightshade which makes me think he doesn't know what it is.

'I am being careful,' he says. 'I intend presenting the whole bike to the constabulary. Yours is a good story, nice and challenging . . . my God, there's tons of incrimination buried here. What are all these toys?'

'More bequests,' I say. 'Interested in the job, inspector? Be nice to have a professional catalogue. You know I so admired your letter of application with its clever allusions to Christian eschatology. The police'd never believe you. I'd only have to show them my manuscript . . . '

'And I'd only have to show them mine,' he says. I feel ineffective against him, the problem unfolds too rapidly for me to keep up. He really means to tell the police. I ask him what purpose it would serve. He can tell I've lost all control of my material and intervenes as detective/editor, asking me what use is an event? What purpose does an event serve, as, he says, I've already demonstrated? Taught him, in fact. My fitness to teach is no longer questioned. In his novel about me, he says, he will demonstrate FICTION AS PIG-IN-THE-MIDDLE, or FICTION VERSUS FICTION. Be a nice coming-out present for Partridge. Don't look so surprised. You knew, he says. That's why you rushed down here to make sure he hadn't guessed. He'll be after you in any case. I've already sent some early chapters to a publisher with favourable results. And what are his opening chapters, I ask? Chapter One, his letter to me, the suicide note. Then my appearance at his kitchen window. He even lets me into a professional secret. His first-person narrator observes us both and we are 'they'. 'I' is Death moving between us and fighting for our souls as advantages swing to and fro, telling us how it's done, right till the end. You don't know who he gets, though you might think it's obvious. What did I think?

Now he's worrying the bike again and I really do feel in the hands of his narrator. I say I don't think much of his idea but admit it's less likely to fail than mine. I remind him of an important fact.

But, perhaps you've guessed it. In any case I can't keep this up much longer. Neither author nor penitent. You should see the night flies battling in the black smoke of my paraffin lamp. Feel the hot night air gather smells from hundreds of braziers. No way can I touch the past, see or hear it, remember or describe it. I still possess a small number of linguistic parts, like those adverts you see in specialist magazines: ABANDONED RESTORATION PROJECT. Do they run out of love or money? Or do they see through it too? Offers, they say. Or TOO MUCH TO LIST. Or, all too frequently: EMIGRATION FORCES SALE.

The parts are the following. Milky doesn't intend to fail. He yanks at the bike's chain and you can tell he's still got those muscles he came to Barratt's Road with. The veins on his hands stick out like bones. His neck is red and taut. He says he's nothing to hide, that's why. His life isn't a mobile graveyard. He doesn't insult the living. He feels comfortable with tradition and knows his place. I didn't, he said. I suggested that he might be building his houses on my land. . . Then the chain snaps and Milky stumbles backwards into the silt margins of the pond, his hand landing nearer the middle. He rights himself but finds nothing to haul himself out with, up to his waist in mud, spitting filth and wiping it from his eyes. He is out of my reach too. 'DAMNATION,' he shouts.

I find a long but fragile stick and tell him to grab the end.

'I don't need your bloody help,' he says. 'I'll find my own way out.'

'Suit yourself,' I tell him, taking my leave from Little Nineveh.

That evening, Milky's brother knocked on my door. 'Ah,' he said, nervous-like, 'alright then, Sedge? Me mum just wondered if Mel was 'ere like, you know. Selina's jis rung me, sez it's urgent.'

'No 'e's not,' I said. 'Should he be?'

'Nah, nah, me mum dunno where 'e is, you know. Couln't fink 'oo e'd be wiv 'cept you, not comin' 'ome fer tea like.'

After he'd gone I walked back to Little Nineveh. The sun wouldn't set till nine thity but once among the trees darkness dropped like a door slamming on the sky. I called out and my own voice put the fear of God through me. 'Milky. MILKY WHITE. UH, MELVYN, ARE YOU THERE?' I had no choice but to go in as far as the pond. He might have sunk. More likely he went round to Wormhole's mum's to wash the mud off or he was sitting in a field by the stream wiping it off systematically. I tried remembering what he'd told his mum about his pissed pants when Partridge ran him over. Then I thought of Partridge strangling me for revenge. There wasn't the slightest trail of damp slime to mark any egress from the pond. He must have sunk. Museum closed for the winter. I ran from that place like I'd run once before.

The Whites had drawn their curtains but the door opened seconds after my knock by Mr White, anxious and disappointed to see me. I was Death and no mistake. His face fell as I interrupted his broken thread about: ' . . . thought it might be Melvyn . . . bit worried . . . not back yet . . . forgotten his key . . . '

'May I come in?' I said and he stood aside. They turned the telly off and Mr White told Margaret, who wasn't married after all, to get up off the best chair so I could sit down. She went into the kitchen and Mrs White came in wiping her hands on an apron. I said, 'Good evening, Mrs White,' an unnatural phrase. Then I told them I knew where Milky was supposed to have been that after-noon but I hoped my suspicions were unfounded. Within ten minutes Mr White parked his car by the iron gate down Little Nineveh.

He took his breakdown lamp from the boot and started shout-ing in a panic.

'Melvyn lad! Melvyn! Give us a toot, son.'

At midnight the police had arc lights up and began to drag the sludge. They got Milky first cast. He came up with the spade, trumps. At dawn I was still sitting in the village sergeant's office, rubbing my eyes and smoking the only fags they could find me, these two detectives from the Maidstone CID. I repeated my story ten times or more and signed a statement in blinding, yellow sunrise. I reproduce this statement.

*

I have known Mr Melvyn White, the deceased, for a number of years. Until last year when I met him by accident in Scotland, I had not been friendly towards him. Over a period of about a month he trusted me with certain confidences about his life. At this time he was depressed and his marriage was failing. His job prospects were also uncertain. One day the subject of Yvonne Sharpe's murder was broached. Melvyn told me about the bicycle, the evidence which led to Partridge's conviction for murder. Melvyn told me that one day an Italian waiter from the Tudor Arms shot him up the backside with an air rifle so he'd stolen the bicycle out of revenge and hidden it down Little Nineveh. I remembered that as a boy he'd puzzled us and some of the strange things he'd said now made sense. For instance, when we'd called him a 'goody gum-drop' he hinted at having done something worse than any of us. After telling me about his theft of the racing bike I asked about his mysterious allusions as a boy. 'No,' he answered. 'I meant something quite different. I meant that I had stolen the Missionary Box from the chip shop, and many other items from shops, all of which I concealed down Little Nineveh along with the bicycle, which, incidentally, I named Bluebird.'

I suggested that this must have been why he'd lied about seeing the bike on the afternoon of the murder and he agreed. He hadn't wanted Partridge to think he'd given evidence against him in case Partridge told the police that Melvyn had stolen the bicycle himself. Because our newly found friendship dwindled a little at this point after an argument, he did not expand upon these facts. There was no exact nature to this argument, but it did have something to do with a book he said he was writing about the past, in which I was the main character. My objection infuriated him. He even showed signs of violent intent, saying he had the right to defend his literary freedom in any way he chose. Soon afterwards, I believe, his wife left him.

On the eve of my departure for London he visited me at my cottage and accused me of covering up for the murderer by lying about the bike. He said he'd seen Yvonne's dog that afternoon, tethered to a stake nearby. Now he'd seen it again in Kildaggie and accused me of planning another murder. Though his state of mind worried me, I returned to London the following day. It was not until three days later that I discovered a note in my rucksack which must have been written and placed there by Melvyn White. On reading it I surmised it to be a suicide note. I have only been able to preserve the last page in which he mentions my responsibility to inform the authorities about his hanging body. This page also contains his views on the plight of the Christian soul at the point of death. I travelled down to the village with the intention of showing this note to his parents. However, Mr Melvyn White, the deceased, opened the door himself and after a brief exchange slammed it in my face.

I saw nothing of him that winter, but in spring he began following me. He later explained this conduct as 'research' and 'defence'. He wanted to see how long it would take me to deduce his part in the murder and the subsequent events. He finally approached me just recently, having learned of Partridge's imminent release on parole. His anxiety for us both was real. Our only option, he said, was to shift the bike so Partridge wouldn't find it. Melvyn White needed a spade but didn't want to draw attention to himself by taking one from the garden shed. His mother works in the only village shop which sells spades so I agreed to purchase it on his behalf. Incidentally, his mother expressed great concern for Melvyn's state of mind and hoped I might intervene on her behalf. Melvyn was also reluctant to be seen carrying the spade through the village so the following day, June sixteenth, I carried it for him down to Little Nineveh, where I had arranged to meet him at 2 o'clock. After waiting over an hour, I left the spade against a tree. I spent the remainder of the afternoon walking. At no point during the day did I see Mr Melvyn White . . .

The police didn't attempt to conceal their suspicions. Everything bothered them, not least my being in Scotland. When I said I was planning on going to Africa, they requested my passport. There was no real pressure on me to confess anything. My only real anxiety was caused by the existence of my manuscript and keeping the police in ignorance. Their intellectual capacity caused me no concern and they did not consider literature as central to the case. Then one day they attempted to trick me into confession but in revealing the attempt they effectively ruined their case against me. I'd been puzzled but relieved by the lack of publicity. The *Courier* had reported 'Local Tragedy,' and my name had only been included as a friend who'd first alerted the parents to Milky's possible whereabouts. For some reason Little Nineveh had been given as Nineveh Farm. There had been no published connection between present and past events. I've no doubt this had much to do with police strategy. They'd effectively minimized the possibility that Partridge would hear of it. They'd prevented connections and questions. So after requesting this photograph of me aged ten, they summoned me to Maidstone Police Station. Perhaps the fact that Milky was a Maidstoner had motivated them. The interview began in the normal way. Several points in my statement needed clearing up. I was confident about my statement and knew I'd kept it simple enough to avoid self-incrimination. This had always disappointed them. They considered it such a complex series of deceits that I was probably as much author as reader, especially as Milky's parents considered it all 'fantastic nonsense', swearing on their son's grave (which had yet to be dug) that Melvyn was incapable of deceit. The official reading of his manuscript alarmed me. Only two things appeared in my favour. One was the miracle of Milky's handwriting. Cramped and cryptic, it gave our detectives a disliking of the contemporary novel. And it did appear to mention me a few times, in strange choruses narrated by Death. In the minds of policemen this queer writing was obsessional. In all good police manuals obsession leads to *felo de se*. And here was Death narrating away at Milky's past and fighting for his soul in Scotland, leaving a trail of false suicide notes and spying on me in the village. And secondly the manuscript was haphazard and incomplete, not having dealt yet with my own part in his turning thus to authorship. My influence as a writer ignored.

So they'd taken the photograph to show an unsuspecting Partridge on the eve of his release from prison, aged forty-one. Is this the boy who stole Bluebird? they asked. The way they told me, I could tell this was their last token and it was already spent. They weren't the sort of blokes used to jackpots either. You wouldn't tell blokes like that the truth, same way you don't let Mormons in or the bloke collecting overdue library books. I had a choice: add one last thing to my statement before they read me Partridge's.

'Why should I add anything?'

'Just think about it for ten minutes,' they said, putting my statement on the table and leaving the room. One of them came in again and smoked a cigarette. Then the other reappears with the pathologist's report and I'm at the Sunday School party charades.

'Yes,' one says, 'it's as we guessed, tut tut tut. Now then Mr Lily, Cedric, quite sure you won't change your mind?'

'About what?' I knew the pathologist's report couldn't matter. They could see I knew that.

'About the bloody bike, lad. Come on, who stole it?'

And the other one sings to the tune of Old Man River: 'Who nicked Blue-Bird . . ?'

It was close. They were too cocky. Partridge had told them.

'Give us a name, Cedric.'

'Lilywhite,' I said. They made faces like empty cupboards.

'Who's 'e?' they asked, but without inspiration.

'Melvyn White, of course. Partridge called him Lilywhite.'

They showed me Partridge's statement. He'd confused us from the start. He even identified both photographs, mine and Milky's, as Lilywhite. They didn't consider we might both have nicked the bike, set him up, strangled Yvonne.

I went home with my passport but remained for the inquest as ordered. The post-mortem results described traces of deadly nightshade in the bloodstream. No signs of violence on the body which were not accidently self-inflicted. The suicide note was referred to. A scene of crimes officer spoke of the considerable pressure under which a bicycle chain would break, the imprints of which were gouged into Milky's hands. Mr and Mrs White were more heartbroken over revelations of their son's childhood criminality than by his death by misadventure. I'd broken their hearts, they said.

It was easy to con his manuscript off them. They didn't want to read it. Milky's dad stood on the landing as I went through folders and shoeboxes. You may have guessed already. You may feel too implicated to cry out. I left England the week after Milky was buried.

*

Someone's torch beam picks over the ground then runs ahead as they lift a hand to switch it off. In my mind I wave to him, and this silence blows into the room which I try and catch like you do a falling leaf just to keep it in the air.